The Dragon and The Raven: Or The Days of King Alfred

G. A. Henty

Contents

THE DRAGON
AND THE RAVEN:
OR THE DAYS OF
KING ALFRED

by

G. A. Henty

PREFACE

MY DEAR LADS,

Living in the present days of peace and tranquillity it is difficult to picture the life of our ancestors in the days of King Alfred, when the whole country was for years overrun by hordes of pagan barbarians, who slaughtered, plundered, and destroyed at will. You may gain, perhaps, a fair conception of the state of things if you imagine that at the time of the great mutiny the English population of India approached that of the natives, and that the mutiny was everywhere triumphant. The wholesale massacres and outrages which would in such a case have been inflicted upon the conquered whites could be no worse than those suffered by the Saxons at the hands of the Danes. From this terrible state of subjection and suffering the Saxons were rescued by the prudence, the patience, the valour and wisdom of King Alfred. In all subsequent ages England has produced no single man who united in himself so many great qualities as did this first of great Englishmen. He was learned, wise, brave, prudent, and pious; devoted to his people, clement to his conquered enemies. He was as great in peace as in war; and yet few English boys know more than a faint outline of the events of Alfred's reign--events which have exercised an influence upon the whole future of the English people. School histories pass briefly over them; and the incident of the burned cake is that which is, of all the actions of a great and glorious reign, the most prominent in boys' minds. In this story I have tried to supply the deficiency. Fortunately in the Saxon Chronicles and in the life of King Alfred written by his friend and counsellor Asser, we have a trustworthy account of the events and battles which first laid Wessex prostrate beneath the foot of the Danes, and finally freed England for many years from the invaders. These histories I have faithfully followed. The account of the siege of Paris is taken from a very full and detailed history of that event by the Abbe D'Abbon, who was a witness of the scenes he described.

Yours sincerely, G. A. HENTY

CHAPTER I:
THE FUGITIVES

A low hut built of turf roughly thatched with rushes and standing on the highest spot of some slightly raised ground. It was surrounded by a tangled growth of bushes and low trees, through which a narrow and winding path gave admission to the narrow space on which the hut stood. The ground sloped rapidly. Twenty yards from the house the trees ceased, and a rank vegetation of reeds and rushes took the place of the bushes, and the ground became soft and swampy. A little further pools of stagnant water appeared among the rushes, and the path abruptly stopped at the edge of a stagnant swamp, though the passage could be followed by the eye for some distance among the tall rushes. The hut, in fact, stood on a hummock in the midst of a wide swamp where the water sometimes deepened into lakes connected by sluggish streams.

On the open spaces of water herons stalked near the margin, and great flocks of wild-fowl dotted the surface. Other signs of life there were none, although a sharp eye might have detected light threads of smoke curling up here and there from spots where the ground rose somewhat above the general level. These slight elevations, however, were not visible to the eye, for the herbage here grew shorter than on the lower and wetter ground, and the land apparently stretched away for a vast distance in a dead flat-- a rush-covered swamp, broken only here and there by patches of bushes and low trees.

The little hut was situated in the very heart of the fen country, now drained and cultivated, but in the year 870 untouched by the hand of man, the haunt of wild-fowl and human fugitives. At the door of the hut stood a lad some fourteen years old. His only garment was a short sleeveless tunic girded in at the waist, his arms and legs were bare; his head was uncovered, and his hair fell in masses on his shoulders. In his hand he held a short spear, and leaning against the wall of the hut close at hand was a bow and quiver of arrows. The lad looked at the sun, which was sinking towards the horizon.

"Father is late," he said. "I trust that no harm has come to him and Egbert. He said he would return to-day without fail; he said three or four days, and this is the fourth. It is dull work here alone. You think so, Wolf, don't you, old fellow? And it is worse for you than it is for me, pent up on this hummock of ground with scarce room to stretch your limbs."

A great wolf-hound, who was lying with his head between his paws by the embers of a fire in the centre of the hut, raised his head on being addressed, and uttered a low howl indicative of his agreement with his master's opinion and his disgust at his present place of abode.

"Never mind, old fellow," the boy continued, "we sha'n't be here long, I hope, and then you shall go with me in the woods again and hunt the wolves to your heart's content." The great hound gave a lazy wag of his tail. "And now, Wolf, I must go. You lie here and guard the hut while I am away. Not that you are likely to have any strangers to call in my absence."

The dog rose and stretched himself, and followed his master down the path until it terminated at the edge of the water. Here he gave a low whimper as the lad stepped in and waded through the water; then turning he walked back to the hut and threw himself down at the door. The boy proceeded for some thirty or forty yards through the water, then paused and pushed aside the wall of rushes which bordered the passage, and pulled out a boat which was floating among them.

It was constructed of osier rods neatly woven together into a sort of basket-work, and covered with an untanned hide with the hairy side in. It was nearly oval in shape, and resembled a great bowl some three feet and a half wide and a foot longer. A broad paddle with a long handle lay in it, and the boy, getting into it and standing erect in the middle paddled down the strip of water which a hundred yards further opened out into a broad half a mile long and four or five hundred yards wide. Beyond moving slowly away as the coracle approached them, the water-fowl paid but little heed to its appearance.

The boy paddled to the end of the broad, whence a passage, through which flowed a stream so sluggish that its current could scarce be detected, led into the next sheet of water. Across the entrance to this passage floated some bundles of light rushes. These the boy drew out one by one. Attached to each was a piece of cord which, being pulled upon, brought to the surface a large cage, constructed somewhat on the plan of a modern eel or lobster pot. They were baited by pieces of dead fish, and from them the boy extracted half a score of eels and as many fish of different kinds.

"Not a bad haul," he said as he lowered the cages to the bottom again. "Now let us see what we have got in our pen."

He paddled a short way along the broad to a point where a little lane of water ran up through the rushes. This narrowed rapidly and the lad got out from his boat into the water, as the coracle could proceed no further between the lines of rushes. The water was knee-deep and the bottom soft and oozy. At the end of the creek it narrowed until the rushes were but a foot apart. They were bent over here, as it would seem to a superficial observer naturally; but a close examination would show that those facing each other were tied together where they crossed at a distance of a couple of feet above the water, forming a sort of tunnel. Two feet farther on this ceased, and the rushes were succeeded by lines of strong osier withies, an inch or two apart, arched over and fastened together. At this point was a sort of hanging door formed of rushes backed with osiers, and so arranged that at the slightest push from without the door lifted and enabled a wild-fowl to pass under, but dropping behind it prevented its exit. The osier tunnel widened out to a sort of inverted basket three feet in diameter.

On the surface of the creek floated some grain which had been scattered there the evening before as a bait. The lad left the creek before he got to the narrower part, and, making a small circuit in the swamp, came down upon the pen.

"Good!" he said, "I am in luck to-day; here are three fine ducks."

Bending the yielding osiers aside, he drew out the ducks one by one, wrung their necks, and passing their heads through his girdle, made his way again to the coracle. Then he scattered another handful or two of grain on the water, sparingly near the mouth of the creek, but more thickly at the entrance to the trap, and then paddled back again by the way he had come.

Almost noiselessly as he dipped the paddle in the water, the hound's quick ear had caught the sound, and he was standing at the edge of the swamp, wagging his tail in dignified welcome as his master stepped on to dry land.

"There, Wolf, what do you think of that? A good score of eels and fish and three fine wild ducks. That means bones for you with your meal to-night--not to satisfy your hunger, you know, for they would not be of much use in that way, but to give a flavour to your supper. Now let us make the fire up and pluck the birds, for I warrant me that father and Egbert, if they return this evening, will be sharp-set. There are the cakes to bake too, so you see there is work for the next hour or two."

The sun had set now, and the flames, dancing up as the boy threw an armful of dry wood on the fire, gave the hut a more cheerful appearance. For some time the lad busied himself with preparation for supper. The three ducks were plucked in readiness for putting over the fire should they be required; cakes of coarse rye-flour were made and placed in the red ashes of the fire; and then the lad threw himself down by the side of the dog.

"No, Wolf, it is no use your looking at those ducks. I am not going to roast them if no one comes; I have got half a one left from dinner." After sitting quiet for half an hour the dog suddenly raised himself into a sitting position, with ears erect and muzzle pointed towards the door; then he gave a low whine, and his tail began to beat the ground rapidly.

"What! do you hear them, old fellow?" the boy said, leaping to his feet. "I wish my ears were as sharp as yours are, Wolf; there would be no fear then of being caught asleep. Come on, old boy, let us go and meet them."

It was some minutes after he reached the edge of the swamp before the boy could hear the sounds which the quick ears of the hound had detected. Then he heard a faint splashing noise, and a minute or two later two figures were seen wading through the water.

"Welcome back, father," the lad cried. "I was beginning to be anxious about you, for here we are at the end of the fourth day."

"I did not name any hour, Edmund," the boy's father said, as he stepped from the water, "but I own that I did not reckon upon being so late; but in truth Egbert and I missed our way in the windings of these swamps, and should not have been back to-night had we not luckily fallen upon a man fishing, who was able to put us right. You have got some supper, I hope, for Egbert and I are as hungry as wolves, for we have had nothing since we started before sunrise."

"I have plenty to eat, father; but you will have to wait till it is cooked, for it was no use putting it over the fire until I knew that you would return; but there is a good fire, and you will not have to wait long. And how has it fared with you, and what is the news?"

"The news is bad, Edmund. The Danes are ever receiving reinforcements from Mercia, and scarce a day passes but fresh bands arrive at Thetford, and I fear that ere long East Anglia, like Northumbria, will fall into their clutches. Nay, unless we soon make head against them they will come to occupy all the island, just as did our forefathers."

"That were shame indeed," Edmund exclaimed. "We know that the people conquered by our ancestors were unwarlike and cowardly; but it would be shame indeed were we Saxons so to be overcome by the Danes, seeing moreover that we have the help of God, being Christians, while the Danes are pagans and idolaters."

"Nevertheless, my son, for the last five years these heathen have been masters of Northumbria, have wasted the whole country, and have plundered and destroyed the churches and monasteries. At present they have but made a beginning here in East Anglia; but if they continue to flock in they will soon overrun the whole country, instead of having, as at present, a mere foothold near the rivers except for those who have come down to Thetford. We have been among the first sufferers, seeing that our lands lie round Thetford, and hitherto I have hoped that there would be a general rising against these invaders; but the king is indolent and unwarlike, and I see that he will not arouse himself and call his ealdormen and thanes together for a united effort until it is too late. Already from the north the Danes are flocking down into Mercia, and although the advent of the West Saxons to the aid of the King of Mercia forced them to retreat for a while, I doubt not that they will soon pour down again."

"'Tis a pity, father, that the Saxons are not all under one leading; then we might surely defend England against the Danes. If the people did but rise and fall upon each band of Northmen as they arrived they would get no footing among us."

"Yes," the father replied, "it is the unhappy divisions between the Saxon kingdoms which have enabled the Danes to get so firm a footing in the land. Our only hope now lies in the West Saxons. Until lately they were at feud with Mercia; but the royal families are now related by marriage, seeing that the King of Mercia is wedded to a West Saxon princess, and that Alfred, the West Saxon king's brother and heir to the throne, has lately espoused one of the royal blood of Mercia. The fact that they marched at the call of the King of Mercia and drove the Danes from Nottingham shows that the West Saxon princes are alive to the common danger of the country, and if they are but joined heartily by our people of East Anglia and the Mercians, they may yet succeed in checking the progress of these heathen. And now, Edmund, as we see no hope of any general effort to drive the Danes off our coasts, 'tis useless for us to lurk here longer. I propose to-morrow, then, to journey north into Lincolnshire, to the Abbey of Croyland, where, as you know, my brother Theodore is the abbot; there we can rest in peace for a time, and watch the progress of events. If we hear that the people of these parts are aroused from their lethargy, we will come back and fight for our home and lands; if not, I will no longer stay in East Anglia, which I see is destined to fall piecemeal into the hands of the Danes; but we will journey down to Somerset, and I will pray King Ethelbert to assign me lands there, and to take me as his thane."

While they had been thus talking Egbert had been broiling the eels and wild ducks over the fire. He was a freeman, and a distant relation of Edmund's father, Eldred, who was an ealdorman in West Norfolk, his lands lying beyond Thetford, and upon whom, therefore, the first brunt of the Danish invasion from Mercia had fallen. He had made a stout resistance, and assembling his people had given battle to the invaders. These, however, were too strong and numerous, and his force having been scattered and dispersed, he had sought refuge with Egbert and his son in the fen country. Here he had remained for two months in hopes that some general effort would be made to drive back the Danes; but being now convinced that at present the Angles were too disunited to join in a common effort, he determined to retire for a while from the scene.

"I suppose, father," Edmund said, "you will leave your treasures buried here?"

"Yes," his father replied; "we have no means of transporting them, and we can at ally time return and fetch them. We must dig up the big chest and take such garments as we may need, and the personal ornaments of our rank; but the rest, with the gold and silver vessels, can remain here till we need them."

Gold and silver vessels seem little in accordance with the primitive mode of life prevailing in the ninth century. The Saxon civilization was indeed a mixed one. Their mode of life was primitive, their dwellings, with the exception of the religious houses and the abodes of a few of the great nobles, simple in the extreme; but they possessed vessels of gold and silver, armlets, necklaces, and ornaments of the same metals, rich and brightly coloured dresses, and elaborate bed furniture while their tables and household utensils were of the roughest kind, and their floors strewn with rushes. When they invaded and conquered England they found existing the civilization introduced by the Romans, which was far in advance of their own; much of this they adopted. The introduction of Christianity further advanced them in the scale.

The prelates and monks from Rome brought with them a high degree of civilization, and this to no small extent the Saxons imitated and borrowed. The church was held in much honour, great wealth and possessions were bestowed upon it, and the bishops and abbots possessed large temporal as well as spiritual power, and bore a prominent part in the councils of the kingdoms. But even in the handsome and well-built monasteries, with their stately services and handsome vestments, learning was at the lowest ebb--so low, indeed, that when Prince Alfred desired to learn Latin he could find no one in his father's dominions capable of teaching him, and his studies were for a long time hindered for want of an instructor, and at the time he ascended the throne he was probably the only Englishman outside a monastery who was able to read and write fluently.

"Tell me, father," Edmund said after the meal was concluded, "about the West Saxons, since it is to them, as it seems, that we must look for the protection of England against the Danes. This Prince Alfred, of whom I before heard you speak in terms of high praise, is the brother, is he not, of the king? In that case how is it that he does not reign in Kent, which I thought, though joined to the West Saxon kingdom, was always ruled over by the eldest son of the king."

"Such has been the rule, Edmund; but seeing the troubled times when Ethelbert came to the throne, it was thought better to unite the two kingdoms under one crown with the understanding that at Ethelbert's death Alfred should succeed him. Their father, Ethelwulf, was a weak king, and should have been born a churchman rather than a prince. He nominally reigned over Wessex, Kent, and Mercia, but the last paid him but a slight allegiance. Alfred was his favourite son, and he sent him, when quite a child, to Rome for a visit. In 855 he himself, with a magnificent retine, and accompanied by Alfred, visited Rome, travelling through the land of the Franks, and it was there, doubtless, that Alfred acquired that love of learning, and many of those ideas, far in advance of his people, which distinguish him. His mother, Osburgha, died before he and his father started on the pilgrimage. The king was received with much honour by the pope, to whom he presented a gold crown of four pounds weight, ten dishes of the purest gold, a sword richly set in gold, two gold images, some silver-gilt urns, stoles bordered with gold and purple, white silken robes embroidered with figures, and other costly articles of clothing for the celebration of the service of the church, together with rich presents in gold and silver to the churches, bishops, clergy, and other dwellers in Rome. They say that the people of Rome marvelled much at these magnificent gifts from a king of a country which they had considered as barbarous. On his way back he married Judith, daughter of the King of the Franks; a foolish marriage, for the king was far advanced in years and Judith was but a girl.

"Ethelbald, Ethelwulf's eldest son, had acted as regent in his father's absence, and so angered was he at this marriage that he raised his standard of revolt against his father. At her marriage Judith had been crowned queen, and this was contrary to the customs of the West Saxons, therefore Ethelbald was supported by the people of that country; on his father's return to England, however, father and son met, and a division of the kingdom was agreed upon.

"Ethelbald received Wessex, the principal part of the kingdom, and Ethelwulf took Kent, which he had already ruled over in the time of his father Egbert. Ethelwulf died a few months afterwards, leaving Kent to Ethelbert, his second surviving son. The following year, to the horror and indignation of the people of the country, Ethelbald married his stepmother Judith, but two years afterwards died, and Ethelbert, King of Kent, again united Wessex to his own dominions, which consisted of Kent, Surrey, and Sussex. Ethelbert reigned but a short time, and at his death Ethelred, his next brother, ascended the throne. Last year Alfred, the youngest brother, married Elswitha, the daughter of Ethelred Mucil, Earl of the Gaini, in Lincolnshire, whose mother was one of the royal family of Mercia.

"It was but a short time after the marriage that the Danes poured into Mercia from the north. Messengers were sent to ask the assistance of the West Saxons.

These at once obeyed the summons, and, joining the Mercians, marched against the Danes, who shut themselves up in the strong city of Nottingham, and were there for some time besieged. The place was strong, the winter at hand, and the time of the soldiers' service nearly expired. A treaty was accordingly made by which the Danes were allowed to depart unharmed to the north side of the Humber, and the West Saxons returned to their kingdom.

"Such is the situation at present, but we may be sure that the Danes will not long remain quiet, but will soon gather for another invasion; ere long, too, we may expect another of their great fleets to arrive somewhere off these coasts, and every Saxon who can bear arms had need take the field to fight for our country and faith against these heathen invaders. Hitherto, Edmund, as you know, I have deeply mourned the death of your mother, and of your sisters who died in infancy; but now I feel that it is for the best, for a terrible time is before us. We men can take refuge in swamp and forest, but it would have been hard for delicate women; and those men are best off who stand alone and are able to give every thought and energy to the defence of their country. 'Tis well that you are now approaching an age when the Saxon youth are wont to take their place in the ranks of battle. I have spared no pains with your training in arms, and though assuredly you lack strength yet to cope in hand-to-hand conflict with these fierce Danes, you may yet take your part in battle, with me on one side of you and Egbert on the other. I have thought over many things of late, and it seems to me that we Saxons have done harm in holding the people of this country as serfs."

"Why, father," Edmund exclaimed in astonishment, "surely you would not have all men free and equal."

"The idea seems strange to you, no doubt, Edmund, and it appears only natural that some men should be born to rule and others to labour, but this might be so even without serfdom, since, as you know, the poorer freemen labour just as do the serfs, only they receive a somewhat larger guerdon for their toil; but had the two races mixed more closely together, had serfdom been abolished and all men been free and capable of bearing arms, we should have been able to show a far better front to the Danes, seeing that the serfs are as three to one to the freemen."

"But the serfs are cowardly and spiritless," Edmund said; "they are not of a fighting race, and fell almost without resistance before our ancestors when they landed here."

"Their race is no doubt inferior to our own, Edmund," his father said, "seeing that they are neither so tall nor so strong as we Saxons, but of old they were not deficient in bravery, for they fought as stoutly against the Romans as did our own hardy ancestors. After having been for hundreds of years subject to the Roman yoke, and having no occasion to use arms, they lost their manly virtues, and when the Romans left them were an easy prey for the first comer. Our fathers could not foresee that the time would come when they too in turn would be invaded. Had they done so, methinks they would not have set up so broad a line of separation between themselves and the Britons, but would have admitted the latter to the rights of citizenship, in which case intermarriage would have taken place freely, and the whole people would have become amalgamated. The Britons, accustomed to our free institutions, and taking part in the wars between the various Saxon kingdoms, would have recovered their warlike virtues, and it would be as one people that we should resist the Danes. As it is, the serfs, who form by far the largest part of the population, are apathetic and cowardly; they view the struggle with indifference, for what signifies to them whether Dane or Saxon conquer; they have no interest in the struggle, nothing to lose or to gain, it is but a change of masters."

Edmund was silent. The very possibility of a state of things in which there should be no serfs, and when all men should be free and equal, had never occurred to him; but he had a deep respect for his father, who bore indeed the reputation of being one of the wisest and most clear-headed of the nobles of East Anglia, and it seemed to him that this strange and novel doctrine contained much truth in it. Still the idea was as strange to him as it would have been to the son of a southern planter in America half a century ago. The existence of slaves seemed as much a matter of course as that of horses or dogs, and although he had been accustomed to see from time to time freedom bestowed upon some favourite serf as a special reward for services, the thought of a general liberation of the slaves was strange and almost bewildering, and he lay awake puzzling over the problem long after his father and kinsman had fallen asleep.

CHAPTER II: THE BATTLE OF KESTEVEN

THE following morning early the little party started. The great chest was dug up from its place of concealment, and they resumed their ordinary dresses. The ealdorman attired himself in a white tunic with a broad purple band round the lower edge, with a short cloak of green cloth. This was fastened with a gold brooch at the neck; a necklet of the same metal and several gold bracelets completed his costume, except that he wore a flat cap and sandals. Edmund had a green tunic and cloak of deep red colour; while Egbert was dressed in yellow with a green cloak--the Saxons being extremely fond of bright colours.

All wore daggers, whose sheaths were incrusted in silver, in their belts, and the ealdorman and his kinsman carried short broad-bladed swords, while Edmund had his boar-spear. Eldred placed in the pouch which hung at his side a bag containing a number of silver cubes cut from a long bar and roughly stamped. The chest was then buried again in its place of concealment among the bushes near the hut, Edmund placed his bows and arrows in the boat--not that in which Edmund had fished, but the much larger and heavier craft which Eldred and Egbert had used-- and then the party, with the hound, took their places in it. The ealdorman and Egbert were provided with long poles, and with these they sent the little boat rapidly through the water.

After poling their way for some eight hours they reached the town of Norwich, to which the Danes had not yet penetrated; here, procuring what articles they needed, they proceeded on their journey to Croyland, making a great circuit to avoid the Danes at Thetford. The country was for the most part covered with thick forests, where the wild boar and deer roamed undisturbed by man, and where many wolves still lurked, although the number in the country had been greatly diminished by the energetic measures which King Egbert had taken for the destruction of these beasts. Their halting-places were for the most part at religious houses, which then served the purpose of inns for travellers, being freely opened to those whom necessity or pleasure might cause to journey. Everywhere they found the monks in a state of alarm at the progress of the Danes, who, wherever they went, destroyed the churches and religious houses, and slew the monks.

Eldred was everywhere received with marked honour; being known as a wise and valiant noble, his opinions on the chances of the situation were eagerly listened to, and he found the monks at all their halting-places prepared, if need be, to take up arms and fight the pagan invaders, as those of Mercia and Wessex had done in the preceding autumn. The travellers, on arriving at Croyland, were warmly welcomed.

"I heard, brother," the abbot said, "that you had bravely fought against the Danes near Thetford, and have been sorely anxious since the news came of the dispersal of your force."

"I have been in hiding," Eldred said, "hoping that a general effort would be made against the invaders. My own power was broken, since all my lands are in their hands. The people of East Anglia foolishly seem to suppose that, so long as the Danes remain quiet, the time has not come for action. They will repent their lethargy some day, for, as the Danes gather in strength, they will burst out over the surrounding country as a dammed-up river breaks its banks. No, brother, I regard East Anglia as lost so far as depends upon itself; its only hope is in the men of Kent and Wessex, whom we must now look upon as our champions, and who may yet stem the tide of invasion and drive back the Danes. This abbey of yours stands in a perilous position, being not far removed from the Humber, where so many of the Danes find entrance to England."

"It is not without danger, Eldred, but the men of the fens are numerous, hardy and brave, and will offer a tough resistance to any who may venture to march hitherward, and if, as I hope, you will stay with us, and will undertake their command, we may yet for a long time keep the Danes from our doors."

For some weeks the time passed quietly. Edmund spent most of his time in hunting, being generally accompanied by Egbert. The Saxon was an exceedingly tall and powerful man, slow and scanty of speech, who had earned for himself the title of Egbert the Silent. He was devoted to his kinsmen and regarded himself as special guardian of Edmund. He had instructed him in the use of arms, and always accompanied him when he went out to hunt the boar, standing ever by his side to aid him to receive the rush of the wounded and furious beasts; and more than once, when Edmund had been borne down by their onslaughts, and would have been severely wounded, if not killed, a sweeping blow of Egbert's sword had rid him of his assailant.

Sometimes Edmund made excursions in the fens, where with nets and snares he caught the fish which swarmed in the sluggish waters; or, having covered his boat with a leafy bower until it resembled a floating bush, drifted close to the flocks of wild-fowl, and with his bow and arrows obtained many a plump wild duck. Smaller birds were caught in snares or traps, or with bird-lime smeared on twigs. Eldred seldom joined his son in his hunting excursions, as he was busied with his brother the abbot in concerting the measures of defence and in organizing a band of messengers, who, on the first warning of danger, could be despatched throughout the fens to call in the fisher population to the defence of the abbey.

It was on the 18th of September, 870, that a messenger arrived at the abbey and craved instant speech with the prior. The latter, who was closeted with his brother, ordered the man to be admitted.

"I come," he said, "from Algar the ealdorman. He bids me tell you that a great Danish host has landed from the Humber at Lindsay. The rich monastery of Bardenay has been pillaged and burned. Algar is assembling all the inhabitants of the marsh lands to give them battle, and he prays you to send what help you can spare, for assuredly they will march hither should he be defeated."

"Return to the ealdorman," the abbot said; "tell him that every lay brother and monk who can bear arms shall march hence to join him under the command of lay brother Toley, whose deeds of arms against the Danes in Mercia are well known to him. My brother here, Eldred, will head all the inhabitants of the marshes of this neighbourhood. With these and the brothers of the abbey, in all, as I reckon, nigh four hundred men, he will to-morrow march to join Algar."

Messengers were at once sent off through the surrounding country bidding every man assemble on the morrow morning at Croyland, and soon after daybreak they began to arrive. Some were armed with swords, some with long sickles, used in cutting rushes, tied to poles, some had fastened long pieces of iron to oars to serve as pikes. They were a rough and somewhat ragged throng, but Eldred saw with satisfaction that they were a hard and sturdy set of men, accustomed to fatigue and likely to stand firm in the hour of battle.

Most of them carried shields made of platted osiers covered with skin. The armoury of the abbey was well supplied, and swords and axes were distributed among the worst armed of the fenmen. Then, with but little order or regularity, but with firm and cheerful countenances, as men determined to win or die, the band moved off under Eldred's command, followed by the contingent of the abbey, eighty strong, under lay brother Toley.

A sturdy band were these monks, well fed and vigorous. They knew that they had no mercy to expect from the Danes, and, regarding them as pagans and enemies of their religion as well as of their country, could be trusted to do their utmost. Late that evening they joined Algar at the place they had appointed, and found that a large number of the people of the marshes had gathered round his banner.

The Danes had not moved as yet from Bardenay, and Algar determined to wait for another day or two before advancing, in order to give time to others farther from the scene of action to arrive.

The next day came the contingents from several other priories and abbeys, and the sight of the considerable force gathered together gave heart and confidence to all. Algar, Eldred, and the other leaders, Morcar, Osgot, and Harding, moved about among the host, encouraging them with cheering words, warning them to be in no way intimidated by the fierce appearance of the Danes, but to hold steadfast and firm in the ranks, and to yield no foot of ground to the onslaught of the enemy. Many priests had accompanied the contingents from the religious houses, and these added their exhortations to those of the leaders, telling the men that God would assuredly fight on their side against the heathen, and bidding each man remember that defeat meant the destruction of their churches and altars, the overthrow of their whole religion, and the restored worship of the pagan gods.

Edmund went about among the gathering taking great interest in the wild scene, for these marsh men differed much in their appearance from the settled inhabitants of his father's lands. The scenes in the camp were indeed varied in their character. Here and there were harpers with groups of listeners gathered round, as they sung the exploits of their fathers, and animated their hearers to fresh fire and energy by relating legends of the cruelty of the merciless Danes. Other groups there were surrounding the priests, who were appealing to their religious feelings as well as to their patriotism.

Men sat about sharpening their weapons, fixing on more firmly the handles of their shields, adjusting arrows to bowstrings, and preparing in other ways for the coming fight. From some of the fires, round which the marsh men were sitting, came snatches of boisterous song, while here and there, apart from the crowd, priests were hearing confessions, and shriving penitents.

The next morning early, one of the scouts, who had been sent to observe the movements of the Danes, reported that these were issuing from their camp, and advancing into the country.

Algar marshalled his host, each part under its leaders, and moved to meet them. Near Kesteven the armies came in sight of each other, and after advancing until but a short distance apart both halted to marshal their ranks anew. Eldred, with the men of the marshes near Croyland and the contingent from the abbey, had their post in the central division, which was commanded by Algar himself, Edmund took post by his father, and Egbert stood beside him.

Edmund had never before seen the Danes, and he could not but admit that their appearance was enough to shake the stoutest heart. All carried great shields covering them from head to foot. These were composed of wood, bark, or leather painted or embossed, and in the cases of the chiefs plated with gold and silver. So large were these that in naval encounters, if the fear of falling into the enemy's hands forced them to throw themselves into the sea, they could float on their shields; and after death in battle a soldier was carried to his grave on his buckler. As they stood facing the Saxons they locked their shields together so as to form a barrier well-nigh impregnable against the arrows.

All wore helmets, the common men of leather, the leaders of iron or copper, while many in addition wore coats of mail. Each carried a sword, a battle-axe, and a bow and arrows. Some of the swords were short and curled like a scimitar; others were long and straight, and were wielded with both hands. They wore their hair long and hanging down their shoulders, and for the most part shaved their cheeks and chins, but wore their moustaches very long.

They were, for the most, tall, lithe, and sinewy men, but physically in no way superior to the Saxons, from whom they differed very widely in complexion, the

Saxons being fair while the Danes were very dark, as much so as modern gypsies; indeed, the Saxon historians speak of them as the black pagans. Upon the other hand many of the Northmen, being Scandinavians, were as fair as the Saxons themselves.

The Danes began the battle, those in front shouting fiercely, and striking their swords on their shields with a clashing noise, while the ranks behind shot a shower of arrows among the Saxons. These at once replied. The combat was not continued long at a distance, for the Danes with a mighty shout rushed upon the Saxons. These stood their ground firmly and a desperate conflict ensued. The Saxon chiefs vied with each other in acts of bravery, and singling out the leaders of the Danes engaged with them in hand-to-hand conflict.

Algar had placed his swordsmen in the front line, those armed with spears in the second; and as the swordsmen battled with the Danes the spearmen, when they saw a shield uplifted to guard the head, thrust under with their weapons and slew many. Edmund, seeing that with his sword he should have but little chance against these fierce soldiers, fell a little behind his father and kinsman, and as these were engaged with the enemy he from time to time, when he saw an opportunity, rushed in and delivered a thrust with his spear at an unguarded point. The Saxon shouts rose louder and louder as the Danes in vain endeavoured to break through their line. The monks fought stoutly, and many a fierce Norseman fell before their blows.

The Danes, who had not expected so firm a resistance, began to hesitate, and Algar giving the word, the Saxons took the offensive, and the line pressed forward step by step. The archers poured their arrows in a storm among the Danish ranks. These fell back before the onslaught. Already three of their kings and many of their principal leaders had fallen, and at last, finding themselves unable to withstand the impetuous onslaught of the Saxons, they turned and fled in confusion towards their camp. The Saxons with exulting shouts pursued them, and great numbers were slaughtered. The Danes had, however, as was their custom, fortified the camp before advancing, and Algar drew off his troops, deeming that it would be better to defer the attack on this position until the following day.

There was high feasting in the Saxon camp that evening, but this was brought to an abrupt conclusion by the arrival of a scout, who reported that a great Danish army marching from the Humber was approaching the camp of the compatriots. The news was but too true. The kings Guthorn, Bergsecg, Oskytal, Halfdene, and Amund, and the Jarls Frene, Hingwar, Hubba, and the two Sidrocs, with all their followers, had marched down from Yorkshire to join the invaders who had just landed.

The news of this immense reinforcement spread consternation among the Angles. In vain their leaders went about among them and exhorted them to courage, promising them another victory as decisive as that they had won that day. Their entreaties were in vain, for when the morning dawned it was found that three-fourths of their number had left the camp during the night, and had made off to the marshes and fastnesses.

A council of the chiefs was held. The chances of conflict appeared hopeless, so vastly were they out-numbered by the Danes. Algar, however, declared that he would die rather than retreat.

"If we fly now," he said, "all East Anglia will fall into the hands of the heathen. Even should we fight and fall, the example of what a handful of brave men can do against the invaders will surely animate the Angles to further resistance; while if we conquer, so great a blow will be dealt to the renown of these Danes that all England will rise against them."

On hearing these words all the chiefs came to the determination to win or die as they stood. Eldred took Edmund aside after this determination had been arrived at.

"My son," he said, "I allowed you yesterday to stand by my side in battle, and well and worthily did you bear yourself, but to-day you must withdraw. The fight is well-nigh hopeless, and I believe that all who take part in it are doomed to perish. I would not that my house should altogether disappear, and shall die more cheerfully in the hope that some day you will avenge me upon these heathen. Therefore, Edmund, I bid you take station at a distance behind the battle, so that when you see the day goes against us you may escape in time. I shall urge our faithful Egbert to endeavour, when he sees that all is lost, to make his way from the fight and rejoin you, and to journey with you to Wessex and there present you to the king. For myself, if the battle is lost I shall die rather than fly. Such is the resolution of Algar and our other brave chiefs, and Eldred the ealdorman must not be the only one of the leaders to run from the fray."

Edmund was deeply touched at his father's words, but the parental rule was so strict in those days that it did not even enter his mind to protest against Eldred's decision.

As the morning went on the Danes were engaged in the funeral ceremonies of their dead kings, while the Saxons, quiet and resolute, received the holy sacrament and prepared for the fight. Algar chose a position on rising ground. He himself with Eldred commanded the centre, Toley and Morcar led the right wing, Osgot and Harding the left.

Each of these wings contained about five hundred men. Algar's centre, which was a little withdrawn from its wings, contained about 200 of his best warriors, and was designed as a reserve, with which, if need be, he could move to the assistance of either of the wings which might be sorely pressed and in danger. The Saxons formed in a solid mass with their bucklers linked together. The Danish array which issued out from their camp was vastly superior in numbers, and was commanded by four kings and eight jarls or earls, while two kings and four earls remained in charge of the camp, and of the great crowd of prisoners, for the most part women and children, whom they had brought with them.

With the Danes who had come down from Yorkshire were a large body of horsemen, who charged furiously down upon the Saxons; but these maintained so firm an array with their lances and spears projecting outward that the Danes failed to break through them, and after making repeated efforts and suffering heavy loss they drew back. Then the Danish archers and slingers poured in a storm of missiles, but these effected but little harm, as the Saxons stooped a little behind their closely packed line of bucklers, which were stout enough to keep out the shower of arrows. All day the struggle continued. Again and again the Danes strove to break the solid Saxon array, and with sword and battle-axe attempted to hew down the hedge of spears, but in vain. At last their leaders, convinced that they could not overcome the obstinacy of the resistance, ordered their followers to feign a retreat.

As the Danes turned to fly the Saxons set up a triumphant shout, and breaking up their solid phalanx rushed after them in complete disorder. In vain Algar, Osgot, Toley, Eldred, and the other leaders shouted to them to stand firm. Weary of their long inactivity, and convinced that the Danes were routed, the Saxons pursued them across the plain. Suddenly the Danish horse, who after failing to break through the ranks had remained apart at a short distance from the conflict, dashed down upon the disordered Saxons, while the flying infantry turning round also fell upon them with exulting shouts.

Taken wholly by surprise, confused and disordered, the Saxons could offer no effectual opposition to the charge. The Danish horse rode among them hewing and slaying, and the swords and battle-axes of the footmen completed the work. In a few minutes of all the Saxon band which had for so many hours successfully resisted the onslaught of the Danes, not one survived save a few fleet-footed young men who, throwing away their arms, succeeded in making their escape, and a little group, consisting of Algar, Toley, Eldred, and the other leaders who had gathered together when their men broke their ranks and had taken up their position on a knoll of ground rising above the plain. Here for a long time they resisted the efforts of the whole of the Danes, surrounding themselves with a heap of slain; but at length one by one they succumbed to the Danish onslaught, each fighting valiantly to the last.

From his position at a distance Edmund watched the last desperate struggle. With streaming eyes and a heart torn by anxiety for his father he could see the Danish foe swarming round the little band who defended the crest. These were lost from his sight, and only the flashing of swords showed where the struggle was still going on in the centre of the confused mass. Edmund had been on his knees for some time, but he now rose.

"Come, old boy," he said to the hound, who lay beside him watching the distant conflict and occasionally uttering deep angry growls. "I must obey my father's last command; let us away."

He took one more glance at the distant conflict before turning. It was plain that it was nearly finished. The swords had well-nigh ceased to rise and fall when he saw a sudden movement in the throng of Danes and suddenly a man burst out from them and started at headlong speed towards him, pursued by a number of Danes. Even at that distance Edmund thought that he recognized the tall figure of his kinsman, but he had no time to assure himself of this, and he at once, accompanied by the hound, set off at the top of his speed from the field of battle. He had fully a quarter of a mile start, and being active and hardy and accustomed to exercise from his childhood, he had no fear that the Danes would overtake him. Still he ran his hardest.

Looking over his shoulder from time to time he saw that at first the Danes who were pursuing the fugitive were gaining upon him also, but after a time he again increased the distance, while, being unencumbered with shield or heavy weapons, the fugitive kept the advantage he had at first gained. Three miles from the battle-field Edmund reached the edge of a wide-spreading wood. Looking round as he entered its shelter he saw that the flying Saxon was still about a quarter of a mile behind him, and that the Danes, despairing of over-taking him, had ceased their pursuit. Edmund therefore checked his footsteps and awaited the arrival of the fugitive, who he now felt certain was his kinsman.

In a few minutes Egbert came up, having slackened his speed considerably when he saw that he was no longer pursued. He was bleeding from several wounds, and now that the necessity for exertion had passed he walked but feebly along. Without a word he flung himself on the ground by Edmund and buried his face in his arms, and the lad could see by the shaking of his broad shoulders that he was weeping bitterly. The great hound walked up to the prostrate figure and gave vent to a long and piteous howl, and then lying down by Egbert's side placed his head on his shoulder.

CHAPTER III: THE MASSACRE AT CROYLAND

EDMUND wept sorely for some time, for he knew that his kinsman's agitation could be only caused by the death of his father. At last he approached Egbert.

"My brave kinsman," he said, "I need ask you no questions, for I know but too well that my dear father has fallen; but rouse yourself, I pray you; let me bandage your wounds, which bleed fast, for you will want all your strength, and we must needs pursue our way well into the forest, for with to-morrow's dawn the Danes will scatter over the whole country."

"Yes," Egbert said, turning round and sitting up, "I must not in my grief forget my mission, and in truth I am faint with loss of blood. It was well the Danes stopped when they did, for I felt my strength failing me, and could have held out but little further. Yes, Edmund," he continued, as the lad, tearing strips from his garments, proceeded to bandage his wounds, "your father is dead. Nobly, indeed, did he fight; nobly did he die, with a circle of dead Danes around him. He, Algar, Toley, and myself were the last four to resist. Back to back we stood, and many were the Danes who fell before our blows. Toley fell first and then Algar. The Danes closed closer around us. Still we fought on, till your father was beaten to his knee, and then he cried to me, 'Fly, Egbert, to my son.' Then I flung myself upon the Danes like a wild boar upon the dogs, and with the suddenness of my rush and the heavy blows of my battle-axe cut a way for myself through them. It was well-nigh a miracle, and I could scarce believe it when I was free. I flung away my shield and helmet as soon as I had well begun to run, for I felt the blood gushing out from a dozen wounds, and knew that I should want all my strength. I soon caught sight of you running ahead of me. Had I found we were gaining upon you I should have turned off and made another way to lead the Danes aside, but I soon saw that you were holding your own, and so followed straight on. My knees trembled, and I felt my strength was well-nigh gone, when, looking round, I found the Danes had desisted from their pursuit. I grieve, Edmund, that I should have left the battle alive when all the others have died bravely, for, save a few fleet-footed youths, I believe that not a single Saxon has escaped the fight; but your father had laid his commands upon me, and I was forced to obey, though God knows I would rather have died with the heroes on that field."

"'Tis well for me that you did not, my good Egbert," Edmund said, drying his eyes, "for what should I have done in this troubled land without one protector?"

"It was the thought of that," Egbert said, "that seemed to give me strength as I dashed at the Danes. And now, methinks, I am strong enough to walk again. Let us make our way far into the forest, then we must rest for the night. A few hours' sleep will make a fresh man of me, and to-morrow morning we will go to Croyland and see what the good abbot your uncle proposes to do, then will we to the hut where we dwelt before coming hither. We will dig up the chest and take out such valuables as we can carry, and then make for Wessex. After this day's work I have no longer any hope that East Anglia will successfully oppose the Danes. And yet the Angles fought well, and for every one of them who has fallen in these two days' fighting at least four Danes must have perished. Have you food, Edmund, for in truth after such a day's work I would not lie down supperless?"

"I have in my pouch here, Egbert, some cakes, which I cooked this morning, and a capon which one of the monks of Croyland gave me. I was tempted to throw it away as I ran."

"I am right glad, Edmund, that the temptation was not too strong for you. If we can find a spring we shall do well."

It was now getting dark, but after an hour's walk through the forest they came upon a running stream. They lit a fire by its side, and sitting down ate the supper, of which both were in much need. Wolf shared the repast, and then the three lay down to sleep. Egbert, overcome by the immense exertions he had made during the fight, was soon asleep; but Edmund, who had done his best to keep a brave face before his kinsman, wept for hours over the loss of his gallant father.

On the following morning Egbert and Edmund started for Croyland. The news of the defeat at Kesteven had already reached the abbey, and terror and consternation reigned there. Edmund went at once to his uncle and informed him of the circumstance of the death of his father and the annihilation of the Saxon army.

"Your news, Edmund, is even worse than the rumours which had reached me, and deeply do I grieve for the loss of my brave brother and of the many valiant men who died with him. This evening or to-morrow the spoilers will be here, and doubtless will do to Croyland as they have done to all the other abbeys and monasteries which have fallen into their hands. Before they come you and Egbert must be far away. Have you bethought you whither you will betake yourselves?"

"We are going to the king of the West Saxons," Edmund replied. "Such was my father's intention, and I fear that all is now lost in East Anglia."

"'Tis your best course, and may God's blessing and protection rest upon you!"

"But what are you going to do, uncle? Surely you will not remain here until the Danes arrive, for though they may spare other men they have no mercy on priests and monks?"

"I shall assuredly remain here, Edmund, at my post, and as my brother Eldred and Earl Algar and their brave companions died at their posts in the field of battle, so I am prepared to die here where God has placed me. I shall retain here with me only a few of the most aged and infirm monks, too old to fly or to support the hardships of the life of a hunted fugitive in the fens; together with some of the children who have fled here, and who, too, could not support such a life. It may be that when the fierce Danes arrive and find nought but children and aged men even their savage breasts may be moved to pity; but if not, God's will be done. The younger brethren will seek refuge in the fens, and will carry with them the sacred relics of the monastery. The most holy body of St. Guthlac with his scourge and psalmistry, together with the most valuable jewels and muniments, the charters of the foundation of the abbey, given by King Ethelbald, and the confirmation thereof by other kings, with some of the most precious gifts presented to the abbey."

Edmund and Egbert set to work to assist the weeping monks in making preparations for their departure. A boat was laden with the relics of the saints, the muniments of the king, and the most precious vessels. The table of the great altar covered with plates of gold, which King Wichtlof had presented, with ten gold chalices, and many other vessels, was thrown into the well of the convent.

In the distance the smoke of several villages could now be seen rising over the plain, and it was clear that the Danes were approaching. The ten priests and twenty monks who were to leave now knelt, and received the solemn benediction of the abbot, then, with Edmund and Egbert, they took their places in the boat and rowed away to the wood of Ancarig, which lay not far from the abbey.

The abbot Theodore and the aged monks and priests now returned to the church, and, putting on their vestments, commenced the services of the day; the abbot himself celebrated high mass, assisted by brother Elfget the deacon, brother Savin the sub-deacon, and the brothers Egelred and Wyelric, youths who acted as taper-bearers. When the mass was finished, just as the abbot and his assistants had partaken of the holy communion, the Danes burst into the church. The abbot was slain upon the holy altar by the hand of the Danish king Oskytal, and the other priests and monks were beheaded by the executioner.

The old men and children in the choir were seized and tortured to disclose where the treasures of the abbey were concealed, and were also put to death with the prior and sub-prior. Turgar, an acolyte of ten years of age; a remarkably beautiful boy, stood by the side of the sub-prior as he was murdered and fearlessly confronted the Danes, and bade them put him to death with the holy father. The young Earl Sidroc, however, struck with the bearing of the child, and being moved with compassion, stripped him of his robe and cowl, and threw over him a long Danish tunic without sleeves, and ordering him to keep close by him, made his way out of the monastery, the boy being the only one who was saved from the general massacre.

The Danes, furious at being able to find none of the treasures of the monastery, broke open all the shrines and levelled the marble tombs, including those of St. Guthlac, the holy virgin Ethelbritha, and many others, but found in these none of the treasure searched for. They piled the bodies of the saints in a heap, and burned them, together with the church and all the buildings of the monastery; then, with vast herds of cattle and other plunder, they moved away from Croyland, and attacked the monastery of Medeshamsted. Here the monks made a brave resistance. The Danes brought up machines and attacked the monastery on all sides, and effected a breach in the walls. Their first assault, however, was repelled, and Fulba, the brother of Earl Hulba, was desperately wounded by a stone.

Hulba was so infuriated at this that when, at the second assault, the monastery was captured, he slew with his own hand everyone of the monks, while all the country people who had taken refuge within the walls were slaughtered by his companions, not one escaping. The altars were levelled to the ground, the monuments broken in pieces. The great library of parchments and charters was burnt. The holy relics were trodden under foot, and the church itself, with all the monastic buildings, burnt to the ground. Four days later, the Danes, having devastated the whole country round and collected an enormous booty, marched away against Huntingdon.

Edmund and Egbert remained but a few hours with the monks who had escaped from the sack of Croyland; for, as soon as they saw the flames mounting up above the church, they knew that the Danes had accomplished their usual work of massacre, and there being no use in their making further stay, they started upon their journey. They travelled by easy stages, for time was of no value to them. For the most part their way lay among forests, and when once they had passed south of Thetford they had no fear of meeting with the Danes. Sometimes they slept at farm-houses or villages, being everywhere hospitably received, the more so when it was known that Edmund was the son of the brave ealdorman Eldred; but the news which they brought of the disastrous battle of Kesteven, and the southward march of the great Danish army, filled everyone with consternation.

The maids and matrons wept with terror at the thought of the coming of these terrible heathen, and although the men everywhere spoke of resistance to the last, the prospect seemed so hopeless that even the bravest were filled with grief and despair. Many spoke of leaving their homes and retiring with their wives and families, their serfs and herds to the country of the West Saxons, where alone there appeared any hope of a successful resistance being made. Wherever they went Edmund and Egbert brought by their news lamentation and woe to the households they entered, and at last Edmund said:

"Egbert, let us enter no more houses until we reach the end of our journey; wherever we go we are messengers of evil, and turn houses of feasting into abodes of grief. Every night we have the same sad story to tell, and have to witness the weeping and wailing of women. A thousand times better were it to sleep among the woods, at any rate until we are among the West Saxons, where our news may cause indignation and rage at least, but where it will arouse a brave resolve to resist to the last instead of the hopelessness of despair."

Egbert thoroughly agreed with the lad, and henceforth they entered no houses save to buy bread and mead. Of meat they had plenty, for as they passed through the forests Wolf was always upon the alert, and several times found a wild boar in his lair, and kept him at bay until Edmund and Egbert ran up and with spears and swords slew him. This supplied them amply with meat, and gave them indeed far more than they could eat, but they exchanged portions of the flesh for bread in the villages. At last they came down upon the Thames near London, and crossing the river journeyed west. They were now in the kingdom of the West Saxons, the most warlike and valiant of the peoples of England, and who had gradually extended their sway over the whole of the country. The union was indeed but little more than nominal, as the other kings retained their thrones, paying only a tribute to the West Saxon monarchs.

As Egbert had predicted, their tale of the battle of Kesteven here aroused no feeling save that of wrath and a desire for vengeance upon the Danes. Swords were grasped, and all swore by the saints of what should happen to the invaders should they set foot in Wessex. The travellers felt their spirits rise at the martial and determined aspect of the people.

"It is a sad pity," Egbert said to Edmund one day, "that these West Saxons had not had time to unite England firmly together before the Danes set foot on the island. It is our divisions which have rendered their task so far easy. Northumbria, Mercia, and East Anglia have one by one been invaded, and their kings have had to fight single-handed against them, whereas had one strong king reigned over the whole country, so that all our force could have been exerted against the invader wherever he might land, the Danes would never have won a foot of our soil. The sad day of Kesteven showed at least that we are able to fight the Danes man for man. The first day we beat them, though they were in superior numbers, the second we withstood them all day, although they were ten to one against us, and they would never have triumphed even then had our men listened to their leaders and kept their ranks. I do not believe that even the West Saxons could have fought more bravely than did our men on that day; but they are better organized, their king is energetic and determined, and when the Danes invade Wessex they will find themselves opposed by the whole people instead of merely a hastily raised assemblage gathered in the neighbourhood."

They presently approached Reading, where there was a royal fortress, in which King Ethelred and his brother Alfred were residing.

"It is truly a fine city," Edmund said as he approached it; "its walls are strong and high, and the royal palace, which rises above them, is indeed a stately building."

They crossed the river and entered the gates of the town. There was great bustle and traffic in the streets, cynings, or nobles, passed along accompanied by parties of thanes, serfs laden with fuel or provisions made their way in from the surrounding country, while freemen, with their shields flung across their shoulders and their swords by their sides, stalked with an independent air down the streets.

The travellers approached the royal residence. The gates were open, and none hindered their entrance, for all who had business were free to enter the royal presence and to lay their complaints or petitions before the king.

Entering they found themselves in a large hall. The lower end of this was occupied by many people, who conversed together in little groups or awaited the summons of the king. Across the upper end of the room was a raised dais, and in the centre of this was a wide chair capable of holding three persons. The back and sides were high and richly carved. A table supported by four carved and gilded legs stood before it. Two persons were seated in the chair.

One was a man of three or four and twenty, the other was his junior by some two years. Both wore light crowns of gold somewhat different in their fashion. Before the younger was a parchment, an inkhorn, and pens. King Ethelred was a man of a pleasant face, but marked by care and by long vigils and rigorous fastings. Alfred was a singularly handsome young prince, with an earnest and intellectual face. Both had their faces shaven smooth. Ethelred wore his hair parted in the middle, and falling low on each side of the face, but Alfred's was closely cut. On the table near the younger brother stood a silver harp.

Edmund looked with great curiosity and interest on the young prince, who was famous throughout England for his great learning, his wisdom, and sweetness of temper. Although the youngest of the king's brothers, he had always been regarded as the future King of England, and had his father survived until he reached the age of manhood, he would probably have succeeded directly to the throne. The law of primogeniture was by no means strictly observed among the Saxons, a younger brother of marked ability or of distinguished prowess in war being often chosen by a father to succeed him in place of his elder brothers.

Alfred had been his father's favourite son. He had when a child been consecrated by the pope as future King of England; and his two journeys to Rome, and his residence at the court of the Frankish king had, with his own great learning and study, given him a high prestige and reputation among his people as one learned in the ways of the world. Although but a prince, his authority in the kingdom nearly equalled that of his brother, and it was he rather than Ethelred whom men regarded as the prop and stay of the Saxons in the perils which were now threatening them.

One after another, persons advanced to the table and laid their complaints before the king; in cases of dispute both parties were present and were often accompanied by witnesses. Ethelred and Alfred listened attentively to all that was said on both sides, and then gave their judgment. An hour passed, and then seeing that no one else approached the table, Egbert, taking Edmund by the hand, led him forward and knelt before the royal table.

"Whom have we here?" the king said. "This youth is by his attire one of noble race, but I know not his face."

"We have come, sir king," Egbert said, "as fugitives and suppliants to you. This is Edmund, the son of Ealdorman Eldred, a valiant cyning of East Anglia, who, after fighting bravely against the Danes near Thetford, joined Earl Algar, and died by his side on the fatal field of Kesteven. He had himself purposed to come hither to you and to ask you to accept him as your thane, and on the morn of the battle he charged me if he fell to bring hither his son to you; and we pray you to accept, in token of our homage to you, these vessels."

And here he placed two handsome goblets of silver gilt upon the table.

"I pray you rise," the king said. "I have assuredly heard of the brave Eldred, and will gladly receive his son as my thane. I had not heard of Eldred's death, though two days since the rumour of a heavy defeat of the East Angles at Kesteven, and the sacrilegious destruction of the holy houses of Bardenay, Croyland, and Medesham-sted reached our ears. Were you present at the battle?"

"I was, sir king," Egbert said, "and fought beside Earl Algar and my kinsman the Ealdorman Eldred until both were slain by the Danes, and I with difficulty cut my way through them and escaped to carry out my kinsman's orders regarding his son."

"You are a stout champion yourself," the king said, regarding with admiration Egbert's huge proportions; "but tell us the story of this battle, of which at present but vague rumours have reached us." Egbert related the incidents of the battle of Kesteven. "It was bravely fought," the king said when he had concluded; "right well and bravely, and better fortune should have attended such valour. Truly the brave Algar has shown that we Saxons have not lost the bravery which distinguished our ancestors, and that, man for man, we are equal to these heathen Danes."

"But methinks," Prince Alfred said, "that the brave Algar and his valiant companions did wrong to throw away their lives when all was lost. So long as there is the remotest chance of victory it is the duty of a leader to set an example of valour to his followers, but when all is lost he should think of his country. What though the brave thanes slew each a score of Danes before they died, their death has left their countrymen without a leader, and by that one battle the Danes have made themselves masters of the north of East Anglia. Better far had they, when the day was lost, retreated, to gather the people together when a better opportunity presented itself, and again to make head against the invaders. It is heathen rather than Christian warfare thus to throw away their lives rather than to retreat and wait for God's time to come again. To stake all on one throw, which if lost loses a whole people, seems to me the act of a gamester. I trust that, should the time ever come, as it is too much to be feared it will ere long, that the Danes invade my brother's kingdom of Wessex, I shall not be found wanting in courage; but assuredly when defeated in battle I would not throw away my life, for that belongs to our people rather than to myself, but would retire to some refuge until I could again gather the Saxons around me and attack the invaders. I like the face of the young ealdorman, and doubt not that he will prove a valiant warrior like his father. My brother will doubtless assign him lands for his maintenance and yours; but if he will let me I will attach him to my person, and will be at once a master and a friend to him. Wouldst thou like this, young Edmund?"

The lad, greatly pleased at the young prince's kindness of speech and manner, replied enthusiastically that he would follow him to the death if he would accept him as his faithful thane.

"Had the times been more peaceful, Edmund," Alfred said, "I would fain have imparted to you some of the little knowledge that I have gained, for I see an intelligence in your face which tells me that you would have proved an apt and eager pupil; but, alas, in the days that are coming it is the sword rather than the book which will prevail, and the cares of state, and the defence of the country, will shortly engross all my time and leave me but little leisure for the studies I love so well."

"There are the lands," the king said, "of Eabald, Ealdorman of Sherborne, in Dorset. He died but last week and has left no children. These lands I will grant to Edmund in return for liege and true service." The lad knelt before the king, and, kissing his hand, swore to be his true and faithful thane, and to spend land, goods, and life in his service.

"And now," the king said, "since the audience is over, and none other comes before us with petitions, we will retire to our private apartments, and there my brother Alfred will present you to the fair Elswitha, his wife."

The room into which Egbert and Edmund followed the king and his brother was spacious and lofty. The walls were covered with hangings of red cloth, and a thick brown baize covered the floor. The ceiling was painted a dark brown with much gilding. Round the sides of the room stood several dressers of carved oak, upon which stood gold and silver cups.

On a table were several illuminated vellums. At Croyland Edmund had seen a civilization far in advance of that to which he had been accustomed in his father's abode; but he saw here a degree of luxury and splendour which surprised him. Alfred had, during his two visits to Rome, learned to appreciate the high degree of civilization which reigned there, and many of the articles of furniture and other objects which met Edmund's eye he had brought with him on his return with his father from that city.

Across the upper end of the room was a long table laid with a white cloth. Elswitha was sitting in a large gilded chair by the great fire which was blazing on the hearth.

Prince Alfred presented Edmund and Egbert to her. Elswitha was well acquainted with the Ealdorman Eldred, as his lands lay on the very border of her native Mercia, and she received the lad and his kinsman with great kindness. In a short time they took their places at table. First the attendance brought in bowls containing broth, which they presented, kneeling, to each of those at table. The broth was drunk from the bowl itself; then a silver goblet was placed by each diner, and was filled with wine. Fish was next served. Plates were placed before each; but instead of their cutting food with their own daggers, as Edmund had been accustomed to see in his father's house, knives were handed round. After the fish came venison, followed by wild boar, chickens, and other meats. After these confections, composed chiefly of honey, were placed on the table. The king and Prince Alfred pledged their guests when they drank. No forks were used, the meat as cut being taken up by pieces of bread to the mouth. During the meal a harper played and sung.

Edmund observed the decorum with which his royal hosts fed, and the care which they took to avoid dipping their fingers into their saucers or their plates. He was also struck with the small amount of wine which they took; for the Saxons in general were large feeders, and drank heavily at their meals.

When the dinner was over a page brought round a basin of warm water, in which lavender had been crushed, and each dipped his fingers in this and then dried them on the cloth. Then at Prince Alfred's request Egbert again related in full the details of the two days' desperate struggle at Kesteven, giving the most minute particulars of the Danes' method of fighting. Egbert and Edmund then retired to the royal guest-house adjoining the palace, where apartments were assigned to them.

After remaining for a week at Reading they took leave of the king and started for the lands which he had assigned to Edmund. They were accompanied by an officer of the royal household, who was to inform the freemen and serfs of the estate that by the king's pleasure Edmund had been appointed ealdorman of the lands. They found on arrival that the house had been newly built, and was large and comfortable. The thanes of the district speedily came in to pay their respects to their new ealdorman, and although surprised to find him so young, they were pleased with his bearing and manner, and knowing that he came of good fighting blood doubted not that in time he would make a valiant leader. All who came were hospitably entertained, and for many days there was high feasting. So far removed was this part of England from the district which the Danes had invaded, that at present but slight alarm had been caused by them; but Edmund and his kinsman lost no time in impressing upon them the greatness of the coming danger.

"You may be sure," he said, "that ere long we shall see their galleys on the coast.

When they have eaten up Mercia and Anglia they will assuredly come hither, and we shall have to fight for our lives, and unless we are prepared it will go hard with us."

After he had been at his new residence for a month Edmund sent out messengers to all the thanes in his district requesting them to assemble at a council, and then formally laid the matter before them.

"It is, above all things," he said, "necessary that we should have some place where we can place the women and children in case of invasion and where we can ourselves retire in extreme necessity. Therefore I propose that we shall build a fort of sufficient size to contain all the inhabitants of the district, with many flocks and herds. My cousin Egbert has ridden far over the country, and recommends that the Roman fortification at Moorcaster shall be utilized. It is large in extent, and has a double circle of earthen banks. These differ from those which we are wont to build, since we Saxons always fill up the ground so as to be flat with the top of the earthen banks, while the Romans left theirs hollow. However, the space is so large that it would take a vast labour to fill it up, therefore I propose that we should merely thicken the banks, and should, in Saxon custom, build a wall with turrets upon them. The sloping banks alone would be but a small protection against the on-slaught of the Danes, but stone walls are another matter, and could only be carried after a long siege. If you fall in with my views you will each of you send half your serfs to carry out the work, and I will do the same, and will, moreover, pay fifty freemen who may do the squaring of the stones and the proper laying of them."

The proposal led to a long discussion, as some thought that there was no occasion as yet to take such a measure; but the thanes finally agreed to carry out Edmund's proposal.

CHAPTER IV: THE INVASION OF WESSEX

EDMUND and Egbert devoted most of their time to the building of the new fort, living very simply, and expended the whole of the revenues of the lands on the payment of the freemen and masons engaged upon the work. The Roman fort was a parallelogram, the sides being about 200 yards long, and the ends half that length. It was surrounded by two earthen banks with wide ditches. These were deepened considerably, and the slopes were cut down more sharply. The inner bank was widened until it was 15 feet across the top.

On this the wall was built. It was faced on both sides with square stones, the space between filled up with rubble and cement, the total thickness being 4 feet. The height of the wall was 8 feet, and at intervals of 30 yards apart towers were raised 10 feet above it, one of these being placed at either side of the entrance. Here the bank was cut away, and solid buttresses of masonry supported the high gates. The opening in the outer bank was not opposite to the gate in the inner, being fifty yards away, so that any who entered by it would have for that distance to follow the ditch between the two banks, exposed to the missiles of those on the wall before arriving at the inner gate.

Five hundred men laboured incessantly at the work. The stone for the walls was fortunately found close at hand, but, notwithstanding this, the work took nearly six months to execute; deep wells were sunk in the centre of the fort, and by this means an ample supply of water was secured, however large might be the number within it.

A very short time after the commencement of the work the news arrived that King Edmund of East Anglia had gathered his forces together and had met the Danes in a great battle near Thetford on Sunday the 20th of November, and had been totally defeated by them, Edmund himself having been taken prisoner. The captive king, after having been for a long time cruelly tortured by the Danes, was shot to death with arrows. It was not long after this that news came that the whole of East Anglia had fallen into the hands of the Danes.

Early in the month of February, 871, just as the walls of his fort had begun to rise, a messenger arrived from the king bidding Edmund assemble all the men in his earlship and march at once to join him near Devizes, as the news had come that a great Danish fleet had sailed up the Thames and had already captured the royal town of Reading.

Messengers were sent out in all directions, and early the next morning, 400 men having assembled, Edmund and his kinsman marched away with them towards Devizes. Upon their arrival at that town they found the king and his brother with 8000 men, and the following day the army moved east towards Reading.

They had not marched many miles before a messenger arrived saying that two of the Danish jarls with a great following had gone out to plunder the country, that they had been encountered by Aethelwulf, Earl of Berkshire, with his men at Englefield, and a fierce battle had taken place. The Saxons had gained the victory, and great numbers of the Danes had been slain, Sidroc, one of their jarls, being among the fallen.

Three days later the royal army arrived in sight of Reading, being joined on their march by Aethelwulf and his men. The Danes had thrown up a great rampart between the Thames and the Kennet, and many were still at work on this fortification. These were speedily slain by the Saxons, but their success was a short one. The main body of the invaders swarmed out from the city and a desperate engagement took place.

The Saxons fought valiantly, led by the king and Prince Alfred; but being wholly undisciplined and unaccustomed to war they were unable to withstand the onslaught of the Danes, who fought in better order, keeping together in ranks: after four hours' hard fighting the Saxons were compelled to fall back.

They rallied again a few miles from Reading. Ethelred and Alfred went among them bidding them be of good cheer, for that another time, when they fought in better order, they would gain the victory; and that their loss had not been greater than the Danes, only that unhappily the valiant Ealdorman Aethelwulf had been slain. Fresh messengers were sent throughout the country bidding all the men of Wessex to rally round their king, and on the fourth morning after the defeat Ethelred found himself at the head of larger forces than had fought with him in the last battle.

The Danes had moved out from Reading and had taken post at Ashdown, and as the Saxon army approached they were seen to be divided into two bodies, one of which was commanded by their two kings and the other by two jarls. The Saxons therefore made a similar division of their army, the king commanding one division and Prince Alfred the other.

Edmund with the men of Sherborne was in the division of Alfred. The Danes advanced to the attack and fell with fury upon them. It had been arranged that this division should not advance to the attack until that commanded by the king was also put in motion. For some time Alfred and his men supported the assaults of the Danes, and then, being hardly pressed, the prince sent a messenger to his brother to urge that a movement should be made. The Saxons were impatient at standing on the defensive, and Alfred saw that he must either allow them to charge the enemy or must retreat.

Presently the messenger returned saying that the king was in his tent hearing mass, and that he had given orders that no man should move or any should disturb him until mass was concluded. Alfred hesitated no longer; he formed his men into a solid body, and then, raising his battle cry, rushed upon the Danes. The battle was a furious one. The Danes were upon higher ground, their standard being planted by the side of a single thorn-tree which grew on the slopes of the hill. Towards this Alfred with his men fought their way.

The lesson of the previous battle had not been lost, the Saxons kept together in a solid body which made its way with irresistible weight through the ranks of the Danes. Still the latter closed in on all sides, and the fight was doubtful until the king, having finished his devotions, led his division into the battle. For a long time a desperate strife continued and great numbers on both sides were killed; but the Saxons, animated at once by love of their country and hatred of the invaders and by humiliation at their previous defeat, fought with such fury that the Danes began to give way. Then the Saxons pressed them still more hotly, and the invaders presently lost heart and fled in confusion, pursued in all directions by the exulting Saxons.

The Danish king Bergsecg and five jarls, the two Sidrocs, Osbearn, Frene, and Hareld, were slain, and many thousands of their followers. Great spoil of arms and armour fell into the hands of the victors.

Edmund had fought bravely in the battle at the head of his men. Egbert had kept beside him, and twice, when the lad had been smitten to his knees by the enemy, covered him with his shield and beat off the foe.

"You are over-young for such a fight as this, Edmund," he said when the Danes had taken to flight. "You will need another four or five years over your head before you can stand in battle against these fierce Northmen. They break down your guard by sheer weight; but you bore yourself gallantly, and I doubt not will yet be as famous a warrior as was your brave father."

Edmund did not join in the pursuit, being too much bruised and exhausted to do so; but Egbert with the men of Sherborne followed the flying Danes until nightfall.

"You have done well, my young ealdorman," Prince Alfred said to the lad after the battle. "I have been wishing much that you could be with me during the past month, but I heard that you were building a strong fort and deemed it better to let you continue your work undisturbed. When it is finished I trust that I shall have you often near me; but I fear that for a time we shall have but little space for peaceful pursuits, for the Danes are coming, as I hear, in great troops westward, and we shall have many battles to fight ere we clear the land of the them."

In those days a defeat, however severe, had not the same decisive effect as it has in modern warfare. There were no cannons to lose, no great stores to fall into the hands of the victors. The army was simply dispersed, and its component parts reassembled in the course of a day or two, ready, when reinforcements arrived, to renew the fight. Thus, decisive as was the victory of Ashdown, Prince Alfred saw that many such victories must be won, and a prolonged and exhausting struggle carried on before the tide of invasion would be finally hurled back from Wessex. The next few days were spent in making a fair distribution of the spoil and arms among the conquerors. Some of the thanes then returned home with their people; but the remainder, on the king's entreaty, agreed to march with him against the Danes, who after the battle had fallen back to Basing, where they had been joined by others coming from the coast. The royal army advanced against them, and fourteen days after the battle of Ashdown the struggle was renewed. The fight lasted for many hours, but towards nightfall the Saxons were compelled to retreat, moving off the field, however, in good order, so that no spoil fell into the hands of the Danes.

This check was a great disappointment to the Saxons, who after their late victory had hoped that they should speedily clear the kingdom of the Danes. These, indeed, taught prudence by the manner in which the West Saxons had fought, for a while refrained from plundering excursions. Two months later the Saxons were again called to arms. Somerled, a Danish chieftain, had again advanced to Reading, and had captured and burned the town. The king marched against him, and the two armies met at Merton. Here another desperate battle took place.

During the first part of the day the Saxons were victorious over both the divisions of the Danish army, but in the afternoon the latter received some reinforcements and renewed the fight. The Saxons, believing that the victory had been won, had fallen into disorder and were finally driven from the field. Great numbers were slain on both sides. Bishop Edmund and many Saxon nobles were killed, and King Ethelred so severely wounded that he expired a few days later, April 23rd, 871, having reigned for five years. He was buried at Wimbourne Minster, and Prince Alfred ascended the throne.

Ethelred was much regretted by his people, but the accession of Alfred increased their hopes of battling successfully against the Danes. Although wise and brave, King Ethelred had been scarcely the monarch for a warlike people in troubled times. Religious exercises occupied too large a share of his thoughts. His rule was kindly rather than strong, and his authority was but weak over his nobles. From Prince Alfred the Saxons hoped better things. From his boyhood he had been regarded with special interest and affection by the people, as his father had led them to regard him as their future king.

The fact that he had been personally consecrated by the pope appeared to invest him with a special authority. His immense superiority in learning over all his people greatly impressed them. Though gentle he was firm and resolute, prompt in action, daring in the field. Thus, then, although the people regretted King Ethelred, there was a general feeling of hope and joy when Alfred took his place on the throne. He had succeeded to the crown but a month when the Danes again advanced in great numbers. The want of success which had attended them in the last two battles had damped the spirit of the people, and it was with a very small force only that Alfred was able to advance against them.

The armies met near Wilton, where the Danes in vastly superior numbers were posted on a hill. King Alfred led his forces forward and fell upon the Danes, and so bravely did the Saxons fight that for some time the day went favourably for them. Gradually the Danes were driven from their post of vantage, and after some hours' fighting turned to fly; but, as at Merton and Kesteven, the impetuosity of the Saxons proved their ruin. Breaking their compact ranks they scattered in pursuit of the Danes, and these, seeing how small was the number of their pursuers, rallied and turned upon them, and the Saxons were driven from the field which they had so bravely won.

"Unless my brave Saxons learn order and discipline," the king said to Edmund and some of his nobles who gathered round him on the evening after the defeat, "our cause is assuredly lost. We have proved now in each battle that we are superior man to man to the Danes, but we throw away the fruits of victory by our impetuosity. The great Caesar, who wrote an account of his battles which I have read in Latin, described the order and discipline with which the Roman troops fought. They were always in heavy masses, and even after a battle the heavy-armed soldiers kept their ranks and did not scatter in pursuit of the enemy, leaving this task to the more lightly armed troops.

"Would that we had three or four years before us to teach our men discipline and order, but alas! there is no time for this. The Danes have fallen in great numbers in every fight, but they are ever receiving reinforcements and come on in fresh waves of invasion; while the Saxons, finding that all their efforts and valour seem to avail nothing, are beginning fast to lose heart. See how small a number assembled round my standard yesterday, and yet the war is but beginning. Truly the look-out is bad for England."

The king made strenuous efforts again to raise an army, but the people did not respond to his call. In addition to the battles which have been spoken of several others had been fought in different parts of Wessex by the ealdormen and their followers against bodies of invading Danes. In the space of one year the Saxons had engaged in eight pitched battles and in many skirmishes. Great numbers had been slain on both sides, but the Danes ever received fresh accessions of strength, and seemed to grow stronger and more numerous after every battle, while the Saxons were dwindling rapidly. Wide tracts of country had been devastated, the men slaughtered, and the women and children taken captives, and the people, utterly dispirited and depressed, no longer listened to the voices of their leaders, and refused again to peril their lives in a strife which seemed hopeless. Alfred therefore called his ealdormen together and proposed to them, that since the people would no longer fight, the sole means that remained to escape destruction was to offer to buy off the Danes.

The proposal was agreed to, for although none of them had any hope that the Danes would long keep any treaty they might make, yet even a little respite might give heart and spirit to the Saxons again. Accordingly negotiations were entered into with the Danes, and these, in consideration of a large money payment, agreed to retire from Wessex. The money was paid, the Danes retired from Reading, which they had used as their headquarters, and marched to London. King Burhred, the feeble King of Mercia, could do nothing to oppose them, and he too agreed to pay them a large annual tribute.

From the end of 872 till the autumn of 875 the country was comparatively quiet. Alfred ruled it wisely, and tried to repair the terrible damages the war had made. Edmund looked after his earldom, and grew into a powerful young man of nineteen years old.

King Alfred had not deceived himself for a moment as to the future. "The Danes," he said, "are still in England. East Anglia and Northumbria swarm with them. Had this army, after being bought off by us and my brother of Mercia, sailed across the seas and landed in France there would have been some hope for us, but their restless nature will not allow them to stay long in the parts which they have conquered.

"In Anglia King Guthrum has divided the land among his jarls, and there they seem disposed to settle down; but elsewhere they care not for the land, preferring to leave it in the hands of its former owners to till, and after to wring from the cultivators the fruits of the harvest; then, as the country becomes thoroughly impoverished, they must move elsewhere. Mercia they can overrun whensoever they choose, and after that there is nothing for them to do but to sweep down again upon Wessex, and with all the rest of England at their feet it is hopeless to think that we alone can withstand their united power."

"Then what, think you, must be the end of this?" Edmund asked.

"'Tis difficult to see the end," Alfred replied. "It would seem that our only hope of release from them is that when they have utterly eaten up and ravaged England they may turn their thoughts elsewhere. Already they are harrying the northern coasts of France, but there are richer prizes on the Mediterranean shores, and it may be that when England is no longer worth plundering they may sail away to Spain and Italy. We have acted foolishly in the way we have fought them. When they first began to arrive upon our coasts we should have laboured hard to build great fleets, so that we could go forth and meet them on the seas.

"Some, indeed, might have escaped our watch and landed, but the fleets could have cut off reinforcements coming to them, and thus those who reached our shores could have been overwhelmed. Even now, I think that something might be done that way, and I purpose to build a fleet which may, when they again invade us, take its station near the mouth of the Thames and fall upon the vessels bringing stores and reinforcements. This would give much encouragement to the people, whose hopelessness and desperation are caused principally by the fact that it seems to be of no use killing the enemy, since so many are ready constantly to take their places."

"I will gladly undertake to build one ship," Edmund said. "The fort is now finished, and with the revenues of the land I could at once commence a ship; and if the Danes give us time, when she is finished I would build another. I will the more gladly do it, since it seems to me that if the Danes entirely overrun our country we must take to the sea and so in turn become plunderers. With this view I will have the ship built large and strong, so that she may keep the sea in all weathers and be my home if I am driven out of England. There must be plenty of ports in France, and many a quiet nook and inlet round England, where one can put in to refit when necessary, and we could pick up many a prize of Danish ships returning laden with booty. With such a ship I could carry a strong crew, and with my trusty Egbert and the best of my fighting men we should be able to hold our own, even if attacked by two or three of the Danish galleys."

"The idea is a good one, Edmund," the king said, "and I would that I myself could carry it into effect. It were a thousand times better to live a free life on the sea, even if certain at last to be overpowered by a Danish fleet, than to lurk a hunted fugitive in the woods; but I cannot do it. So long as I live I must remain among my people, ready to snatch any chance that may offer of striking a blow against the invader. But for you it is different."

"I should not, of course, do it," Edmund said, "until all is lost here, and mean to defend my fort to an extremity; still should it be that the Danes conquer all our lands, it were well to have such a refuge."

Edmund talked the matter over with Egbert, who warmly entered into the plan. "So long as I have life I will fight against the Danes, and in a ship at least we can fight manfully till the end. We must not build her on the sea-coast, or before the time when we need her she may be destroyed by the Danes. We will build her on the Parrot. The water is deep enough far up from the sea to float her when empty, and if we choose some spot where the river runs among woods we might hide her so that she may to the last escape the attention of the Danes.

"We must get some men crafty in ship-building from one of the ports, sending down a body of our own serfs to do the rough work. We will go to Exeter first and there choose us the craftsman most skilled in building ships, and will take council with him as to the best form and size. She must be good to sail and yet able to row fast with a strong crew, and she must have room to house a goodly number of rowing and fighting men. You, Edmund, might, before we start, consult King Alfred. He must have seen at Rome and other ports on the Mediterranean the ships in use there, which are doubtless far in advance of our own. For we know from the Holy Bible that a thousand years ago St. Paul made long voyages in ships, and doubtless they have learned much since those days."

Edmund thought the idea a good one, and asked the king to make him a drawing of the vessels in use in the Mediterranean. This King Alfred readily did, and Egbert and Edmund then journeyed to Exeter, where finding out the man most noted for his skill in building ships, they told him the object they had in view, and showed him the drawings the king had made. There were two of them, the one a long galley rowed with double banks of oars, the other a heavy trading ship.

"This would be useless to you," the shipwright said, laying the second drawing aside. "It would not be fast enough either to overtake or to fly. The other galley would, methinks, suit you well. I have seen a drawing of such a ship before. It is a war galley such as is used by the Genoese in their fights against the African pirates. They are fast and roomy, and have plenty of accommodation for the crews. One of them well manned and handled should be a match for six at least of the Danish galleys, which are much lower in the water and smaller in all ways. But it will cost a good deal of money to build such a ship."

"I will devote all the revenues of my land to it until it is finished," Edmund said. "I will place a hundred serfs at your service, and will leave it to you to hire as many craftsmen as may be needed. I intend to build her in a quiet place in a deep wood on the river Parrot, so that she may escape the eyes of the Danes."

"I shall require seasoned timber," the shipwright urged.

"That will I buy," Edmund replied, as you shall direct, and can have it brought up the river to the spot."

"Being so large and heavy," the shipwright said, "she will be difficult to launch. Methinks it were best to dig a hole or dock at some little distance from the river; then when she is finished a way can be cut to the river wide enough for her to pass out. When the water is turned in it will float her up level to the surface, and as she will not draw more than two feet of water the cut need not be more than three feet deep."

"That will be the best plan by far," Edmund agreed, "for you can make the hole so deep that you can build her entirely below the level of the ground. Then we can, if needs be, fill up the hole altogether with bushes, and cover her up, so that she would not be seen by a Danish galley rowing up the river, or even by any of the enemy who might enter the wood, unless they made special search for her; and there she could lie until I chose to embark."

The shipwright at once set to work to draw out his plans, and a week later sent to Edmund a messenger with an account of the quantity and size of wood he should require. This was purchased at once. Edmund and Egbert with their serfs journeyed to the spot they had chosen, and were met there by the shipwright, who brought with him twenty craftsmen from Exeter. The wood was brought up the river, and while the craftsmen began to cut it up into fitting sizes, the serfs applied themselves to dig the deep dock in which the vessel was to be built.

CHAPTER V: A DISCIPLINED BAND

THE construction of the ship went on steadily. King Alfred, who was himself building several war vessels of ordinary size, took great interest in Edmund's craft and paid several visits to it while it was in progress.

"It will be a fine ship," he said one day as the vessel was approaching completion, "and much larger than any in these seas. It reminds me, Edmund, not indeed in size or shape, but in its purpose, of the ark which Noah built before the deluge which covered the whole earth. He built it, as you know, to escape with his family from destruction. You, too, are building against the time when the deluge of Danish invasion will sweep over this land, and I trust that your success will equal that of the patriarch."

"I shall be better off than Noah was," Edmund said, "for he had nothing to do, save to shut up his windows and wait till the floods abated, while I shall go out and seek my enemies on the sea."

The respite purchased by the king from the Danes was but a short one. In the autumn of 875 their bands were again swarming around the borders of Wessex, and constant irruptions took place. Edmund received a summons to gather his tenants, but he found that these no longer replied willingly to the call. Several of his chief men met him and represented to him the general feeling which prevailed.

"The men say," their spokesman explained, "that it is useless to fight against the Danes. In 872 there were ten pitched battles, and vast numbers of the Danes were slain, and vast numbers also of Saxons. The Danes are already far more numerous than before, for fresh hordes continue to arrive on the shores, and more than fill up the places of those who are killed; but the places of the Saxons are empty, and our fighting force is far smaller than it was last year. If we again go out and again fight many battles, even if we are victorious, which we can hardly hope to be, the same thing will happen. Many thousands will be slain, and the following year we shall in vain try to put an army in the field which can match that of the Danes, who will again have filled up their ranks, and be as numerous as ever. So long as we continue to fight, so long the Danes will slay, burn, and destroy wheresoever they march, until there will remain of us but a few fugitives hidden in the woods. We should be far better off did we cease to resist, and the Danes become our masters, as they have become the masters of Northumbria, Mercia, and Anglia.

"There, it is true, they have plundered the churches and thanes' houses and have stolen all that is worth carrying away; but when they have taken all that there is to take they leave the people alone, and unmolested, to till the ground and to gain their livelihood. They do not slay for the pleasure of slaying, and grievous as is the condition of the Angles they and their wives and children are free from massacre and are allowed to gain their livings. The West Saxons have showed that they are no cowards; they have defeated the Northmen over and over again when far out-numbering them. It is no dishonour to yield now when all the rest of England has yielded, and when further fighting will only bring ruin upon ourselves, our wives, and children."

Edmund could find no reply to this argument. He knew that even the king despaired of ultimately resisting the Danish invasion, and after listening to all that the thanes had to say he retired with Egbert apart.

"What say you, Egbert? There is reason in the arguments that they use. You and I have neither wives nor children, and we risk only our own lives; but I can well understand that those who have so much to lose are chary of further effort. What say you?"

"I do not think it will be fair to press them further," Egbert answered; "but me-thinks that we might raise a band consisting of all the youths and unmarried men in the earldom. These we might train carefully and keep always together, seeing that the lands will still be cultivated and all able to pay their assessment, and may even add to it, since you exempt them from service. Such a band we could train and practise until we could rely upon them to defeat a far larger force of the enemy, and they would be available for our crew when we take to the ship."

"I think the idea is a very good one, Egbert; we will propose it to the thanes." The proposition was accordingly made that all married men should be exempt from service, but that the youths above the age of sixteen and the unmarried men should be formed into a band and kept permanently under arms. Landowners who lost the services of sons or freemen working for them should pay the same assessment only as before, but those who did not contribute men to the levy should pay an additional assessment. Edmund said he would pay the men composing the band the same wages they would earn in the field, and would undertake all their expenses. "So long as the king continues the struggle," he said, "it is our duty to aid him, nor can we escape from the dangers and perils of invasion. Should the Danes come near us all must perforce fight, but so long as they continue at a distance things can go on here as if we had peace in the land."

The proposal was, after some discussion, agreed to, and the news caused gladness and contentment throughout the earldom. The younger men who had been included in the levy were quite satisfied with the arrangement. The spirit of the West Saxons was still high, and those without wives and families who would suffer by their absence or be ruined by their death were eager to continue the contest. The proposal that they should be paid as when at work was considered perfectly satisfactory.

The men of Sherborne had under their young leader gained great credit by their steadiness and valour in the battles four years before, and they looked forward to fresh victories over the invader. The result was that ninety young men assembled for service. Edmund had sent off a messenger to the king saying that the people were utterly weary of war and refused to take up arms, but that he was gathering a band of young men with whom he would ere long join him; but he prayed for a short delay in order that he might get them into a condition to be useful on the day of battle.

After consultation with Egbert, Edmund drew up a series of orders somewhat resembling those of modern drill. King Alfred had once, in speaking to him, described the manner in which the Thebans, a people of Northern Greece, had fought, placing their troops in the form of a wedge. The formation he now taught his men. From morning to night they were practised at rallying from pursuit or flight, or changing from a line into the form of a wedge. Each man had his appointed place both in the line and wedge. Those who formed the outside line of this formation were armed with large shields which covered them from chin to foot, and with short spears; those in the inner lines carried no shields, but bore spears of increasing length, so that four lines of spears projected from the wedge to nearly the same distance. Inside the four lines were twenty men armed with shields, bows, and arrows. The sides of the wedge were of equal length, so that they could march either way.

Egbert's place was at the apex of the wedge intended generally for attack. He carried no spear, nor did those at the other corners, as they would be covered by those beside and behind them; he was armed with a huge battle-axe. The other leaders were also chosen for great personal strength. Edmund's place was on horseback in the middle of the wedge, whence he could overlook the whole and direct their movements.

In three weeks the men could perform their simple movements to perfection, and at a sound from Edmund's horn would run in as when scattered in pursuit or flight, or could form from line into the wedge, without the least confusion, every man occupying his assigned place.

The men were delighted with their new exercises, and felt confident that the weight of the solid mass thickly bristling with spears would break through the Danish line without difficulty, or could draw off from the field in perfect order and safety in case of a defeat, however numerous their foes. The two front lines were to thrust with their pikes, the others keeping their long spears immovable to form a solid hedge. Each man carried a short heavy sword to use in case, by any fatality, the wedge should get broken up.

When assured that his band were perfect in their new exercise Edmund marched and joined the king. He found on his arrival that the summons to arms had been everywhere disregarded. Many men had indeed come in, but these were in no way sufficient to form a force which would enable him to take the field against the Danes.

Edmund therefore solicited and obtained permission to march with his band to endeavour to check the plundering bands of Danes, who were already committing devastations throughout the country.

"Be not rash, Edmund," the monarch said, "you have but a handful of men, and I should grieve indeed did aught of harm befall you. If you can fall upon small parties of plunderers and destroy them you will do good service, not only by compelling them to keep together but by raising the spirits of the Saxons; but avoid conflict with parties likely to defeat you."

"You shall hear of us soon, I promise you," Edmund replied, "and I trust that the news will be good."

The little party set out towards the border, and before long met numbers of fugitives, weeping women carrying children, old men and boys, making their way from the neighbourhood of the Danes. The men had for the most part driven their herds into the woods, where they were prepared to defend them as best they could against roving parties. They learned that Haffa, a Danish jarl, with about 600 followers, was plundering and ravaging the country about twelve miles away. The force was a formidable one, but after consultation with Egbert, Edmund determined to advance, deeming that he might find the Danes scattered and cut off some of their parties.

As they neared the country of which the Danes were in possession the smoke of burning villages and homesteads was seen rising heavily in the air. Edmund halted for the night in a wood about a mile distant from a blazing farm, and the band lay down for some hours.

Before daybreak three or four of the swiftest-footed of the men were sent out to reconnoitre. They learned, from badly wounded men whom they found lying near the burning farms, that the Danes had been plundering in parties of twenty or thirty, but that the main body under Haffa lay five miles away at the village of Bristowe.

A consultation was held, and it was agreed that the party should remain hidden in the wood during the day, and that upon the following night they should fall upon the Danes, trusting to the surprise to inflict much damage upon them, and to be able to draw off before the enemy could recover sufficiently to rally and attack them.

Accordingly about nine o'clock in the evening they started, and marching rapidly approached Bristowe an hour and a half later. They could see great fires blazing, and round them the Danes were carousing after their forays of the day. Great numbers of cattle were penned up near the village.

Edmund and Egbert having halted their men stole forward until close to the village in order to learn the nature of the ground and the position of the Danes. Upon their return they waited until the fires burned low and the sound of shouting and singing decreased. It was useless to wait longer, for they knew that many of the Danes would, according to their custom, keep up their revelry all night. Crawling along the ground the band made for the great pen where were herded the cattle which the Danes had driven in from the surrounding country, and over which several guards had been placed. Before starting Egbert assigned to each man the special duties which he was to fulfil.

The Saxons crept up quite close to the Danish guards unobserved. To each of these three or four bowmen had been told off, and they, on nearing the sentries lay prone on the ground with bows bent and arrows fixed until a whistle from Edmund gave the signal. Then the arrows were loosed, and the distance being so short the Danish sentries were all slain. Then a party of men removed the side of the pen facing the village; the rest mingled with the cattle, and soon with the points of their spears goaded them into flight. In a mass the herd thundered down upon the village, the Saxons keeping closely behind them and adding to their terror by goading the hindermost.

The Danes, astonished at the sudden thunder of hoofs bearing down upon them, leaped to their feet and endeavoured to turn the course of the herd, which they deemed to have accidentally broken loose, by loud shouts and by rattling their swords against their shields. The oxen, however, were too terrified by those in their rear to check their course, and charged impetuously down upon the Danes.

Numbers of these were hurled to the ground and trampled under foot, and the wildest confusion reigned in the camp. This was increased when, as the herds swept along, a number of active men with spear and sword fell suddenly upon them. Scores were cut down or run through before they could prepare for defence, or recover from their surprise at the novel method of attack.

At last, as the thunder of the herd died away in the distance, and they became aware of the comparative fewness of their foes, they began to rally and make head against their assailants. No sooner was this the case than the note of a horn was heard, and as if by magic their assailants instantly darted away into the night, leaving the superstitious Danes in some doubt whether the whole attack upon them had not been of a supernatural nature.

Long before they recovered themselves, and were ready for pursuit, the Saxons were far away, no less than 200 of the Danes having been slain or trampled to death, while of Edmund's band not one had received so much as a wound.

The Saxons regained the wood in the highest state of exultation at their success, and more confident than before in themselves and their leader.

"I am convinced," Edmund said, "that this is the true way to fight the Danes, to harry and attack them by night assaults until they dare not break up into parties, and become so worn out by constant alarms that they will be glad to leave a country where plunder and booty are only to be earned at so great a cost."

Knowing that Haffa's band would for some time be thoroughly on the alert Edmund moved his party to another portion of the country, where he inflicted a blow, almost as heavy as he had dealt Haffa, upon Sigbert, another of the Danish jarls. Three or four more very successful night attacks were made, and then the Danes, by this time thoroughly alarmed, obtained from some Saxon country people whom they took prisoners news as to the strength of Edmund's band.

Furious at the heavy losses which had been inflicted upon them by so small a number, they determined to unite in crushing them. By threats of instant death, and by the offers of a high reward, they succeeded in persuading two Saxon prisoners to act as spies, and one day these brought in to Haffa the news that the band had that morning, after striking a successful blow at the Danes ten miles away, entered at daybreak a wood but three miles from his camp.

The Northman, disdaining to ask for assistance from one of the other bands against so small a foe, moved out at once with 300 of his men towards the wood. The Saxons had posted guards, who on the approach of the Danes roused Edmund with the news that the enemy were close at hand. The Saxons were soon on their feet.

"Now, my friends," Edmund said to them, "here is the time for trying what benefit we have got from our exercise. We cannot well draw off, for the Danes are as fleet-footed as we; therefore let us fight and conquer them."

The men formed up cheerfully, and the little body moved out from the wood to meet the Danes. The latter gave a shout of triumph as they saw them. The Saxon force, from its compact formation, appeared even smaller than it was, and the Norsemen advanced in haste, each eager to be the first to fall upon an enemy whom they regarded as an easy prey. As they arrived upon the spot, however, and saw the thick hedge of spears which bristled round the little body of Saxons, the first comers checked their speed and waited till Haffa himself came up, accompanied by his principal warriors.

Without a moment's hesitation the jarl flung himself upon the Saxons. In vain, however, he tried to reach them with his long sword. As he neared them the front line of the Saxons dropped on one knee, and as the Danes with their shields dashed against the spears and strove to cut through them, the kneeling men were able with their pikes to thrust at the unguarded portions of the bodies below their shields, and many fell grievously wounded. After trying for some time in vain, Haffa, finding that individual effort did not suffice to break through the Saxon spears, formed his men up in line four deep, and advanced in a solid body so as to overwhelm them.

The Saxons now rose to their feet. The spears, instead of being pointed outwards, were inclined towards the front, and the wedge advanced against the Danes. The Saxon war cry rose loud as they neared the Danish line, and then, still maintaining their close formation, they charged upon it. The assault was irresistible. The whole weight was thrown upon a point, and preceded, as it was, by the densely-packed spears, it burst through the Danish line as if the latter had been composed of osier twigs, bearing down all in its way.

With shouts of surprise the Danes broke up their line and closed in a thick mass round the Saxons, those behind pressing forward and impeding the motions of the warriors actually engaged. The Saxons no longer kept stationary. In obedience to Edmund's orders the triangle advanced, sometimes with one angle in front, sometimes with another, but whichever way it moved sweeping away the Danes opposed to it, while the archers from the centre shot fast and strong into the mass of the enemy.

Haffa himself, trying to oppose the advance of the wedge, was slain by a blow of Egbert's axe, and after half an hour's fierce fighting, the Danes, having lost upwards of fifty of their best men, and finding all their efforts to produce an impression upon the Saxons vain, desisted from the attack and fled.

At once the wedge broke up, and the Saxons followed in hot pursuit, cutting down their flying enemies. Obedient, however, to Edmund's repeated shouts they kept fairly together, and when the Danes, thinking them broken and disordered, turned to fall upon them, a single note of the horn brought them instantly together again, and the astonished Danes saw the phalanx which had proved so fatal to them prepared to receive their attack. This they did not attempt to deliver, but took to flight, the Saxons, as before, pursuing, and twice as many of the Danes were slain in the retreat as in the first attack.

The pursuit was continued for many miles, and then, fearing that he might come across some fresh body of the enemy, Edmund called off his men. Great was the triumph of the Saxons. A few of them had suffered from wounds more or less serious, but not one had fallen. They had defeated a body of Danes four times their own force, and had killed nearly half of them, and they felt confident that the tactics which they had adopted would enable them in future to defeat any scattered bodies of Danes they might meet.

For a week after the battle they rested, spending their time in further improving themselves in their drill, practicing especially the alterations of the position of the spears requisite when changing from a defensive attitude, with the pikes at right angles to each face, to that of an attack, when the spears of both faces of the advancing wedge were all directed forward. A messenger arrived from the king, to whom Edmund had sent the news of his various successes, and Alfred sent his warmest congratulations and thanks for the great results which had been gained with so small a force, the king confessing that he was unable to understand how with such disproportionate numbers Edmund could so totally have routed the force of so distinguished a leader as Haffa.

For some weeks Edmund continued the work of checking the depredations of the Danes, and so successful was he that the freebooters became seized with a superstitious awe of his band. The rapidity of its maneuvering, the manner in which men, at one moment scattered, were in another formed in a serried mass, against which all their efforts broke as waves against a rock, seemed to them to be something superhuman. In that part of Wessex, therefore, the invaders gradually withdrew their forces across the frontier; but in other parts of the country, the tide of invasion being unchecked, large tracts of country had been devastated, and the West Saxons could nowhere make head against them. One day a messenger reached Edmund telling him that a large Danish army was approaching Sherborne, and urging him to return instantly to the defence of his earldom.

With rapid marches he proceeded thither, and on arriving at his house he found that the Danes were but a few miles away, and that the whole country was in a state of panic. He at once sent off messengers in all directions, bidding the people hasten with their wives and families, their herds and valuables, to the fort. His return to some extent restored confidence. The news of the victories he had gained over the Danes had reached Sherborne, and the confidence of their power to defeat the invaders which his followers expressed as they scattered to their respective farms again raised the courage of the people.

All through the night bands of fugitives poured into the fort, and by morning the whole of the people for many miles round were assembled there. Egbert and Edmund busied themselves in assigning to each his duty and station. All the men capable of bearing arms were told off to posts on the walls. The old men and young boys were to draw water and look after the cattle; the women to cook and attend to the wounded. The men of his own band were not placed upon the walls, but were held in readiness as a reserve to move to any point which might be threatened, and to take part in sorties against the enemy.

Soon smoke was seen rising up in many directions, showing that the enemy were at their accustomed work. Cries broke from the women, and exclamations of rage from the men, as they recognized by the direction of the smoke that their own homesteads and villages were in the hands of the spoilers. About mid-day a party of mounted Danes rode up towards the fort and made a circuit of it. When they had satisfied themselves as to the formidable nature of its defences they rode off again, and for the rest of the day none of the enemy approached the fort.

CHAPTER VI: THE SAXON FORT

Astrict watch was kept all night, and several scouts were sent out. These on their return reported that the Danes were feasting, having slain many cattle and broached the casks of mead which they found in the cellars of Edmund's house. This they had not burned nor the houses around it, intending, as the scouts supposed, to make it their headquarters while they attacked the fort.

Edmund and Egbert agreed that it would be well to show the Danes at once that they had an active and enterprising foe to deal with; they therefore awakened their band, who were sleeping on skins close to the gate, and with them started out.

It was still two hours before dawn when they approached the house. Save a few men on watch, the great Danish host, which the messengers calculated to amount to ten thousand men, were asleep. Cautiously making their way so as to avoid stumbling over the Danes, who lay scattered in groups round the house, the Saxons crept forward quietly until close to the entrance, when a sleepy watchman started up.

"Who are ye?"

The answer was a blow from Egbert's battle-axe. Then the leaders with twenty of their men rushed into the house, while the rest remained on guard at the entrance.

The combat was short but furious, and the clashing of arms and shouts of the Danes roused those sleeping near, and the men who escaped from the house spread the alarm. The fight lasted but three or four minutes, for the Danes, scattered through the house, and in many cases still stupid from the effects of the previous night's debauch, were unable to gather and make any collective resistance. The two jarls fought in a manner worthy of their renown, but the Saxon spears proved more than a match for their swords, and they died fighting bravely till the last. Between Saxon and Dane there was no thought of quarter; none asked for mercy on either side, for none would be granted. The sea rovers never spared an armed man who fell into their hands, and the Saxons were infuriated by the sufferings which the invaders had inflicted upon them, and had no more pity upon their foes than if they had been wild animals. Besides the jarls some thirty of their minor leaders were in the house, and but five or six of them escaped. It was well for the Danes that the detachment which lay there was not their principal body, which was still a few miles in the rear, for had it been so two of their kings and six jarls, all men of famed valour, would have been slain. The instant the work was done the Saxons rejoined those assembled at the entrance.

Already the Danes were thronging up, but at present in confusion and disorder, coming rather to see what was the matter than to fight, and hardly believing that the Saxons could have had the audacity to attack them. In an instant the Saxons fell into their usual formation, and overturning and cutting down those who happened to be in their path, burst through the straggling Danes, and at a trot proceeded across the country.

It was still quite dark, and it was some time before the Danes became thoroughly aware of what had happened; then missing the voices of their leaders, some of them rushed into the house, and the news that the two jarls and their companions had been slain roused them to fury. At once they set off in pursuit of the Saxons in a tumultuous throng; but the band had already a considerable start, and had the advantage of knowing every foot of the country, of which the Danes were ignorant. When once fairly through the enemy, Edmund had given the word and the formation had broken up, so that each man could run freely and without jostling his comrades. Thus they were enabled to proceed at a rapid pace, and reached the fort just as day was breaking, without having been discovered or overtaken by the Danes.

The news of this successful exploit raised the spirits of the garrison of the fort. The Danes swarmed nearly up to the walls, but seeing how formidable was the position, and being without leaders, they fell back without making an attack, some of the more impetuous having fallen from the arrows of the bowmen.

About mid-day a solid mass of the enemy were seen approaching, and the banners with the Black Raven on a blood-red field showed that it contained leaders of importance, and was, in fact, the main body of the Danes. It was an imposing sight as it marched towards the fort, with the fluttering banners, the sun shining upon the brass helmets and shields of the chiefs, and the spear-heads and swords of the footmen. Here and there parties of horsemen galloped about the plain.

"Their number has not been exaggerated," Egbert said to Edmund, "there must be ten thousand of them. There are full twice as many as attacked us on the field of Kesteven."

The sight of the great array struck terror into the minds of a great part of the defenders of the fort; but the confident bearing of their young ealdorman and the thought of the strength of their walls reassured them. The Danes halted at a distance of about a quarter of a mile from the walls, and three or four of their chiefs rode forward. These by the splendour of their helmets, shields, and trappings were clearly men of great importance. They halted just out of bowshot distance, and one of them, raising his voice, shouted:

"Dogs of Saxons, had you laid down your arms, and made submission to me, I would have spared you; but for the deed which you did last night, and the slaying of my brave jarls, I swear that I will have revenge upon you, and, by the god Wodin, I vow that not one within your walls, man, woman, or child, shall be spared. This is the oath of King Uffa."

"It were well, King Uffa," Edmund shouted back, "to take no rash oaths; before you talk of slaying you have got to capture, and you will need all the aid of your false gods before you take this fort. As to mercy, we should as soon ask it of wolves. We have God and our good swords to protect us, and we fear not your host were it three times as strong as it is."

The Saxons raised a great shout, and the Danish king rode back to his troops. The lesson which had been given them of the enterprise of the Saxons was not lost, for the Danes at once began to form a camp, raising an earthen bank which they crowned with stakes and bushes as a defence against sudden attacks. This work occupied them two days, and during this time no blow was struck on either side, as the Danes posted a strong body of men each night to prevent the Saxons from sallying out. On the third day the work was finished, and the Danish kings with their jarls made a circuit round the walls, evidently to select the place for attack.

The time had passed quietly in the fort. In one corner the priests had erected an altar, and here mass was said three times a day. The priests went among the soldiers exhorting them to resist to the last, confessing them, and giving them absolution.

The pains which the Danes had taken in the preparation of their camp was a proof of their determination to capture the fort, however long the operation might be. It showed, too, that they recognized the difficulty of the task, for had they believed that the capture could be easily effected they would at once upon their arrival have advanced to the attack.

"To-morrow morning early," Egbert said, "I expect that they will assault us. In the first place probably they will endeavour to carry the fort by a general attack; if they fail in this they will set to construct engines with which to batter the wall."

At daybreak the following morning the Danes issued from their camp. Having formed up in regular order, they advanced towards the castle. They divided into four bands; three of these wheeled round to opposite sides of the fort, the fourth, which was as large as the other three together, advanced towards the entrance. The Saxons all took the posts previously assigned to them on the walls. Edmund strengthened the force on the side where the gate was by posting there in addition the whole of his band. Altogether there were nearly 350 fighting men within the walls, of whom the greater part had fought against the Danes in the battles of the previous year. The attack commenced simultaneously on all sides by a discharge of arrows by the archers of both parties. The Saxons, sheltered behind the parapet on the walls, suffered but slightly; but their missiles did considerable execution among the masses of the Danes. These, however, did not pause to continue the conflict at a distance, but uttering their battle-cry rushed forward.

Edmund and Egbert had but little fear of the attack on the other faces of the fort proving successful; the chief assault was against the gate, and it was here that the real danger existed.

The main body of the Danes covered themselves with their shields and rushed forward with the greatest determination, pouring through the gap in the outer bank in a solid mass, and then turned along the fosse towards the inner gate. Closely packed together, with their shields above their heads forming a sort of testudo or roof which protected them against the Saxons' arrows, they pressed forward in spite of the shower of missiles with which the Saxons on the walls assailed them. Arrows, darts, and great stones were showered down upon them, the latter breaking down the shields, and affording the archers an opportunity of pouring in their arrows.

Numbers fell, but the column swept along until it gained the gate. Here those in front began an attack upon the massive beams with their axes, and when they had somewhat weakened it, battered it with heavy beams of timber until it was completely splintered. While this was going on the Saxons had continued to shoot without intermission, and the Danish dead were heaped thickly around the gate. The Danish archers, assisted by their comrades, had scrambled up on to the outer bank and kept up a heavy fire on the defenders of the wall. The Saxons sheltered their heads and shoulders which were above the parapet with their shields; and between these, as through loopholes, their archers shot at the Danes.

Edmund and Egbert had debated much on the previous days whether they would pile stones behind the gate, but had finally agreed not to do so. They argued that although for a time the stones would impede the progress of the Danes, these would, if they shattered the door, sooner or later pull down the stones or climb over them; and it was better to have a smooth and level place for defence inside. They had, however, raised a bank of earth ten feet high in a semicircle at a distance of twenty yards within the gate.

When it was seen that the gates were yielding Edmund had called down his own band from the walls and formed them in a half-circle ten yards from the gate. They were four deep, as in their usual formation, with the four lines of spears projecting towards the gate. The mound behind them he lined with archers.

At last the gates fell, and with an exulting shout the Danes poured in. As they did so the archers on the mound loosed their arrows, and the head of the Danish column melted like snow before the blast of a furnace. Still they poured in and flung themselves upon the spearmen, but they strove in vain to pierce the hedge of steel. Desperately they threw themselves upon the pike-heads and died there bravely, but they were powerless to break a passage.

The archers on the mound still shot fast among them, while those on the wall, turning round, smote them in the back, where, unprotected by their shields, they offered a sure and fatal mark. Soon the narrow semicircle inside the gate became heaped high with dead, impeding the efforts of those still pressing in. Several of the bravest of the Danish leaders had fallen. The crowd in the fosse, unaware of the obstacle which prevented the advance of the head of the column and harassed by the missiles from above, grew impatient, and after half an hour of desperate efforts, and having lost upwards of three hundred of his best men, the Danish king, furious with rage and disappointment, called off his men.

On the other three sides the attack equally failed. The Danes suffered heavily while climbing the steep side of the inner mound. They brought with them faggots, which they cast down at the foot of the wall, but this was built so near the edge of the slope that they were unable to pile sufficient faggots to give them the height required for a successful assault upon it. Many climbed up on their comrades' shoulders, and so tried to scale the wall, but they were thrust down by the Saxon spears as they raised themselves to its level, and in no place succeeded in gaining a footing. Over two hundred fell in the three minor attacks.

There were great rejoicings among the Saxons, on whose side but twenty-three had been killed. A solemn mass was held, at which all save a few look-outs on the walls attended, and thanks returned to God for the repulse of the pagans; then the garrison full of confidence awaited the next attack of the enemy.

Stones were piled up in the gateway to prevent any sudden surprise being effected there. The Danes in their retreat had carried off their dead, and the next morning the Saxons saw that they were busy with the ceremonies of their burial. At some little distance from their camp the dead were placed in a sitting position, in long rows back to back with their weapons by their sides, and earth was piled over them until a great mound fifty yards long and ten feet high was raised.

Three jarls and one of their kings were buried separately. They were placed together in a sitting position, with their helmets on their heads, their shields on their arms, and their swords by their sides. Their four war-horses were killed and laid beside them; twenty slaves were slaughtered and placed lying round them, for their spirits to attend them in the Walhalla of the gods. Golden drinking-vessels and other ornaments were placed by them, and then a mound forty feet in diameter and twenty feet high was piled over the whole.

The whole force were occupied all day with this work. The next day numbers of trees were felled and brought to the camp, and for the next two days the Danes were occupied in the manufacture of war-engines for battering down the walls. Edmund and Egbert utilized the time in instructing the soldiers who did not form part of the regular band, in the formation of the quadruple line of defence which the Danes had found it so impossible to break through, so that if more than one breach was effected, a resistance similar to that made at the gate could be offered at all points. The skins of the oxen killed for the use of the garrison were carefully laid aside, the inside being thickly rubbed with grease.

The Danish preparations were at length completed, the war-engines were brought up and began to hurl great stones against the wall at three points. The Saxons kept up a constant fire of arrows at those employed at working them, but the Danes, though losing many men, threw up breastworks to protect them.

The Saxons manufactured many broad ladders, and in the middle of the night, lowering these over the walls, they descended noiselessly, and three strong bodies fell upon the Danes guarding the engines. These fought stoutly, but were driven back, the engines were destroyed, and the Saxons retired to their walls again and drew up their ladders before the main body of Danes could arrive from the camp. This caused a delay of some days in the siege, but fresh engines having been constructed, the assault on the walls was recommenced, this time the whole Danish army moving out and sleeping at night close to them.

After three days' battering, breaches of from thirty to fifty feet wide were effected in the walls. The Saxons had not been idle. Behind each of the threatened points they raised banks of earth ten feet high, and cut away the bank perpendicularly behind the shattered wall, so that the assailants as they poured in at the gaps would have to leap ten feet down.

Each night the masses of wall which fell inside were cleared away, and when the breach was complete, and it was evident that the assault would take place the next morning, the hides which had been prepared were laid with the hairy side down, on the ground below. Through them they drove firmly into the ground numbers of pikes with the heads sticking up one or two feet, and pointed stakes hardened in the fire. Then satisfied that all had been done the Saxons lay down to rest.

In the morning the Danes advanced to the assault. This time they were but little annoyed in their advance by the archers. These were posted on the walls at each side of the gaps to shoot down at the backs of the Danes after they had entered. On the inner semicircular mounds the Saxon force gathered four deep.

With loud shouts the Danes rushed forward, climbed the outer mounds, and reached the breaches. Here the leaders paused on seeing the gulf below them, but pressed by those behind they could not hesitate long, but leapt down from the breach on to the slippery hides below.

Not one who did so lived. It was impossible to keep their feet as they alighted, and as they fell they were impaled by the pikes and stakes. Pressed by those behind, however, fresh men leapt down, falling in their turn, until at length the hides and stakes were covered, and those leaping down found a foothold on the bodies of the fallen. Then they crowded on and strove to climb the inner bank and attack the Saxons. Now the archers on the walls opened fire upon them, and, pierced through and through with the arrows which struck them on the back, the Danes fell in great numbers. Edmund commanded at one of the breaches, Egbert at another, and Oswald, an old and experienced warrior, at the third.

At each point the scene was similar. The Danes struggled up the mounds only to fail to break through the hedge of spears which crowned them, fast numbers dying in the attempt, while as many more fell pierced with arrows. For an hour the Danes continued their desperate efforts, and not until fifteen hundred had been slain did they draw off to their camp, finding it impossible to break through the Saxon defences.

Loud rose the shouts of the triumphant Saxons as the Danes retired, and it needed all the efforts of their leaders to prevent them from pouring out in pursuit; but the events of the preceding year had taught the Saxon leaders how often their impetuosity after success had proved fatal to the Saxons, and that once in the plain the Danes would turn upon them and crush them by their still greatly superior numbers. Therefore no one was allowed to sally out, and the discomfited Danes retired unmolested.

The next morning to their joy the Saxons saw that the invaders had broken up their camp, and had marched away in the night. Scouts were sent out in various directions, and the Saxons employed themselves in stripping and burying the Danes who had fallen within the fort, only a few of the most distinguished having been carried off. The scouts returned with news that the Danes had made no halt, but had departed entirely from that part of the country. Finding that for the present they were free of the invaders, the Saxons left the fort and scattered again, to rebuild as best they might their devastated homes.

But if in the neighbourhood of Sherborne the Danes had been severely repulsed, in other parts of the kingdom they continued to make great progress, and the feeling of despair among the Saxons increased. Great numbers left their homes, and taking with them all their portable possessions, made their way to the sea-coast, and there embarked for France, where they hoped to be able to live peaceably and quietly.

Edmund placed no hindrance in the way of such of his people who chose this course, for the prospect appeared well-nigh hopeless. The majority of the Saxons were utterly broken in spirit, and a complete conquest of the kingdom by the Danes seemed inevitable. In the spring, however, of 877 King Alfred again issued an urgent summons. A great horde of Danes had landed at Exeter and taken possession of that town, and he determined to endeavour to crush them. He sent to Edmund begging him to proceed at once to Poole, where the king's fleet was ready for sea, and to embark in it with what force he could raise, and to sail and blockade the entrance to the river Exe, and so prevent the Danes from reinforcing their countrymen, while he with his forces laid siege to Exeter.

Edmund would have taken his own vessel, but some time would have been lost, and the king's ships were short of hands. He was not sorry, indeed, that his men should have some practise at sea, and taking his own band, in which the vacancies which had been caused in the defence of the fort had been filled up, he proceeded to Poole. Here he embarked his men in one of the ships, and the fleet, comprising twenty vessels, put to sea.

The management of the vessels and their sails was in the hands of experienced sailors, and Edmund's men had no duties to perform except to fight the enemy when they met them.

The news of the siege of Exeter reached the Danes at Wareham, which was their head-quarters, and 120 vessels filled with their troops sailed for the relief of Exeter.

The weather was unpropitious, heavy fogs lay on the water, dissipated occasionally by fierce outbursts of wind. The Saxon fleet kept the sea. It was well that for a time the Danish fleet did not appear in sight, for the Saxons, save the sailors, were unaccustomed to the water, and many suffered greatly from the rough motion; and had the Danes appeared for the first week after the fleet put to sea a combat must have been avoided, as the troops were in no condition to fight.

Presently, however, they recovered from their malady and became eager to meet the enemy; Edmund bade his men take part in the working of the ship in order to accustom themselves to the duties of seamen. The fleet did not keep the sea all the time, returning often to the straits between the Isle of Wight and the mainland, where they lay in shelter, a look-out being kept from the top of the hills, whence a wide sweep of sea could be seen, and where piles of wood were collected by which a signal fire could warn the fleet to put to sea should the enemy's vessels come in sight.

A full month passed and the Saxons began to fear that the Danes might have eluded them, having perhaps been blown out to sea and having made the land again far to the west. One morning, however, smoke was seen to rise from the beacon fire. The crews who were on shore instantly hurried on board. From the hills the Danish fleet was made out far to the west and was seen to be approaching the land from seaward, having been driven far out of its course by the winds.

The weather was wild and threatening and the sailors predicted a great storm. Nevertheless the fleet put to sea and with reefed sails ran to the west. Their vessels were larger than the Danish galleys and could better keep the sea in a storm. Many miles were passed before, from the decks, the Danish flotilla could be seen. Presently, however, a great number of their galleys were discerned rowing in towards Swanage Bay.

In spite of the increasing fury of the wind the Saxons spread more sail and succeeded in intercepting the Danes. A desperate fight began, but the Danes in their low, long vessels had all they could do to keep afloat on the waves. Many were run down by the Saxons. The showers of arrows from their lofty poops confused the rowers and slew many. Sweeping along close to them they often broke off the oars and disabled them. Sometimes two or three of the Danish galleys would try to close with a Saxon ship, but the sea was too rough for the boats to remain alongside while the men tried to climb up the high sides, and the Saxons with their spears thrust down those who strove to do so. Confusion and terror soon reigned among the Danes, and fearing to try to escape by sea in such a storm made for the shore, hotly pursued by the Saxons.

But the shore was even more inhospitable than their foes. Great rocks bordered the coast, and upon these the galleys were dashed into fragments. The people on shore, who had gathered at the sight of the approaching fleets, fell upon such of the Danes as succeeded in gaining the coast, and everyone who landed was instantly slain. Thus, partly from the effects of the Saxon fleet but still more from that of the storm, the whole of the Danish fleet of one hundred and twenty vessels was destroyed, not a single ship escaping the general destruction.

CHAPTER VII: THE DRAGON

THE Danes at Exeter, being now cut off from all hope of relief, asked for terms, and the king granted them their lives on condition of their promising to leave Wessex and not to return. This promise they swore by their most solemn oaths to observe, and marching northward passed out of Wessex and settled near Gloucester. Some of the Saxons thought that the king had been wrong in granting such easy terms, but he pointed out to the ealdormen who remonstrated with him that there were many other and larger bands of Danes in Mercia and Anglia, and that had he massacred the band at Exeter--and this he could not have done without the loss of many men, as assuredly the Danes would have fought desperately for their lives--the news of their slaughter would have brought upon him fresh invasions from all sides.

By this time all resistance to the Danes in Mercia had ceased. Again and again King Burhred had bought them off, but this only brought fresh hordes down upon him, and at last, finding the struggle hopeless, he had gone as a pilgrim to Rome, where he had died. The Danes acted in Mercia as they had done in Northumbria. They did not care, themselves, to settle down for any length of time, and therefore appointed a weak Saxon thane, Ceolwulf, as the King of Mercia. He ruled cruelly and extorted large revenues from the land-owners, and robbed the monasteries, which had escaped destruction, of their treasures.

The Danes suffered him to pursue this course until he had amassed great wealth, when they swooped down upon him, robbed him of all he possessed, and took away the nominal kingship he had held. As there was now but little fresh scope for plundering in England many of the Danes both in Anglia and Mercia settled down in the cities and on the lands which they had taken from the Saxons.

The Danes who had gone from Exeter were now joined by another band which had landed in South Wales. The latter, finding but small plunder was to be obtained among the mountains of that country, moved to Gloucester, and joining the band there proposed a fresh invasion of Wessex. The Danes, in spite of the oaths they had sworn to Alfred, and the hostages they had left in his hands, agreed to the proposal; and early in the spring of 878 the bands, swollen by reinforcements from Mercia, marched into Wiltshire and captured the royal castle of Chippenham on the Avon. From this point they spread over the country and destroyed everything with fire and sword. A general panic seized the inhabitants. The better class, with the bishops, priests, and monks, made for the sea-coasts and thence crossed to France, taking with them all their portable goods, with the relics, precious stones, and ornaments of the churches and monasteries.

Another party of Danes in twenty-three ships had landed in Devonshire. Here the ealdorman Adda had constructed a castle similar to that which Edmund had built. It was fortified by nature on three sides and had a strong rampart of earth on another. The Danes tried to starve out the defenders of the fort; but the Saxons held out for a long time, although sorely pressed by want of water. At last they sallied out one morning at daybreak and fell upon the Danes and utterly defeated them, only a few stragglers regaining their ships.

A thousand Danes are said to have been slain at Kynwith; but this was an isolated success; in all other parts of the kingdom panic appeared to have taken possession of the West Saxons. Those who could not leave the country retired to the woods, and thence, when the Danes had passed by, leaving ruin and desolation behind them, they sallied out and again began to till the ground as best they could. Thus for a time the West Saxons, formerly so valiant and determined, sank to the condition of serfs; for when all resistance ceased the Danes were well pleased to see the ground tilled, as otherwise they would speedily have run short of stores.

At the commencement of the invasion Edmund had marched out with his band and had inflicted heavy blows upon parties of plunderers; but he soon perceived that the struggle was hopeless. He therefore returned to Sherborne, and collecting such goods as he required and a good store of provisions he marched to the place where the ship had been hidden. No wandering band of Danes had passed that way, and the bushes with which she had been covered were undisturbed. These were soon removed and a passage three feet deep, and wide enough for the ship to pass through, was dug from the deep hole in which she was lying to the river.

When the last barrier was cut the water poured in, and the Saxons had the satisfaction of seeing the vessel rise gradually until the water in the dock was level with that in the river. Then she was taken out into the stream, the stores and fittings placed aboard, and she was poled down to the mouth of the river. Egbert had gone before and had already engaged fifteen sturdy sailors to go with them. The Danes had not yet reached the sea-coast from the interior, and there was therefore no difficulty in obtaining the various equipments necessary. In a week her masts were up and her sails in position.

The Dragon, as she was called, excited great admiration at the port, all saying that she was the finest and largest ship that had ever been seen there. While her fitting out had been going on she was hove up on shore and received several coats of paint. Edmund was loath to start on his voyage without again seeing the king, but no one knew where Alfred now was, he, on finding the struggle hopeless, having retired to the fastnesses of Somerset to await the time when the Saxons should be driven by oppression again to take up arms.

At last all was ready, and the Dragon put out to sea. She was provided with oars as well as sails, but these were only to be used when in pursuit, or when flying from a superior enemy. As soon as she had been long enough at sea to enable the band again to recover from the effects of sickness the oars were got out and the men practised in their use.

As in the models from which she had been built, she rowed two banks of oars, the one worked by men upon deck, the others through small port-holes. The latter could only be used when the weather was fine; when the sea was high they were closed up and fastened. The lower-deck oars were each rowed by one man, while the upper bank, which were longer and heavier, had each two men to work it.

Before starting Edmund had increased the strength of his band to ninety men, that number being required for the oars, of which the Dragon had fifteen on each bank on each side. At first there was terrible splashing and confusion, but in time the men learned to row in order, and in three weeks after putting to sea the oars worked well in time together, and the Dragon, with her ninety rowers, moved through the water at a great rate of speed.

During this time she had never been far from land keeping but a short distance from the port from which she had sailed, as Edmund did not wish to fall in with the Danes until his crew were able to maneuver her with the best effect. When, at last, satisfied that all knew their duty he returned to port, took in a fresh supply of provisions, and then sailed away again in search of the enemy. He coasted along the shore of Hampshire and Sussex without seeing a foe, and then sailing round Kent entered the mouth of the Thames. The Dragon kept on her way until she reached the point where the river begins to narrow, and there the sails were furled and the anchor thrown overboard to wait for Danish galleys coming down the river.

On the third day after they had anchored they perceived four black specks in the distance, and these the sailors soon declared to be Danish craft. They were rowing rapidly, having ten oars on either side, and at their mast-heads floated the Danish Raven. The anchor was got up, and as the Danes approached, the Golden Dragon, the standard of Wessex, was run up to the mast-head, the sails were hoisted, the oars got out, and the vessel advanced to meet the approaching Danes.

These for a moment stopped rowing in astonishment at seeing so large a ship bearing the Saxon flag. Then they at once began to scatter in different directions; but the Dragon, impelled both by the wind and her sixty oars, rapidly overtook them. When close alongside the galley nearest to them the men on the upper deck, at an order from Edmund, ran in their oars, and seizing their bows poured a volley of arrows into the galley, killing most of the rowers. Then the Dragon was steered alongside, and the Saxons, sword in hand, leaped down into the galley. Most of the Danes were cut down at once; the rest plunged into the water and swam for their lives. Leaving the deserted galley behind, the Dragon continued the pursuit of the others, and overtook and captured another as easily as she had done the first.

The other two boats reached the shore before they were overtaken, and those on board leaping out fled. The Saxons took possession of the deserted galleys. They found them, as they expected, stored full of plunder of all kinds--rich wearing apparel, drinking goblets, massive vessels of gold and silver which had been torn from some desecrated altar, rich ornaments and jewels and other articles. These were at once removed to the Dragon. Fire was applied to the boats, and they were soon a mass of flames. Then the Dragon directed her course to the two galleys she had first captured. These were also rifled of their contents and burned. The Saxons were delighted at the success which had attended their first adventure.

"We shall have rougher work next time," Egbert said. "The Danes who escaped will carry news to London, and we shall be having a whole fleet down to attack us in a few days."

"If they are in anything like reasonable numbers we will fight them; if not, we can run. We have seen to-day how much faster we are than the Danish boats; and though I shall be in favour of fighting if we have a fair chance of success, it would be folly to risk the success of our enterprise by contending against overwhelming numbers at the outset, seeing that we shall be able to pick up so many prizes round the coast."

"We can beat a score of them," Egbert grumbled. "I am in favour of fighting the Danes whenever we see them."

"When there is a hope of success, Egbert, yes; but you know even the finest bull can be pulled down by a pack of dogs. The Dragon is a splendid ship, and does credit alike to King Alfred's first advice, to the plans of the Italian shipbuilders, and to the workmanship and design of the shipwright of Exeter, and I hope she will long remain to be a scourge to the Danes at sea as they have been a scourge to the Saxons on shore; and it is because I hope she is going to do such good service to England that I would be careful of her. You must remember, too, that many of the Danish galleys are far larger than those we had to do with to-day. We are not going to gobble them all up as a pike swallows minnows."

The Dragon had now anchored again, and four days elapsed before any Danish galleys were seen. At the end of that time six large Danish war-ships were perceived in the distance. Edmund and Egbert from the top of the lofty poop watched them coming.

"They row thirty oars each side," Egbert said, "and are crowded with men. What say you, Edmund, shall we stop and fight them, or shall the Dragon spread her wings?"

"We have the advantage of height," Edmund said, "and from our bow and stern castles can shoot down into them; but if they lie alongside and board us their numbers will give them an immense advantage. I should think that we might run down one or two of them. The Dragon is much more strongly built than these galleys of the Danes, and if when they close round us we have the oars lashed on both sides as when we are rowing, it will be next to impossible for them to get alongside except at the stern and bow, which are far too high for them to climb."

"Very well," Egbert said, "if you are ready to fight, you may be sure I am."

The anchor was got up and the oars manned, and the Dragon quietly advanced towards the Danish boats. The men were instructed to row slowly, and it was not until within a hundred yards of the leading galley that the order was given to row hard.

The men strained at the tough oars, and the Dragon leapt ahead to meet the foe. Her bow was pointed as if she would have passed close by the side of the Danish galley, which was crowded with men. When close to her, however, the helmsman pushed the tiller across and the Dragon swept straight down upon her. A shout of dismay rose from the Danes, a hasty volley of arrows and darts was hurled at the Dragon, and the helmsman strove to avoid the collision, but in vain. The Dragon struck her on the beam, the frail craft broke up like an egg-shell under the blow, and sank almost instantly under the bows of the Dragon.

Without heeding the men struggling thickly in the water, the Dragon continued her course. Warned by the fate of the first boat, the next endeavoured to avoid her path. Her commander shouted orders. The rowers on one side backed while those on the other pulled, but she was not quite quick enough. The Dragon struck her a few feet from the stern, cutting her in two.

The other galleys now closed in alongside. The Saxons hastily fastened their oars as they had been rowing and then betook themselves to their posts, those with spears and swords to the sides to prevent the enemy from climbing up, the archers to the lofty castles at either end. The Danes had the greatest difficulty in getting alongside, the oars keeping the galleys at a distance. For some time the combat was conducted entirely by the archers on both sides, the Danes suffering much the most heavily, as the Saxons were protected by the bulwarks, while from their lofty positions they were enabled to fire down into the galleys.

At last one of the Danish vessels rowed straight at the broadside of the Dragon, and breaking her way through the oars her bow reached the side. Then the Danes strove to leap on board, but the Saxons pursued the tactics which had succeeded so well on land, and forming in a close mass where the Danish vessel touched the Dragon, opposed a thick hedge of spears to those who strove to board her.

The Danes fought desperately. Several notable leaders, hearing that a great Saxon ship had appeared on the Thames, had come down to capture her, and leading their followers, strove desperately to cut their way to the deck of the Dragon. Taking advantage of the strife, the other galleys repeated the maneuver which had succeeded, and each in turn ran their stem through the Saxon oars, and reached the side of the Dragon. In this position, however, they had the immense disadvantage that only a few men at once could strive to board, while the Saxons were able to oppose all their strength at these four points.

For a time the Saxons repulsed every effort, but as the lashings of the oars gave way under the pressure of the Danish ships, these drifted alongside, and they were thus able to attack along the whole length of the bulwarks between the castles. The Saxons were now hard put to it, but their superior height still enabled them to keep the Danes in check.

All this time the five vessels had been drifting down the river together. Presently, when the conflict was hottest, the chief of the sailors made his way to Edmund.

"If we get up the sails we may be able to draw out from the galleys."

"Do so," Edmund said, "and at once, for we are hardly pressed; they are four to one against us."

The sailors at once sprang to the halliards, and soon the great sail rose on the mast. Almost instantly the Dragon began to glide away from the galleys. The Danes with ropes endeavoured to lash themselves to her sides, but these were severed as fast as thrown, and in two or three minutes the Dragon had drawn herself clear of them. The Danes betook themselves to their oars, but many of these had been broken between the vessels, and rowing their utmost they could only just keep up with the Dragon, for the wind was blowing freely. Fully half the oars of the Dragon were broken, but the rest were soon manned, and she then rapidly drew away from her pursuers.

"I am not going to run further," Edmund said. "Now that we have once shaken them off, let us turn and meet them again."

As the vessel's head was brought up into the wind the Danes ceased rowing. The fate which had befallen their two galleys at the commencement of the fight was still before them. They had lost great numbers of men in the attempt to board from the Saxon pikes and arrows, and their desire to renew the fight vanished when they saw that the Saxons were equally ready. Therefore, as the Dragon approached them, they sheered off on either side of her and rowed for the mouth of the Medway.

The Saxons did not pursue. They had lost eight men killed, and seventeen wounded by the Danish arrows, and were well content to be quit of their opponents, upon whom they had inflicted a severe blow, as each of the galleys sunk had contained fully a hundred and fifty men, and great numbers of the Danes on board the other ships had fallen.

They now left the Thames and sailed to Sandwich. The town had been shortly before burned by the Danes, but these had left, and some of the inhabitants had returned. Here the Dragon waited for a week, by the end of which time the traces of the conflict had been obliterated, and new oars made. Edmund found no difficulty in filling up the vacancies caused in the fight, as many of the young Saxons were burning to avenge the sufferings which the Danes had inflicted, and could have obtained several times the number he required had there been room for them. He was therefore enabled to pick out sturdy fellows accustomed to the sea. When the Dragon again set sail her head was laid to the northward, as Edmund intended to cruise off East Anglia, from whose shores fleets were constantly crossing and recrossing to Denmark.

They picked up several prizes at the mouths of the eastern rivers, scarcely having to strike a blow, so surprised were the Danes at the appearances of the great Saxon galley. Whenever the Danes surrendered without resistance Edmund gave them quarter and landed them in small boats on the shore; their ships, after being emptied of the booty they contained, were burned. When off Yarmouth, where they had captured four Danish vessels sailing out unsuspicious of danger, the wind veered round to the north-east and began to blow very strongly.

The long line of sandbanks off the coast broke somewhat the violence of the sea, and the Dragon rode all night to her anchors; but in the morning the wind continued to rise. The sea became more and more violent, and the anchors began to drag. Edmund and Egbert, after a consultation, agreed that their only chance of saving the vessel was to enter the river. The tide was running in, but the sea was so heavy on the bar of the river that the efforts of the crew at the oars barely sufficed to keep her on her course. At length, however, she made her way safely between the posts which marked the entrance, and rowing up until they passed a turn, and were sheltered from the force of the gale, they again anchored.

The oars were all lashed out firmly to keep any boats from approaching her sides. Bales of goods with which her hold was filled were brought on deck, and piled high along the bulwarks so as to afford a shelter from missiles. Even as they entered the harbour numbers of Danes had assembled at the point; for the capture and destruction of their ships had of course been seen, and the crews set ashore had spread the news that the strange vessel was a Saxon. The Norfolk bank being somewhat higher than the Suffolk, the boat was anchored rather nearer to the latter, as it was from the town of Yarmouth that an attack was anticipated.

As soon as the anchors were let go the Danes began to fire their arrows; but so powerful was the gale that the greater part of them were swept far away. As the day went on the numbers of Danes on the bank increased largely, and vast numbers of arrows were discharged at the Dragon. The crew kept under shelter, and although she was often struck no damage was done.

In the afternoon a fleet of galleys was seen coming down the river. The Danes possessed a large number of these boats at Yarmouth, and in these they navigated the inland waters far into the interior. The wind had shifted until it was blowing nearly due east, and Edmund and Egbert had agreed upon the best course to be pursued. In case of attack they could hardly hope finally to beat off the assault of a large fleet of galleys, and would besides be exposed to attack by boats laden with combustibles. Therefore as soon as the galleys were seen approaching the oars were unlashed, the great sail hoisted, and at her best speed the Dragon advanced up the river to meet her foes. The Danes gave a shout of alarm as the vessel advanced to meet them with the water surging in a white wave from her bows, and the greater part of them hurried towards one bank or the other to escape the shock. Some, slower in movement or stouter in heart, awaited the attack, while from all a storm of missiles was poured upon the advancing boat.

Heedless of these she continued her way. Her sharp bow crashed right through the side of the Danish boats, and having destroyed seven of them on her way she passed through the flotilla and continued her course. The dragon waved triumphantly from her mast as she passed under the walls of Yarmouth. These were crowded with Danes, who vainly showered arrows and javelins as she flew past, with the fleets of galleys rowing in her wake. A few minutes and she was out on the broad sheet of water beyond. The Danish galleys paused at the entrance. In so wild a storm they would have had difficulty in keeping their boats straight, while the great galley with her sails and oars would be able to maneuver freely, and could strike and run them down one by one.

"What is that pile of buildings on the rising knoll of ground some three miles away?" Edmund asked.

"It is Bamborough Castle," Egbert replied, "a Roman stronghold of immense strength."

"Let us run up thither," Edmund said. "If, as is likely enough, it is unoccupied, we will land there and take possession. Are the walls complete?"

"Assuredly they are," Egbert said. "They are of marvellous strength, such as we cannot build in our days. They run in a great semicircle from the edge of the water round the crest of the knoll and down again to the water. There is but one gateway in the wall on the land side, and this we can block up. We need not fear an attack from the land, for between the river and the castle there are wide swamps; so that unless they row up and attack us from the water we are safe."

"I think that they will not do that," Edmund said, "after the taste which the Dragon has given them of her quality. At any rate I think we are safe till the storm abates."

By this time, running rapidly before the wind, the Dragon was approaching the great Roman fort, whose massive walls struck Edmund with astonishment. No one was to be seen moving about in the space inclosed by them. The sail was lowered and the vessel brought to the bank. The anchors were taken ashore and she was soon solidly moored. Then the crew leapt on to the land and ascended the bank to the great level inclosure.

The walls were, as Egbert had said, intact--and indeed, except on the side facing the river, remained almost unbroken to the present day. An hour's labour sufficed to block the gateway, where a pair of massive doors were in position, for the place had been defended by the Saxons against the Danes at their first landing on the coast. A few men were placed as sentries on the walls, and, feeling now perfectly safe from any attack on the land side, Edmund and his followers returned on board the Dragon for the night.

CHAPTER VIII: THE CRUISE OF THE DRAGON

THE night passed without alarm. The gale continued to blow with fury, and until it abated Edmund had little fear that the Danes would venture upon an attack. They had indeed no reason for haste. The Saxon vessel was in their waters, and could not return so long as the storm continued to blow from the east. The next day parties of Danes were seen making their way across the swampy country from the direction of Yarmouth.

As soon, however, as these approached near enough to see the Saxons in readiness on the walls of the castle they retired at once, knowing that the place could be captured by nothing short of a prolonged and desperate siege. On the fourth day the storm abated, and the Saxons prepared to make their way seaward again. The wind still blew, but lightly, from the same quarter, and the sails would therefore be of no use. With their great oar-power they were confident that, once through the Danish flotilla, they could defy pursuit.

Accordingly they again embarked, and loosing their moorings rowed down towards Yarmouth. They had chosen a time when the tide was running in; for although this would hinder their progress it would equally impede their pursuers, while it would enable them to check their vessel in time did they find any unforeseen obstacle in their way. They entered the river and rowed along quietly until they neared the walls of the town. Here the river was at its narrowest, and they saw the Danish galleys gathered thickly in the stream.

Edmund and Egbert were on the forecastle, and presently gave the signal for the men to cease rowing.

"It is just as I expected," Egbert said; "they have formed a boom across the river of trunks of trees and beams lashed together. We cannot make our way down until that obstacle is removed. What say you Edmund?"

"I agree with you," Edmund replied.

"We had best keep along close to the right bank until within a short distance of the boom; then we must land the greater part of our men. These must march along the bank in their phalanx; the others must keep the boat moving close alongside, and from the forecastle they will be able to fire down upon the Danes and aid those on shore to drive them back and make their way to the end of the boom. They have but to cut the lashings there and the whole will swing round. But now we see the nature of the obstacle, and what is to be done, it were best to wait until the tide turns. In the first place, fewer men will be needed on board the ship, as she will advance by herself abreast of the men on shore. In the second place, when the lashing is cut the boom will then swing down the stream, will cause confusion among the boats behind it, and will open a clear space for us to make our way down."

Edmund agreed, a light anchor was dropped, and the Dragon rode quietly in the stream. Great animation was evident among the Danes, large numbers crossed the river, and a strong force gathered at either end of the boom and in boats close behind it, to prevent the Saxons from attempting to cut the lashings. There was little uneasiness on board the Dragon, the Saxons were confident now of the power of their close formation to force its way through any number of the enemy, and they would gain such assistance from the fire from the lofty forecastle that they doubted not that they should be able to drive back the Danes and destroy the boom. In an hour the tide no longer rose. They waited till it ran down with full force, then the anchor was hauled up, and the Dragon rowed to the bank.

Sixty of the fighting men headed by Egbert leapt on shore. Edmund with the remainder took his place on the forecastle. The oars next to the bank were drawn in, and some of those on the outward side manned by the sailors. Then in its usual order the phalanx moved slowly forward while the ship floated along beside them close to the bank. The Danes with loud shouts advanced to meet them, and the arrows soon began to fly thickly. Covered by the long shields of the front rank the Saxons moved forward steadily, while, as the Danes approached, the archers on the forecastle opened a destructive fire upon them.

The confidence of the Saxons was justified, for the combat was never in doubt. Although the Northmen fought bravely they were unable to withstand the steady advance of the wedge of spears, and very many fell beneath the rain of arrows from above. Steadily the wedge made its way until it reached the end of the boom. A few blows with their axes sufficed to cut the cables which fastened it in its place. As soon as this was done Edmund gave a shout, and the Saxons at once sprang on board the ship, which before the Danes could follow them was steered out into the stream.

As Egbert had foreseen, the boom as it swung round swept before it a number of the Danish boats, and imprisoned them between it and the shore. The oars were soon run out, and while the men on the forecastle continued their fire at the Danish boats, the others seizing the oars swept the Dragon along the stream. The Danes strove desperately to arrest her progress. Some tried to run alongside and board, others dashed in among the oars and impeded the work of the rowers, while from the walls of the town showers of missiles were poured down upon her. But the tide was gaining every moment in strength, and partly drifting, partly rowing, the Dragon, like a bull attacked by a pack of dogs, made her way down the river. Every effort of the Danes to board was defeated, and many of their boats sunk, and at last she made her way into the open sea. There her sails were hoisted, and she soon left her pursuers behind. Once at sea her course was again turned north, and picking up some prizes on the way she took up her station off the mouth of the Humber.

Several ships were captured as they sailed out from the river. After the spoil on board was taken out, these, instead of being burnt, as had always been the case before, were allowed to proceed on their way, since had they been destroyed the crews must either have been slain or landed. The first course was repugnant to Edmund, the second could not be adopted, because they would have carried the news to the Danes, that the Dragon was off the river and no more ships would have put to sea; and indeed, so large was the number of Danish vessels always up the Humber that a fleet could easily have been equipped and sent out, before which the Dragon must have taken flight.

One day a large sailing ship was seen coming out. The Dragon remained with lowered sail until she had passed; then started in pursuit, and speedily came up with the Danish vessel. Edmund summoned her to surrender, and was answered by a Norseman of great stature and noble appearance, who from the poop hurled a javelin, which would have pierced Edmund had he not leapt quickly aside. A few other darts were thrown and then the Dragon ran alongside the enemy and boarded her.

The opposition of the Northmen was speedily beaten down, but their leader desperately defended the ladder leading to the poop. He was struck by two arrows, and fell on one knee, and Edmund was about to climb the ladder when the door of the cabin in the poop opened, and a Norse maiden some sixteen years old sprang out. Seeing her father wounded at the top of the ladder and the Saxons preparing to ascend it, while others turned their bows against the wounded Northman, she sprang forward and throwing herself upon her knees before Edmund besought him to spare her father's life. Edmund raised his hand and the bows were lowered.

"I have no wish to slay your father, maiden," he said gently; "we slay only those who resist, and resistance on the part of a single man, and he wounded, against a whole ship's crew is madness. We are no sea-wolves who slay for the pleasure of slaying, but are Saxons, who fight for our country against the oppressions and rapine of your people. Little right have they to mercy seeing they show none; but our religion enjoins us to have pity even upon our enemies. You had best ascend to your father and see to his wounds, none will harm you or him."

The girl with an exclamation of thanks sprang up the ladder. Edmund superintended the searching of the ship. She contained a great store of valuables, which were speedily transferred to the Dragon. When this had been done Edmund ascended to the poop. The jarl was sitting in a great chair placed there. Edmund had already learnt from the crew that he was Jarl Siegbert, a noted leader of the Northmen. His daughter had drawn out the arrows and bandaged the wounds.

"Jarl Siegbert," Edmund said as he approached him, "you have been a bitter enemy of the Saxons, and small mercy have you shown to those who have fallen into your hands, but learn now that we Christian Saxons take no vengeance on a defenceless foe. You are free to pursue your voyage with your daughter and your ship to Norway. Your stores we have made free with, seeing that they are all plunder taken from the Saxons, and we do but reclaim our own."

"And who are you, young sir?" the jarl asked.

"I am one of King Alfred's ealdormen of Wessex, Edmund by name."

"I have heard of you," the Dane said, "as one who has taught the Saxons new tactics, fighting in a close body which has more than once pierced our lines and caused our overthrow; but you are a mere lad."

"I am young," Edmund replied, "and had it not been for the invasions and oppressions of your countrymen, might have still accounted myself as scarce a man; but you have made warriors of every West Saxon capable of bearing a sword. Remember, jarl, that your life has been in Saxon hands, and that they have spared it, so come not hither to our shores again."

"I purpose not doing so," the Northman replied. "I have seen enough of stricken fields, and was returning to my own country to hang up my sword, content with the fame I have gained, until Woden called me to join his warriors and feast in his halls. Since we may not meet there, young Saxon--for they say that you Christians look to a place where arms will be laid aside and the sound of feasting be unheard--I will say farewell. For myself, I thank you not for my life, for I would rather have died as I have lived with my sword in my hand; but for my daughter's sake I thank you, for she is but young to be left unprotected in the world."

A few minutes later, the Danish vessel continued on her way, and the Dragon again took her station on the look-out. She was now deep in the water, and after picking up one or two more small prizes, Edmund and Egbert determined to return home.

It was probable that the Danes would soon take the alarm and despatch a fleet to attack them. Laden down as the Dragon was, her speed under oars was materially affected, and it was advisable to stow away their booty before proceeding with further adventures. Her head was turned south, and she coasted down the eastern shores of England without adventure. Several Danish vessels were seen arriving at or quitting the coast, but the Dragon continued her course without heeding them, and rounding the Forelands, sailed along the south coast and made her way up the Parrot.

Upon inquiry they learnt that no event of any importance had taken place during their absence. The Danes were complete masters of the country. King Alfred was in hiding, none knew where. The greater portion of the Danes were at their camp at Chippenham, but parties roamed here and there through the land.

Dressed as countrymen, Edmund and Egbert made their way to Exeter, and there arranged with some traders for the purchase of the less valuable portion of the Dragons cargo. This consisted of rich clothing, silks and other stuffs, wine, vestments, and altar hangings from churches, arms and armour, hides and skins. The prices obtained were far below the real value of the articles, for money was scarce,

and none could say when the Danes might again swoop down and clear out the contents of the warehouses. Nevertheless the sum obtained was a large one for those
days, and this did not include the value of the gold and silver goblets, salvers, vases,
and utensils used in the celebration of religious services.

Of these, spoiled from the houses of the wealthy, and the churches and monasteries, they had obtained a considerable number. These were buried in the wood
near the lonely spot at which the Dragon was moored, the rest of the cargo was
sent in wagons--the more valuable portions hidden under the hides and skins--to
Exeter. The amount which had been obtained from the cargo was divided as agreed
before starting: twenty-five shares were set apart for the king, twenty-five shares
were divided between the two leaders, and each soldier and sailor had one share.
All were well satisfied with the success of the adventure, and with the damage
which they had inflicted upon the Danes.

A fortnight's leave was given, for the men to visit their homes, and the money
which they had gained in their trip was of great use to their friends in enabling
them to repair the damages effected by the Danes. Not a man was absent at the appointed time, and the Dragon again made her way down to the sea.

It was midwinter now, and they cruised along the southern coast of England
without perceiving a single hostile sail. They lay for a week off the mouth of the
Thames, and then saw four large Danish vessels making their way down the river.
They were all vessels of the largest size, strongly built, and full of men, and the
Saxons judged them to be too strong to be attacked in company. The Northmen, on
seeing the golden dragon flying at the mast-head of the Saxon ship, at once made
towards her, keeping in a close body; but the Dragon with sails and oars easily left
them behind, and the Danes giving up the pursuit continued on their way.

The Dragon fell into their wake and followed at a distance, hoping that one
might prove slower than the others, or that they might in the night get separated.
At nightfall, however, the Danes lit cressets of tar and hemp, which enabled them
not only to keep close together, but sent out a wide circle of light, so that they could
perceive the Dragon should she venture to approach.

For two days and nights the Dragon followed patiently.

"The weather is about to change," Egbert said on the third morning. "Methinks
that there is a storm brewing, and if this be so the Northmen may well get sepa-

rated, and we may pick up one away from her fellows."

Darker and darker grew the sky, and the wind soon blew in furious gusts, raising a sea so heavy that the Saxons were obliged to lay in their oars. By nightfall it was blowing a furious gale. In the gathering darkness and the flying scud the ships of the Danes were lost sight of; but this was of little consequence now, for the attention of the Saxons was directed to their own safety.

For the next three days their position was one of the greatest danger. With only a rag of sail set they ran before the gale from the south-west. Every wave as it overtook them threatened the destruction of the ship; but the Dragon, light and buoyant, and ably handled, rode safely over the waves. On the fourth morning the wind was still blowing fiercely, although its force had in some degree moderated. As the daylight dawned Edmund and Egbert, who had hardly left the poop since the storm began, looked anxiously ahead.

"Surely, Edmund, I see a dark mass ahead?" Egbert exclaimed.

For a minute or two Edmund gazed silently ahead.

"It is so, Egbert," he said; "it is a rocky coast. Do you not see a white fringe below where the waves strike against it?"

As the light became clearer the imminence of their peril grew more distinct. A lofty iron-bound coast rose in front of them, and extended as far as the eye could reach on either hand. The seas broke with terrible force against its base, sending its spray far up on the cliffs.

"Could we bring her about?" Edmund asked the chief of the sailors.

"It would be useless," the man said. "She could not make her way in the teeth of this gale."

"That I see," Edmund said; "but at present we are rushing on to destruction. If we bring her to the wind we may run some distance along the coast before we are driven ashore, and may perceive some spot towards which we may direct her with a chance of making land ere she goes to pieces."

The sail was still further lessened and the ship's head brought round parallel with the coast.

The Dragon laboured tremendously as the sea struck her full on the beam, and every wave flooded her low waist. Each sea which struck her lifted her bodily to leeward, and for every foot she sailed forward she was driven one towards the coast.

This was now but three miles distant, and another hour would ensure her destruction; for none there hoped that the anchors, even should they find bottom, could hold her for an instant in the teeth of the gale. Every eye was directed towards the shore, but no break could be seen in the wall of rock which rose almost perpendicularly from the water.

"I fear it is hopeless," Edmund said to Egbert; "the strongest swimmer would be dashed to pieces in an instant against those rocks."

"He would indeed," Egbert replied. "I wish now that we had boldly engaged the four Danish ships. Far better would it have been for us to have died fighting for England on her decks than to have perished here."

The time passed slowly. Every minute the Dragon was swept nearer and nearer towards the rocks.

"She will just make that headland," the master sailor said, "and that is all. Once round it we had best turn her head to the rocks. If the cliffs rise as here sheer from the water, the moment she strikes will be the last for all of us; but if the rocks are, as in some places, piled high at the foot of the cliffs, a few may possibly manage to leap from her forecastle as she strikes and to clamber up."

Scarce a word was spoken on board the Dragon as she came abreast of the headland. It was but a few hundred yards away. The roar of the seas as they struck its base sounded high above the din of the storm. Great sheets of foam were thrown up to a vast height, and the turmoil of the water from the reflux of the waves was so great that the Dragon was tossed upon it like a cock-boat, and each man had to grasp at shroud or bulwark to retain his footing.

Suddenly a cheer burst from end to end of the ship. Beyond the headland a great gap was visible a quarter of a mile wide, as if the cliffs had been rent in sunder by some tremendous convulsion, and a fiord was seen stretching away in the bosom of the hills as far as the eye could reach. The Dragon's head was turned, and soon she was flying before the wind up the inlet. A mile farther and the fiord widened to a lake some two miles across between steep hills clothed from foot to summit with trees.

Its course was winding and they were soon sheltered from the gale and were gliding quietly over comparatively tranquil water. Ten miles up the anchor was let go in a sheltered inlet, and Edmund summoned the whole crew to return thanks to

God for their marvellous escape.

The Dragon had suffered severely in her conflict with the elements, her large sails had been split or blown away, the bulwarks at her waist had been shattered, and considerable damage done to her gear and fittings. Four-and-twenty hours were allowed to the men for rest after their labours, and then all hands were set to work to refit.

The next morning Edmund said to his kinsman:

"I will take two of the men and go ashore to hunt; there should be wild boar and deer in these forests, and all would be glad of some fresh meat."

"Be careful, Edmund; remember you are in the country of our enemies, for without doubt this land to which we have been blown is Norway; and although we can see no signs of habitations there may well be villages somewhere among these hills."

"I will be careful," Edmund said, laughing; "and if I do not return in two days do you set sail without me. I should like to discover the abode of some Northern jarl; it would indeed be a grand retaliation to give them a taste of the sufferings they have inflicted upon us."

"That would be good work," Egbert said; "nevertheless I own that at present I am anxious to be at sea again."

"Two days will be sufficient to refit," Edmund said, "and then we will spread our wings. Good-bye, Egbert, I will be back by sunset, and I hope with a deer or two."

Selecting a couple of followers, both skilled with the bow, and all being armed with spears, Edmund leapt ashore, for the water was deep up to the rocks, and the Dragon had been moored alongside for the convenience of taking on board the wood for the repairs.

Although those on board the Dragon guessed it not, many eyes were watching them. A small fishing village lay at the edge of the fiord a mile or two beyond the inlet in which the ship was moored. Hidden as they were among the trees the huts had not been noticed by the Saxons, but the strange ship had been seen by some of those in the village, and the fishermen at once pronounced that whencesoever she might have come she was assuredly no Northman's ship. Messengers had immediately been sent to the villages among the hills. These were widely scattered, and it was not until the day after the ship's arrival that a force was collected which was deemed sufficient to attack it. Already, as Edmund leapt ashore, the Norsemen were making their way quietly through the forest towards the Dragon.

Edmund had advanced but a few hundred yards up the hillside when a large party of Norsemen suddenly sprang upon him. Two Saxon arrows flew true to their marks, then the Danes rushed upon them. So far no words had been spoken, but Edmund placed to his lips the whistle with which he gave orders on board the ship and blew a long shrill note, and then shouted at the top of his voice:

"The Danes! the Danes! push off!"

The instant afterwards he was attacked. He and his men fought bravely, but in a few seconds the latter were cut down and Edmund was levelled to the ground by a tremendous blow from a club.

A minute later the din of battle rose by the water's side; Edmund's whistle and shout had been heard, and the Saxons on shore sprang on board and seized their spears and bows just as the Danes poured down through the trees. For a time the Saxons defended the ship against the desperate attempts of the Danes to gain footing on her; but seeing the number of its assailants, and being certain that Edmund was killed or captured, Egbert ordered the ropes to be cut, and the Dragon was thrust away from the rocks. The oars were then got out and she rowed out of bowshot from the shore. Then Egbert held a consultation with the leading men among the Saxons.

All on board were filled with grief at the loss of their young leader, but they felt that nothing could be done for him, and it would be but courting danger to remain longer in the fiord. Since so large a force had been collected in the forest news might have been sent to the ports, and at any moment they might see a fleet of the Northmen's galleys barring their retreat; therefore with bitter grief and lamentation the Dragon's sails were hoisted and she made her way to sea.

"My only consolation is," Egbert said, "that if the brave lad is not killed at once he may yet find his way back to England. He is ready of wit and full of invention that, if any can possibly extricate themselves from such a strait, it is assuredly he; but I fear that he fell in the first onslaught. Brave lad, even in the moment of his own peril he thought first of us. Had it not been for his timely warning we should have been taken unawares, and many must have been killed even if the Dragon herself escaped capture."

The storm had entirely abated, and the waters sparkled brightly in the cold January sun as the Dragon sailed out between the two headlands into the sea. Very different were the feelings of the crew to those which had animated them when, two days before, they had passed through the channel; then every heart beat with joy and thankfulness; now the deepest depression and grief reigned on board.

Edmund was adored by his followers. His kindness as their ealdorman, his skill and bravery as a leader, his cheerfulness and brightness under every danger and peril had immensely endeared him to their hearts, and each man felt that he had sustained an irretrievable loss, and that with their chief the spirit which had animated the Dragon and directed their enterprises was gone.

Egbert was a valiant warrior, and was an admirable second to an enterprising leader; but he was altogether without initiative, and, except when excited by danger, was dull and silent. Although all esteemed him and honoured him for his strength and bravery, they felt that he would be a poor substitute indeed for the leader they had lost.

CHAPTER IX: A PRISONER

WHEN Edmund recovered his senses he found that he was being carried along on a rough litter through the forest. It was some little time before he realized his position and recalled the circumstances of the attack. After the Dragon had moved safely out into the fiord, its assailants had returned to the spot where they had attacked the three Saxons who had landed. Two of them were without life, but they found that the third, who, from his habiliments was evidently of higher rank, and whom they judged, although still but a youth, to be the commander of the Saxon party, had only been stunned by the blow of the club which had felled him.

It was at once resolved to carry him to the jarl of the district, who would assuredly wish to learn from him the meaning of the coming of the strange ship. That the Dragon was a Saxon vessel the Northmen were sure. Many of them had been on expeditions across the seas, and knew the Saxons both from their dress and manner of wearing their hair, but the ship was unlike anything they had seen before, and it seemed above all things strange that when, as they understood, England had been completely conquered, Saxon warships should be entering a northern fiord.

For many hours Edmund was carried through the forest. He wondered to himself whether he would be slain on his arrival or kept as a slave, for the Norse and Saxon tongues were so similar that he was perfectly able to understand the language of his captors. A party of twelve men accompanied him, four of whom bore the litter, and were relieved at intervals by the others. After some hours the feeling of giddiness and weakness passed off, and on the men stopping to change bearers he expressed his readiness to walk.

Hitherto he had lain with his eyes closed, as he thought it better to remain as he was until he felt perfectly able to keep up with his captors in a journey which might, for aught he knew, be a long one. The Northmen expressed their satisfaction at finding that their burden need no longer be carried, and throwing aside the boughs which had formed the litter, proceeded with him on their way. They asked him many questions concerning the Dragon. Most of these he answered readily enough, but he evaded those as to the place where she had been built, or the port from which she had sailed. It was not until late in the afternoon that they arrived at the abode of the Jarl Bijorn.

It was a rough abode constructed of timber, thatched with rushes, for as yet the Northmen were scarcely a settled people, the tribes for the most part wandering in the forests hunting when not engaged in those warlike expeditions which they loved above all other things. Only the leaders dwelt in anything like permanent abodes, the rest raising huts of boughs at such places as they might make any stay at.

One of Edmund's conductors had gone on ahead, and as the party approached the building Bijorn came out from his house to meet them. He was, like almost all Northmen, a man of great stature and immense strength. Some fifty years had passed over his head, but he was still in the prime of his life; for the Northmen, owing to their life of constant activity, the development of their muscles from childhood, and their existence passed in the open air, retained their strength and vigour to a great age.

So assiduous was their training, and so rapidly did their figures develop in consequence, that at the age of fifteen a young Northman received arms and was regarded as a man, although he did not marry until many years afterwards, early wedlock being strongly discouraged among them. By Bijorn's side stood his son, who, though but twenty-two years old, rivalled him in stature and in muscular development, although lacking the great width of shoulder of the jarl.

As Edmund approached, a war-horse of the jarl fastened up to a post close to the entrance of the house neighed loudly. Bijorn looked surprised. The neighing of a horse among the Northmen was regarded as the happiest of auguries, and in their sacred groves horses were tied up, as the neighing of these animals was considered an infallible proof that a propitious answer would be given by the gods to the prayer of any petitioner who sought their aid.

"By Thor!" Bijorn exclaimed, "my good war-horse welcomes the stranger. As I said to you anon, Sweyn, I had intended to offer him as a sacrifice to Odin; but as the gods have thus declared him welcome here I must needs change my intentions. Who are you, young Saxon?" he asked as Edmund was brought before him, "and whence do you come? And how is it that a war-ship of your people is found upon our coasts?"

"I am Edmund," the young man said steadily, "an ealdorman of King Alfred of the West Saxons. The ship which was seen on your coast is mine; I built it to attack the Northmen who harry our coasts. I am here because, when in chase of four of your ships, a storm arose and blew us hither."

"You speak boldly," the jarl said, "for one in the hands of his foes. How old are you?"

"I am twenty-two," Edmund replied.

"The same age as you, Sweyn. Stand side by side and let me compare you. Ay," he went on, "he lacks nigh three inches of your height, but he is more than that bigger across the shoulders--a stalwart young champion, indeed, and does brave credit to his rearing. These West Saxons have shown themselves worthy foemen, and handled us roughly last year, as this will testify," and he pointed to the scar of a sword-cut across his face. "Doubtless this is the son of that Saxon earl who more than once last summer inflicted heavy losses upon us. Is that so, young Saxon?"

"I am the Ealdorman Edmund himself," the young man replied quietly. "My successes were won not by my own strength or courage, but by the valour of those under me, who, fighting in a novel manner, gained advantage over your Northmen."

"By Thor!" Bijorn exclaimed, "and this is the youth who attacked us at night and drove off the cattle we had taken and slew many of our followers, Sweyn! Truly he would be a rare sacrifice to offer to Odin; but the god has himself welcomed him here."

"It may be that he welcomed him as a sacrifice, father," Sweyn suggested.

"Ah! that may be so," the jarl replied. "We must consult the omens to find out the true meaning of my charger's neighing. Nevertheless in either case I shall be content, for if he be not welcomed as a sacrifice he is welcome as bringing good fortune; and in truth he will make a noble cup-bearer to me. It is not every jarl who is waited upon by a Saxon ealdorman. But till the omens have spoken let him be set aside and carefully watched. In a day or two we will journey to Odin's temple and there consult the auguries."

Three days passed, during which Edmund was well fed and treated. At the end of that time he was ordered to accompany the jarl on a journey. Two days' travelling brought them to a temple of Odin. It was a rough structure of unhewn stones situated in a wood. Bijorn and his son entered, while Edmund remained without under a guard. Presently the jarl and his son came out with a priest. The latter carried a white bag in his hand with twelve small pieces of wood. On half of these four small nicks were cut, on the others five nicks. All were placed in the bag, which was then shaken.

"Now," the priest said, "you will see the will of Odin; the first three sticks drawn out will declare it. If two of the three bear an even number of nicks, the neigh of your horse signifies that Odin accepted the sacrifice; if two of them bear unequal numbers, then it meant that his coming was propitious to you."

The bag was again shaken. Edmund looked on calmly, for Saxons and Northmen alike disdained to show the slightest fear of death; even the colour did not fade from his cheek as he watched the trial upon which his life depended.

The first stick drawn out bore five marks; the priest showed it to the jarl, and without a word dropped it in the bag again. This was again shaken and another stick drawn out; this bore but four notches; the chances were even. The silence was unbroken until the third twig was drawn.

"Odin has spoken," the priest said. "The neigh of the horse indicated that the coming of this Saxon was propitious to your house."

The jarl gave an exclamation of satisfaction, while Sweyn's brow darkened. Bijorn had indeed set his heart upon retaining this famous young Saxon leader as his slave and cup-bearer, and it was probable that in his interview with the priest before the drawing his inclinations had been clearly shown, for a slight difference between the thickness of the sticks might well have existed and served as an index to the priest in drawing them.

Bijorn, in his gratification at the answer of the god, bestowed a handsome present upon the priest, and then rode back to his abode well content with his journey. Edmund was at once installed in his new duties. Hitherto he had not entered the house nor seen the females of the family. Ulfra, the jarl's wife, was a woman of commanding stature and appearance. Like most of the northern women she had accompanied her husband in his many wanderings, and shared his dangers and privations. The wives of the Norsemen occupied a far more exalted position in the households of their lords than did those of the people of southern Europe; they were not only mistresses of the house, but were treated with respect as well as with affection; they were not, as in the south, regarded as puppets for the amusements of an idle hour, but were the companions and advisers of their husbands, occupying a position at least as free and respected as at the present day.

There were two daughters, who both bade fair to resemble their mother in stature and dignity of demeanour, for both were models of female strength and activity. Edmund's duties were light. In the morning he gathered firewood for the household; at the meals he handed the dishes, and taking his station behind the jarl's chair, refilled his goblet with mead as often as it was empty. Usually a large party sat down to supper, for an expedition to France was talked of in the spring, and the jarls and warriors often met to discuss the place of starting, the arrangements for the voyage, and the numbers which each leader would place in the field. The feasts were kept up to a late hour, and, as was the invariable custom of the Northmen, the arrangements decided upon overnight were rediscussed at a morning meeting; for they held that while over the wine-cup each man would speak the truth frankly and honestly, the colder counsels and greater prudence which the morning brought were needed before any matter could be finally settled.

A month thus passed, and Bijorn, his family and followers then moved south, as there was to be a great conference near the southern point of the country, at which a large number of the chiefs from Denmark were to be present.

Edmund observed that for some reason Sweyn was looking forward anxiously to this meeting, and his sisters more than once joked him about his anxiety.

"Pooh! pooh!" the jarl said one day in answer to such an observation. "Sweyn is but a lad yet. I know what you are driving at, and that Sweyn is smitten with the charms of my old companion's daughter, the pretty Freda; I noted it when we were in camp together; but it will be fully another ten years yet before Sweyn can think of marrying. He has got to win for himself the name of a great warrior before a jarl's daughter of proper spirit would so much as think of him. When he has the spoils of France to lay at her feet it will be time enough."

Sweyn made no reply, but Edmund saw that he was far from pleased at his father's words, and a look of surly determination on his face showed the young Saxon that he would go his own way in the matter if it lay in his power.

After ten days' travelling the party arrived at the rendezvous. Here drawn up on the shore were a vast number of galleys of all sizes, for the greater part of those who had assembled had journeyed by sea. Great numbers of huts of boughs and many tents constructed of sails had been erected. Edmund and the other slaves, these being either Saxon or Franks captured in war, soon erected bowers for the jarl and his family.

Edmund had been looking forward to the meeting with much anxiety, for he had judged that some mode of escape might there open to him. Among the Saxon slaves were several young men of strength and vigour, and Edmund had confided to them his project of stealing a boat and sailing away in it, and they, knowing that he had experience in navigation, had readily consented to join him in making an effort for freedom.

The jarl and his family were warmly welcomed by many of their companions in arms, and the day after their arrival Bijorn told Edmund to accompany him to a banquet at which he and his family were to be present. At four in the afternoon they set out and presently arrived at a large tent. Edmund waited without until the attendants carried in the dishes, when he entered with them and prepared to take his place behind his master's seat. From a few words which had passed between Sweyn and his sisters Edmund doubted not that the companion with whom Bijorn was going to dine was the father of the maiden about whom they had joked him. He was not surprised when on entering he saw Sweyn talking earnestly with a damsel somewhat apart from the rest.

The entrance of the viands was the signal for all to take their places at the table. There were in all sixteen in number, and as nearly half were women the meeting was evidently of a family character, as upon occasions of importance or when serious discussions were to take place men alone sat down. As Edmund advanced to take his place, his eye fell upon the jarl who seated himself at the head of the table, and as he did so he gave a slight start of surprise, for he at once recognized in him the Northman Siegbert, whose ship he had stopped at the mouth of the Humber. From him his eye glanced at the girl by whose side Sweyn was on the point of seating himself, and recognized in her the maiden who had besought her father's life.

The dinner commenced and proceeded for some little time, when Edmund saw the girl looking fixedly at him.

"Who is that who is standing behind your father's chair?" she asked Sweyn.

"A Saxon slave," he answered. "His vessel was well-nigh wrecked on our coast. Our people captured him and slew some of his followers, and the ship speedily took to flight."

"Father," the girl said in a clear voice, which at once attracted the attention of all, "unless my eyes deceive me the young Saxon standing behind Jarl Bijorn is he whose ship captured us as we left England, and who suffered no harm to be done to us."

The Northman turned in his chair.

"It is he, Freda, surely enough, though how he comes to be a slave here to my comrade Bijorn I know not. Bijorn, my friend, I owe this youth a deep debt of gratitude; he had my life and the life and honour of Freda in his hands, and he spared both, and, slave though he may be of yours at present, yet I hail him as my friend. Tell me how came he in your hands? He is Edmund, the valiant young Saxon who smote us more than once so heavily down in Wessex."

"I know it," Bijorn replied, "and will tell you how he came into my hands, and in truth he was captured by accident and not by any valour of my arm." The jarl then related the circumstances under which Edmund had been captured, and the narrow escape he had had of being offered as a sacrifice to Odin. And Siegbert then told his guests at length the incidents of his capture by the Dragon.

"He let me go free and without a ransom," he concluded, "and that part of my obligation I should be glad to repay, though for his gentleness to Freda I must still remain his debtor. What say you, Bijorn, will you sell him to me? Name your price in horses, arms, and armour, and whatever it be I will pay it to you."

"In truth, Siegbert," Bijorn said, "I like not to part with the lad; but since you are so urgent, and seeing that you cannot otherwise discharge the obligation under which, as you say, he has laid you, I cannot refuse your prayer. As to the price, we will arrange that anon."

"Then it is settled," Siegbert said. "You are a free man, Ealdorman Edmund," and he held out his hand to the youth. "Now seat yourself at the table with my guests; there are none here but may feel honoured at dining with one of King Alfred's bravest thanes."

The transformation in Edmund's position was sudden indeed; a moment since he was a slave, and although he had determined upon making an effort for freedom, he had known that the chances of escape were small, as swift galleys would have been sent off in pursuit, and it was probable that he would have been speedily over-taken and brought back. Now he was free, and would doubtless be allowed to return home with the first party who sailed thither.

Siegbert at once tried to make Edmund feel at home, addressing much of his conversation to him. Bijorn, too, spoke in a friendly manner with him, but Sweyn was silent and sullen; he was clearly ill-pleased at this change of fortune which had turned his father's slave into a fellow-guest and equal. His annoyance was greatly heightened by the fact that it was Freda who had recognized the young Saxon, and the pleasure which her face evinced when her father proposed to purchase him from Bijorn angered him still more. In his heart he cursed the horse whose wel-coming neigh had in the first instance saved Edmund's life, and the trial by augury which had confirmed the first omen. After the banquet was over Siegbert requested Edmund to relate his various adventures.

The telling of tales of daring was one of the favourite amusements of the Danes; Siegbert and his friends quaffed great bumpers of mead; and the ladies sat apart lis-tening while Edmund told his story.

"You have a brave record, indeed," Siegbert said when he had finished, "for one so young; and fond as are our youths of adventure there is not one of them of your age who has accomplished a tithe of what you have done. Why, Freda, if this youth were but one of us he would have the hearts of all the Norse maidens at his feet. In the eyes of a Danish girl, as of a Dane, valour is the highest of recommendations."

"I don't know, father," Freda said, colouring at being thus addressed, "that we should be as bold as that, although assuredly it is but right that a maiden should esteem valour highly. It is to her husband she has to look for protection, and she shares in the honour and spoil which he gains by his valiant deeds, so you have always taught me."

"And rightly too, girl. Next to being a great hero, the greatest honour is to be the wife of one. I pledge you, Ealdorman Edmund, and should be right proud were you a son of mine. You have told your story modestly, for many of the battles and adventures of which you have spoken are known to me by report, and fame has given you a larger share in the successes than you claim for yourself. 'Tis a pity you were not born a Northman, for there is little for you to do in Saxon England now."

"I do not despair yet," Edmund replied. "Things have gone badly with us, but the last blow is not struck yet. You will hear of King Alfred in the spring, unless I am mistaken."

"But they say your King Alfred is half a monk, and that he loves reading books more than handling the sword, though, to do him justice, he has shown himself a brave warrior, and has given us far more trouble than all the other Saxon kings together."

"King Alfred fights bravely," Edmund said, "because he is fighting for his country and people; but it is true that he loves not war nor strife. He reads much and thinks more, and should he ever come to his kingdom again he will assuredly be one of the wisest and best monarchs who has ever sat on a throne. He has talked to me much of the things which he has at heart, and I know he intends to draw up wise laws for the ruling of his people."

"We love not greatly being ruled, we Northmen," Bijorn said, "but for each to go his own way as he wills, provided only he inflicts no ill upon his neighbour. We come and we go each as it pleases him. Our fleets traverse the sea and bring home plunder and booty. What need we of laws?"

"At present you have no great need of laws," Edmund replied, "seeing that you lead a wandering life; but when the time shall come--and it must come to you as it has come to other nations--when you will settle down as a rich and peaceful community, then laws will become necessary."

"Well," Bijorn said, "right glad am I that I live before such times have come. So far as I can see the settling down you speak of, and the abandonment of the ancient gods has done no great good either to you Saxons or to the Franks. Both of you were in the old time valiant people, while now you are unable to withstand our arms. You gather goods, and we carry them off; you build cities, and we destroy them; you cultivate the land, and we sweep off the crops. It seems to me that we have the best of it."

"It seems so at present," Edmund said, "but it will not last. Already in Northumbria and in East Anglia the Danes, seeing that there is no more plunder to be had, are settling down and adopting the customs of the Saxons, and so will it be in Mercia and Wessex if you keep your hold of them, and so will it be in other places. The change is but beginning, but it seems to me certain to come; so I have heard King Alfred say."

"And does he think," Sweyn said scoffingly, speaking almost for the first time, "that we shall abandon the worship of our gods and take to that of your Christ?"

"He thinks so and hopes so," Edmund replied quietly. "So long as men's lives are spent wholly in war they may worship gods like yours, but when once settled in peaceful pursuits they will assuredly recognize the beauty and holiness of the life of Christ. Pardon me," he said, turning to Siegbert, "if it seems to you that I, being still young, speak with over-boldness, but I am telling you what King Alfred says, and all men recognize his wisdom and goodness."

"I know not of your religion myself," Siegbert replied, "but I will own willingly that though its teachings may be peaceful, it makes not cowards of those who believe in it. I have seen over and over again old men and young men die on the altars of their churches as fearlessly and calmly as a Viking should do when his time comes. No Northman fears death, for he knows that a joyous time awaits him; but I am bound to say that your Christians meet death to the full as calmly. Well, each his own way, I say, and for aught I know there may be a Christian heaven as well as the Halls of Odin, and all may be rewarded in their own way for their deeds."

Bijorn and his party now rose to take leave. "I will come across to your tent in the morning," Siegbert said, "and we can then discuss what payment I shall make you for this young Saxon. I fear not that you will prove over hard to your old comrade."

After Bijorn had departed Siegbert assigned to Edmund a place in his tent as an honoured guest. Slaves brought in bundles of rushes for the beds. Freda retired to a small tent which had been erected for her adjoining the larger one, and the jarl and Edmund lay down on their piles of rushes at the upper end of the tent. Siegbert's companions and followers stretched themselves along the sides, the slaves lay down without, and in a few minutes silence reigned in the tent.

CHAPTER X: THE COMBAT

I was thinking much of what you said last night," Freda said at breakfast. "How is it that you, whose religion is as you say a peaceful one, can yet have performed so many deeds of valour and bloodshed?"

"I am fighting for my home, my country, and my religion," Edmund said. "Christianity does not forbid men to defend themselves; for, did it do so, a band of pagans might ravage all the Christian countries in the world. I fight not because I love it. I hate bloodshed, and would rather die than plunder and slay peaceful and unoffending people. You have been in England and have seen the misery which war has caused there. Such misery assuredly I would inflict on none. I fight only to defend myself and my countrymen and women. Did your people leave our land I would gladly never draw sword again."

"But what would you do with yourself?" Freda asked in tones of surprise. "How would you pass your time if there were no fighting?"

"I should have plenty to do," Edmund said smiling; "I have my people to look after. I have to see to their welfare; to help those who need it; to settle disputes; to rebuild the churches and houses which have been destroyed. There would be no difficulty in spending my time."

"But how could a man show himself to be a hero," the Danish girl asked, "if there were no fighting?"

"There would be no occasion for heroes," Edmund said, "at least of heroes in the sense you mean--that is, of men famous principally for the number they have slain, and the destruction and misery they have caused. Our religion teaches us that mere courage is not the highest virtue. It is one possessed as much by animals as by men. Higher virtues than this are kindness, charity, unselfishness, and a desire to benefit our fellow-creatures. These virtues make a man a truer hero than the bravest Viking who ever sailed the seas. Even you, Freda, worshipper of Odin as you are, must see that it is a higher and a better life to do good to your fellow-creatures than to do evil."

"It sounds so," the girl said hesitatingly; "but the idea is so new to me that I must think it over before I can come to any conclusion."

Freda then went about her occupations, and Edmund, knowing that Siegbert would not return for some time, as he was going with Bijorn to a council which was to be held early in the day, strolled down to look at the galleys ranged along on the beach. These varied greatly in form and character. Some of the sailing ships were large and clumsy, but the galleys for rowing were lightly and gracefully built. They were low in the water, rising to a lofty bow, which sometimes turned over like the neck of a swan, at other times terminated in a sharp iron prow, formed for running down a hostile boat. Some of them were of great length, with seats for twenty rowers on either side, while all were provided with sails as well as oars. When the hour for dinner approached he returned to Siegbert's tent. The jarl had not yet come back from the council. When he did so Edmund perceived at once that he was flushed and angry.

"What has disturbed you, father?" Freda asked, as on hearing his voice she entered the tent. "Has aught gone wrong at the council?"

"Yes," the jarl replied, "much has gone wrong. Bijorn and I had not concluded our bargain when we went to the council. We had, indeed, no difficulty about the terms, but we had not clasped hands over them, as I was going back to his tent after the council was over. At the council the expedition against France was discussed, and it was proposed that we should consult the gods as to the chances of the adventure. Then the Jarl Eric rose and proposed that it should be done in the usual way by a conflict between a Dane and a captive. This was of course agreed to.

"He then said that he understood that there was in the camp a young Saxon of distinguished valour, and that he proposed that Sweyn, the son of Bijorn, should fight with him. Sweyn had expressed to him his willingness to do so should the council agree. I rose at once and said that the Saxon was no longer a captive, since I had ransomed him because he had once done me a service; but upon being pressed I was forced to admit that the bargain had not been concluded. I must acquit Bijorn of any share in the matter, for it came upon him as much by surprise as it did upon me. It seems that it is all Sweyn's doing. He must have taken the step as having a private grudge against you. Have you had any quarrel with him?"

"No," Edmund replied. "He has ever shown himself haughty and domineering, but we have come to no quarrel."

"At any rate he wants to kill you," Siegbert said. "I did my best to prevent it, pointing out that the combat ought to take place between a Frank and a Dane. However, the Northmen are always glad to see a good fight, and having satisfied themselves that in point of age and strength you were not unfairly matched, they decided that the conflict should take place. He is taller, and I think somewhat stronger than you, and has proved himself a valiant fighter, and I would give much if the combat could be avoided."

"I fear him not," Edmund said quietly, "though I would fain that this could be avoided. Had I met Sweyn upon a battle-field in England I would have slain him as a natural enemy; but to fight him in cold blood, either as a matter of augury or to furnish amusement for the assembly, likes me not. However, I must of course defend myself, and if harm comes to him it is no blame of mine."

"You will have no easy victory, I can tell you," Siegbert said, "for none among our young Danes bears a higher reputation."

"But after the combat is over how shall I stand?" Edmund asked; "for if I defeat or slay Sweyn I shall still be his father's slave."

"That will you not," Siegbert replied. "In these cases the captive if victorious is always restored to liberty; but at any rate you shall fight as a free man, for when I have finished my dinner I will go to Bijorn and conclude our bargain. Do not look so cast down, Freda; a Northman's daughter must not turn pale at the thought of a conflict. Sweyn is the son of my old friend, and was, before he took to arms, your playfellow, and since then has, methought, been anxious to gain your favour, though all too young yet for thinking of taking a wife; but never mind, there are as good as he to be found; and if our young Saxon here proves his conqueror other suitors will come, never fear."

Freda was silent, but her face flushed painfully, and Edmund saw the tears falling down her cheeks as she bent over her plate.

After the meal was over Siegbert again went out, and Edmund, approaching Freda, said, "Do not fret, Freda; if it should be that I find my skill in arms greater than that of Sweyn, I promise you that for your sake I will not wound him mortally."

"I care not," the girl said passionately; "spare him not for my sake, for I hate him, and were there no other Norseman in the world I would never be wife of his."

So saying she left the tent. Edmund now regretted the chance which had assigned him to Siegbert, for he would rather have taken his chance of escape by sea than have awaited the conflict with Sweyn. But he could not carry his plan of escape into effect now, for it would seem as if he had fled the conflict. That this would be a desperate one he did not doubt. The course which Sweyn had taken showed a bitter feeling of hatred against him, and even were it not so the young Northman would, fighting in the presence of the leaders of his nation, assuredly do his best to conquer. But Edmund had already tried his strength with older and more powerful men than his adversary and had little fear of results.

The news of the approaching conflict caused considerable excitement in the Danish camp, and Edmund's figure was narrowly scrutinized as he wandered through it. All who had been engaged in the war in Wessex had heard of Edmund, and there was no slight curiosity, when the news went abroad that the Saxon leader was a captive in the camp, to see what he was like.

At first when it was bruited abroad that Sweyn, the son of Jarl Bijorn, was to fight this noted Saxon champion the idea was that the enterprise was a rash one, strong and valiant as Sweyn was known to be for a young man; but when it was seen that Edmund was no older than he, and to the eye less strong and powerful, they felt confident in the power of their champion to overcome him.

Siegbert spared no pains to see that his guest had an even equal chance. He procured for him a strong and well-made helmet which fitted him comfortably, and gave him the choice out of a large number of shields and swords. Edmund selected a weapon which answered nearly in weight and balance that which he was accustomed to wield. There was feasting again that night in Siegbert's tent; but he did not allow Edmund to join in it, insisting after the meal was over that he should retire to a small hut hard by.

"You will want your head and your nerves in good order to-morrow," he said. "Feasting is good in its way, and the night before battle I always drink deeply, but for a single combat it were best to be prudent." As Edmund left the tent Freda, who had not appeared at dinner, came up to him.

"I have been crying all day," she said simply. "I know not why, for I have often seen my father go out to battle without a tear. I think you must have upset me with your talk this morning. I hope that you will win, because it was wrong and unfair of Sweyn to force this battle upon you; and I hate him for it! I shall pray Odin to give you victory. You don't believe in him, I know; still my prayers can do you no harm."

"Thank you," Edmund said. "I shall pray to One greater and better than Odin. But weep not any longer, for I trust neither of us will be killed. I shall do my best to guard myself, and shall try not to slay him; for this fight is not for my nation or for my religion, but concerns myself only."

The following morning the Northmen assembled. The jarls and other leading men formed the inner line of a circle some thirty yards in diameter, the others stood without; Jarl Eric entered the ring with Sweyn, while Edmund, accompanied by Siegbert, entered at the other side of the circle.

"I protest," Siegbert cried in a loud voice, "against this conflict taking place. Edmund the Saxon is no captive here, but a free man, and my guest; moreover, being a Saxon, the issue of this fight between him and a Northman can serve no purpose as an augury as to the success of our expedition against the Franks. Therefore do I protest against the conflict."

There was again a consultation between the leaders, for a murmur of approbation had run round the ranks of the spectators, who it was evident were impressed in favour of the young Saxon, and considered that the jarl's words were just and reasonable. Eric spoke for a minute with Sweyn.

"I feel," he said in a loud voice, "that what Jarl Siegbert says is reasonable, that no augury can be drawn from the fight, and that, since Edmund is no longer a captive, and a friend of Siegbert's, he cannot be forced into fighting in order that we may have an augury. But the Saxon, though so young, has won a reputation even among us, the enemies of his race; and my friend Sweyn, who has shown himself one of the bravest of our young men, considers that he has cause of quarrel with him, and challenges him to fight--not necessarily to the death, or till one is slain, but till the jarls here assembled do pronounce one or the other to be the victor. This is a fair challenge--first, there is a private quarrel; next, there is emulation between these young men, who may fairly claim to be the champions of the youth of the two races. Such a challenge the Saxon will hardly refuse."

In accordance with the customs of the day it would have been impossible for Edmund to have refused such a challenge without disgrace, and he did not for a moment think of doing so.

"I am ready to fight Sweyn," he said. "I have no great cause of quarrel with him; but if he conceives that he has grounds of quarrel with me, that is enough. As to championship of the Saxons, we have no champions; we fight not for personal honour or glory, but for our homes, our countries, and our religion, each doing his best according to the strength God has given him, and without thought of pride on the one hand or envy on the other because the strength or courage of one may be somewhat greater than that of another. Still, as a Saxon standing here as the only representative of my nation in an assembly of Northmen, I cannot refuse such a challenge, for to do so would be to infer that we Saxons are less brave than you. Therefore I am ready for the combat."

The Northmen clashed their weapons against their shields in token of their approval of the young Saxon's words, and the young champions prepared for the combat. They were naked to the waist save for shield and helmet; below the waist each wore a short and tightly-fitting garment covered with plates of brass; the legs were naked, and each wore a pair of light sandals; their weapons were long straight swords. The weapon Edmund had chosen was considerably lighter than that of his opponent, but was of toughest steel, on which were engraved in rough characters, "Prayers to Woden for victory."

The difference in height between the combatants was considerable. Edmund stood five feet ten, but looked shorter from the squareness and width of his shoulders. Sweyn was nearly four inches taller, and he too was very strongly built. His muscles indeed stood out in stronger development than did those of Edmund, and if pure strength was to win the day few of those who looked on doubted that the Dane would be the victor.

The combat was a long one. For some time Edmund contented himself with standing upon the defensive and guarding the tremendous blows which Sweyn rained upon him. In spite of the efforts of the Northman, he could neither beat down the Saxon's guard nor force him to fall back a single step.

Again and again the rattle of the spectators' arms clashed an approval of Edmund's steady resistance to his opponent's assaults. The Norsemen delighted beyond all things in a well-fought encounter. Each man, himself a warrior, was able to appreciate the value of the strokes and parries. The betting at the commencement had run high upon Sweyn, and horses, armour, arms, and slaves had been freely wagered upon his success; but as the fight went on the odds veered round, and the demeanour of the combatants had as much to do with this as the skill and strength shown by Edmund in his defence. The Dane was flushed and furious; his temper gave way under the failure of his assaults. The Saxon, on the contrary, fought as calmly and coolly as if practicing with blunted weapons; his eyes never left those of his adversary, a half smile played on his lips, and although drops of perspiration from his forehead showed how great were his exertions, his breathing hardly quickened.

Twice Sweyn drew back for breath, and Edmund each time, instead of pressing him, dropped the point of his sword and waited for him to renew the combat. At present he had scarce struck a blow, and while his own shield was riven in several places and his helmet dinted, those of Sweyn were unmarked.

At the third assault Sweyn came up determined to end the conflict, and renewed the attack with greater fury than before. Three times his sword descended with tremendous force, but each time it met the blade of the Saxon; the fourth time his arm was raised, then there was a flash and a sudden shout from the crowd.

With a mighty blow Edmund had smitten full on his opponent's uplifted arm, and, striking it just above the elbow, the sword clove through flesh and bone, and the severed limb, still grasping the sword, fell to the ground.

A loud shout of approval burst from the Danes. Although the conqueror was their enemy they appreciated so highly the virtues of coolness and courage that their applause was no less hearty than if the victor had been a countryman. Sweyn had fallen almost the instant the blow had been struck. The ring was at once broken up, and his friends ran to him. The Norsemen were adepts at the treatment of wounds, and everything had been prepared in case of emergencies.

A bandage was instantly tied tightly round the upper part of the arm to stop the rush of blood, and the stump was then dipped into boiling pitch, and Sweyn, who had become almost instantly insensible from the loss of blood, was carried to his father's tent. According to custom handsome presents of swords and armour were made to Edmund by those who had won by his success.

It would have been considered churlish to refuse them, and Edmund had no thought of doing so, for he needed money, and these things in those days were equivalent to wealth.

"You have done well and gallantly indeed, my young friend," Siegbert said as, followed by several slaves bearing Edmund's presents, they returned to the tent. "I am glad you did not slay him, for I think not that he will die. Such a blow given in battle would assuredly have been fatal, but here the means of stanching the blood were at hand, and I trust for Bijorn's sake that he will recover; but whether or no he brought it on himself."

On reaching the tent Freda ran out radiant.

"I hear that you have conquered," she said, "and I am glad indeed; it serves him right, for all say that he forced the fight upon you."

"I did not know that your sympathies were so strongly against Sweyn," Siegbert said in a somewhat reproachful tone. "He has always been your devoted follower."

"He has always been my tyrant, father, for he has always insisted on my doing his pleasure; but if he had been ten times my follower, and had been a valiant warrior instead of a youth, and I a maiden of twenty instead of a girl of fifteen, I should still be glad that he was conquered, because without any reason for quarrel he has sought to slay this Saxon youth who did us such great service, and to whom as he knew we were so indebted."

Siegbert smiled. "Hitherto I have wondered, daughter mine, at the reason which induced Sweyn to challenge Edmund, but now methinks I understand it. Sweyn has, as his father has told me, youth as he is, set his heart on winning your hand when you shall reach the age of womanhood, and it is just because Edmund has done you and me service that he hates him. You are young, child, for your bright eyes to have caused bloodshed; if you go on like this there will be no end to the trouble I shall have on your account before I get you fairly wedded."

Freda coloured hotly.

"That is nonsense, father; another five years will be soon enough to begin to think of such things. At any rate," she said with a laugh, "I am rid of Sweyn, for he can hardly expect me ever to love a one-armed man."

"There have been brave warriors," Seigbert said, "with but one arm."

"It makes no difference," Freda laughed; "if he had fifty arms I should never love him."

Edmund now entreated Siegbert to repay himself from the presents he had received for the goods he had the evening before given to Bijorn as the price of his liberty, but this the jarl would not hear of. Edmund then begged him to buy with them, of Bijorn, the four Saxon slaves with whom he had agreed to attempt an escape, and to expend the rest of the presents in freeing as many other Saxon prisoners as he could.

This Siegbert did, and by the evening Edmund had the satisfaction of finding around him twelve Saxons whose freedom he had purchased. He remained as the guest of Siegbert until the expedition sailed in the last week of March. Then with the twelve Saxons he embarked in Siegbert's ship, which, instead of keeping with the others, sailed for the mouth of the Thames. The wind was favourable and the passage quick, and three days after sailing Edmund and his companions were disembarked on the coast of Kent. His adieus with Siegbert were hearty and earnest.

"I would you had been a Northman," the jarl said, "for I love you as a son, and methinks that when the time comes, had you been so inclined, you might have really stood in that relation to me, for I guess that my little Freda would not have said no had you asked her hand; but now our paths are to part. I shall never war again with the Saxons, for indeed there is but scant booty to be gained there, while you are not likely again to be cast upon our shores; but should the fates ever throw us together again, remember that you have a friend for life in Jarl Siegbert."

Freda, who had accompanied her father as usual, wept bitterly at the parting, which, however, she did not deem to be as final as it appeared to her father; for the evening before, as she was standing on the poop with Edmund, he had said to her, "You will not forget me, Freda; we are both very young yet; but some day, when the wars are over, and England no longer requires my sword, I will seek you again."

"Is that a promise, Edmund?"

"Yes, Freda, a solemn promise."

"I will wait for you," she said simply, "if it were till the end of my life."

The youth and girl ratified the promise by a kiss, and Freda, as through her tears she watched the boat which conveyed Edmund and his companions to shore, felt sure that some day she should see her Saxon hero again.

On landing, Edmund soon learned that the Danes were everywhere masters, and that since the autumn nothing had been heard of the king, who was supposed to be somewhere in hiding.

In every village through which they passed they found evidence of the mastership of the Danes. Many of the houses were burnt or destroyed, the people were all dressed in the poorest garb, and their sad faces and listless mien told of the despair which everywhere prevailed. In every church the altars had been thrown down, the holy emblems and images destroyed, the monks and priests had fled across the sea or had been slain.

The Danish gods, Thor and Woden, had become the divinities of the land, and the Saxons, in whom Christianity had but recently supplanted the superstitions of paganism, were fast returning to the worship of the pagan gods. Edmund and his companions were shocked at the change. On reaching home they found that the ravages of the Danes had here been particularly severe, doubtless in revenge for the heavy loss which had been sustained by them in their attack upon Edmund's fortification. His own abode had been completely levelled to the ground, and the villages and farm-houses for the most part wholly destroyed. His people were lying in rude shelters which they had raised, but their condition was very much better than that of the people in general.

The news of Edmund's return spread like wildfire, and excited the most extreme joy among his people, who had long given him up for lost. He found to his delight that the Dragon had returned safely, and that she was laid up in her old hiding-place. The great amount of spoil with which she was loaded had enabled her crew largely to assist their friends, and it was this which had already raised the condition of the people above that of their neighbours. Houses were being gradually rebuilt, animals had been brought from districts which had been less ravaged by the Danes, and something approaching comfort was being rapidly restored.

Upon the day after Edmund's return Egbert arrived. Feeling sure of Edmund's death he had taken no steps towards rebuilding the house, but was living a wild life in the woods, when the news reached him that Edmund had reappeared. His own large share of the booty with that of Edmund he had buried, with the portion set aside for the king, in the wood near the spot where the Dragon was laid up.

They had passed up the Parrot at night unobserved by the Danes, and after taking the masts out of the Dragon, and dismantling her, they had laid her up in the hole near the river where she was built. There was little fear of her discovery there, for the Danes were for the most part gathered in winter quarters at the great camp near Chippenham.

Egbert's delight at the reappearance of Edmund was unbounded, for he loved him as a son, and it was a long time before their joy at the meeting was sufficiently calmed down to enable them to tell each other the events which had happened since they parted three months before. Egbert's narrative was indeed brief. He had remained two or three days off the coast of Norway in the lingering hope that Edmund might in some way have escaped death, and might yet come off and join him. At the end of a week this hope had faded, and he sailed for England. Being winter, but few Danish galleys were at sea, and he had encountered none from the time he set sail until he arrived off the coast at the mouth of the Parrot.

He had entered the river at night so as to be unseen by any in the village at its mouth, and had, after the Dragon was laid up, passed his time in the forest. Edmund's narration was much more lengthy, and Egbert was surprised indeed to find that his kinsman owed his freedom to the jarl whose vessel they had captured at the mouth of the Humber.

CHAPTER XI: THE ISLE OF ATHELNEY

EDMUND spent a month on his lands, moving about among his vassals and dwelling in their abodes. He inspired them by his words with fresh spirit and confidence, telling them that this state of things could not last, and that he was going to join the king, who doubtless would soon call them to take part in a fresh effort to drive out their cruel oppressors. Edmund found that although none knew with certainty the hiding-place of King Alfred, it was generally reported that he had taken refuge in the low lands of Somersetshire, and Athelney was specially named as the place which he had made his abode.

"It is a good omen," Edmund said, "for Athelney lies close to the Parrot, where my good ship the Dragon is laid away."

After visiting all the villages in his earldom Edmund started with Egbert and four young men, whom he might use as messengers, for the reported hiding-place of the king. First they visited the Dragon, and found her lying undisturbed; then they followed the river down till they reached the great swamps which extended for a considerable distance near its mouth. After much wandering they came upon the hut of a fisherman. The man on hearing the footsteps came to his door with a bent bow. When he saw that the new-comers were Saxons he lowered the arrow which was already fitted to the string.

"Can you tell us," Edmund said, "which is the way to Athelney? We know that it is an island amidst these morasses, but we are strangers to the locality and cannot find it."

"And you might search for weeks," the man said, "without finding it, so thickly is it surrounded by deep swamps and woods. But what want ye there?"

"Men say," Edmund replied, "that King Alfred is hidden there. We are faithful followers of his. I am Ealdorman Edmund of Sherborne, and have good news for the king."

"If ye are indeed the Ealdorman of Sherborne, of whose bravery I have heard much, I will right willingly lead you to Athelney if you will, but no king will you find there. There are a few fugitives from the Danes scattered here and there in these marshes, but none, so far as I know, of any rank or station. However, I will lead you thither should you still wish to go."

Edmund expressed his desire to visit the island even if the king were not there. The man at once drew out a small boat from a hiding-place near his hut. It would hold four at most. Edmund and Egbert stepped in with one of their followers, charging the others to remain at the hut until they received further instructions. The fisherman with a long pole took his place in the bow of the boat and pushed off. For some hours they made their way through the labyrinth of sluggish and narrow channels of the morass. It was a gloomy journey. The leafless trees frequently met overhead; the long rushes in the wetter parts of the swamp rustled as the cold breezes swept across them, and a slight coating of snow which had fallen the previous night added to the dreary aspect of the scene. At last they came upon sharply rising ground.

"This is Athelney," the fisherman said, "a good hiding-place truly; for, as you see, it rises high over the surrounding country, which is always swampy from the waters of the Parrot and Theme, and at high tides the salt water of the sea fills all these waterways, and the trees rise from a broad sheet of sea. No Dane has ever yet set foot among these marshes; and were there but provisions to keep them alive, a safe refuge might be found on this island for hundreds of fugitives. Will you be returning to-night?"

"That I cannot tell you," Edmund replied; "but at any rate I will hire you and your boat to remain at my service for a week, and will pay you a far higher price than you can obtain by your fishing."

The fisherman readily agreed, and Edmund and his companions made their way into the heart of the island. It was of some extent, and rose above the tree-tops of the surrounding country. Presently they came to a cottage. A man came out.

"What do you seek?" he asked.

"You have fugitives in refuge here," Edmund said. "Know you if among them is our good King Alfred?" The man looked astonished.

"A pretty place to seek for a king!" he replied. "There are a few Saxons in hiding here. Some live by fishing, some chop wood; but for the most part they are an idle and thriftless lot, and methinks have fled hither rather to escape from honest work or to avoid the penalties of crimes than for any other reason."

"How may we find them?" Edmund asked.

"They are scattered over the island. There are eight or ten dwellers here like myself, and several of them have one or more of these fellows with them; others have built huts for themselves and shift as they can; but it is a hard shift, I reckon, and beech-nuts and acorns, eked out with an occasional fish caught in the streams, is all they have to live upon. I wonder that they do not go back to honest work among their kinsfolk."

"Ah!" Edmund said, "you do not know here how cruel are the ravages of the Danes; our homes are broken up and our villages destroyed, and every forest in the land is peopled with fugitive Saxons. Did you know that you would speak less harshly of those here. At any rate the man I seek is young and fair-looking, and would, I should think"--and he smiled as he remembered Alfred's studious habits--"be one of the most shiftless of those here."

"There is such a one," the man replied, "and several times friends of his have been hither to see him. He dwells at my next neighbour's, who is often driven well-nigh out of her mind--for she is a dame with a shrewish tongue and sharp temper--by his inattention. She only asks of him that he will cut wood and keep an eye over her pigs, which wander in the forest, in return for his food; and yet, simple as are his duties, he is for ever forgetting them. I warrant me, the dame would not so long have put up with him had he not been so fair and helpless. However bad-tempered a woman may be, she has always a tender corner in her heart for this sort of fellow. There, you can take this path through the trees and follow it on; it will take you straight to her cottage."

The description given by the man tallied so accurately with that of the king that Edmund felt confident that he was on the right track. The fact, too, that from time to time men had come to see this person added to the probability of his being the king. Presently they came upon the hut. A number of pigs were feeding under the trees around it; the door was open, and the shrill tones of a woman's voice raised in anger could be heard as they approached.

"You are an idle loon, and I will no longer put up with your ways, and you may seek another mistress. You are worse than useless here. I do but ask you to watch these cakes while I go over to speak with my neighbour, and inquire how she and the child born yestereven are getting on, and you go to sleep by the fire and suffer the case to burn.

"You were not asleep, you say? then so much the worse. Where were your eyes, then? And where was your nose? Why, I smelt the cakes a hundred yards away, and you sitting over them, and as you say awake, neither saw them burning nor smelt them! You are enough to break an honest woman's heart with your mooning ways. You are ready enough to eat when the meal-time comes, but are too lazy even to watch the food as it cooks. I tell you I will have no more of you. I have put up with you till I am verily ashamed of my own patience; but this is too much, and you must go your way, for I will have no more of you."

At this moment Edmund and Egbert appeared at the door of the hut. As he had expected from the nature of the colloquy Edmund saw King Alfred standing contrite and ashamed before the angry dame.

"My beloved sovereign!" he cried, running in and falling on his knees.

"My trusted Edmund," Alfred exclaimed cordially, "right glad am I to see you, and you too, my valiant Egbert; truly I feared that the good ship Dragon had long since fallen into the hands of our enemy."

"The Dragon lies not many miles hence, your majesty, in the hole in which she was built, by the river Parrot; she has done bravely and has brought home a rich store of booty, a large share of which has been hidden away for your majesty, and can be brought here in a few hours should you wish it."

"Verily I am glad to hear it, Edmund, for I have long been penniless; and I have great need of something at least to pay this good woman for all the trouble she has been at with me, and for her food which my carelessness has destroyed, as you may have heard but now."

Edmund and Egbert joined in the king's merry laugh. The dame looked a picture of consternation and fell upon her knees.

"Pardon me, your majesty," she cried; "to think that I have ventured to abuse our good King Alfred, and have even in mine anger lifted my hand against him!"

"And with right good-will too," the king said laughing. "Never fear, good dame, your tongue has been rough but your heart has been kindly, or never would you have borne so long with so shiftless a serving-man. But leave us now, I pray ye, for I have much to say to my good friends here. And now, Edmund, what news do you bring? I do not ask after the doings of the Dragon, for that no doubt is a long story which you shall tell me later, but how fares it with my kingdom? I have been in correspondence with several of my thanes, who have from time to time sent me news of what passes without. From what they say I deem that the time for action is at last nigh at hand. The people are everywhere desperate at the oppression and exactions of the Danes, and are ready to risk everything to free themselves from so terrible a yoke. I fled here and gave up the strife because the Saxons deemed anything better than further resistance. Now that they have found out their error it is time to be stirring again."

"That is so," Edmund said; "Egbert and I have found the people desperate at their slavery, and ready to risk all did a leader but appear. My own people will all take up arms the instant they receive my summons; they have before now proved their valour, and in my crew of the Dragon you have a body which will, I warrant me, pierce through any Danish line."

"This tallies with what I have heard," Alfred said, "and in the spring I will again raise my banner; but in the meantime I will fortify this place. There are but two or three spots where boats can penetrate through the morasses; were strong stockades and banks erected at each landing-place we might hold the island in case of defeat against any number of the enemy."

"That shall be done," Edmund said, "and quickly. I have a messenger here with me, and others waiting outside the swamp, and can send and bring my crew of the Dragon here at once."

"Let that be one man's mission," the king said; "the others I will send off with messages to the thanes of Somerset, who are only awaiting my summons to take up arms. I will bid them send hither strong working parties, but to make no show in arms until Easter, at which time I will again spread the Golden Dragon to the winds. The treasure you speak of will be right welcome, for all are so impoverished by the Danes that they live but from hand to mouth, and we must at least buy provisions to maintain the parties working here. Arms, too, must be made, for although many have hidden their weapons, the Danes have seized vast quantities, having issued an order that any Saxon found with arms shall be at once put to death. Money will be needed to set all the smithies to work at the manufacture of pikes and swords. Hides must be bought for the manufacture of shields. It will be best to send orders to the ealdormen and thanes to send hither privately the smiths, armourers, and shield-makers in the villages and towns. They cannot work with the Danes ever about, but must set up smithies here. They must bring their tools and such iron as they can carry; what more is required we must buy at the large towns and bring privately in carts to the edge of the morass. The utmost silence and secrecy must be observed, that the Danes may obtain no news of our preparations until we are ready to burst out upon them."

A fortnight later Athelney presented a changed appearance. A thousand men were gathered there. Trees had been cut down, a strong fort erected on the highest ground, and formidable works constructed at three points where alone a landing could be effected. The smoke rose from a score of great mounds, where charcoal-burners were converting timber into fuel for the forges. Fifty smiths and armourers were working vigorously at forges in the open air, roofs thatched with rushes and supported by poles being erected over them to keep the rain and snow from the fires. A score of boats were threading the mazes of the marshes bringing men and cattle to the island. All was bustle and activity, every face shone with renewed hope. King Alfred himself and his thanes moved to and fro among the workers encouraging them at their labours.

Messengers came and went in numbers, and from all parts of Wessex King Alfred received news of the joy which his people felt at the tidings that he was again about to raise his standard, and of the readiness of all to obey his summons. So well was the secret kept that no rumour of the storm about to burst upon them reached the Danes. The people, rejoicing and eager as they were, suffered no evidence of their feelings to be apparent to their cruel masters, who, believing the Saxons to be finally crushed, were lulled into a false security. The king's treasure had been brought from its hiding-place to Athelney, and Edmund and Egbert had also handed over their own share of the booty to the king. The golden cups and goblets he had refused to take, but had gladly accepted the silver.

Edmund and Egbert had left Athelney for a few days on a mission. The king had described to them minutely where he had hidden the sacred standard with the Golden Dragon. It was in the hut of a charcoal-burner in the heart of the forests of

Wiltshire. Upon reaching the hut, and showing to the man the king's signet-ring, which when leaving the standard he had told him would be the signal that any who might come for it were sent by him, the man produced the standard from the thatch of his cottage, in which it was deeply buried, and hearing that it was again to be unfurled called his two stalwart sons from their work and at once set out with Edmund and Egbert to join the army.

Easter came and went, but the preparations were not yet completed. A vast supply of arms was needed, and while the smiths laboured at their work Edmund and Egbert drilled the fighting men who had assembled, in the tactics which had on a small scale proved so effective. The wedge shape was retained, and Edmund's own band claimed the honour of forming the apex, but it had now swollen until it contained a thousand men, and as it moved in a solid body, with its thick edge of spears outward, the king felt confident that it would be able to break through the strongest line of the Danes.

From morning till night Edmund and Egbert, assisted by the thanes of Somerset who had gathered there, drilled the men and taught them to rally rapidly from scattered order into solid formation. Unaccustomed to regular tactics the ease and rapidity with which these movements came to be carried out at the notes of Edmund's bugle seemed to all to be little less than miraculous, and they awaited with confidence and eagerness their meeting with the Danes on the field.

At the end of April messengers were sent out bidding the Saxons hold themselves in readiness, and on the 6th of May Alfred moved with his force from Athelney to Egbertesstan (now called Brixton), lying to the east of the forest of Selwood, which lay between Devonshire and Somerset. The Golden Dragon had been unfurled. On the fort in Athelney, and after crossing the marshes to the mainland it was carried in the centre of the phalanx.

On the 12th they reached the appointed place, where they found a great multitude of Saxons already gathered. They had poured in from Devonshire, Somerset, and Wiltshire, from Dorset and Hants. In spite of the vigorous edicts of the Danes against arms a great proportion of them bore weapons, which had been buried in the earth, or concealed in hollow trees or other hiding-places until the time for action should again arrive.

As they saw the king approaching at the head of his band, with the Golden Dragon fluttering in the breeze, a great shout of joy arose from the multitude, and they crowded round the monarch with shouts of welcome at his reappearance among them, and with vows to die rather than again to yield to the tyranny of the Northmen. The rest of the day was spent in distributing the newly fashioned arms to those who needed them, and in arranging the men in bands under their own thanes, or, in their absence, such leaders as the king appointed.

Upon the following morning the army started, marching in a north-easterly direction against the great camp of the Danes at Chippenham. That night they rested at Okeley, and then marched on until in the afternoon they came within sight of the Danes gathered at Ethandune, a place supposed to be identical with Edington near Westbury.

As the time for Alfred's reappearance approached the agitation and movement on the part of the people had attracted the attention of the Danes, and the news of his summons to the Saxons to meet him at Egbertesstan having come to their ears, they gathered hastily from all parts under Guthorn their king, who was by far the most powerful viking who had yet appeared in England, and who ruled East Anglia as well as Wessex. Confident of victory the great Danish army beheld the approach of the Saxons. Long accustomed to success, and superior in numbers, they regarded with something like contempt the approach of their foes.

In the centre Alfred placed the trained phalanx which had accompanied him from Athelney, in the centre of which waved the Golden Dragon, by whose side he placed himself. Its command he left in the hands of Edmund, he himself directing the general movements of the force. On his right were the men of Somerset and Hants; on the left those of Wilts, Dorset, and Devon.

His orders were that the advance was to be made with regularity; that the whole line were to fight for a while on the defensive, resisting the onslaught of the Danes until he gave the word for the central phalanx to advance and burst through the lines of the enemy, and that when these had been thrown into confusion by this attack the flanks were to charge forward and complete the rout. This plan was carried out. The Danes advanced with their usual impetuosity, and for hours tried to break through the lines of the Saxon spears. Both sides fought valiantly, the Danes inspired by their pride in their personal prowess and their contempt for the Saxons; the Saxons by their hatred for their oppressors, and their determination to die rather than again submit to their bondage. At length, after the battle had raged some hours, and both parties were becoming wearied from their exertions, the king gave Edmund the order.

Hitherto his men had fought in line with the rest; but at the sound of his bugle they quitted their places, and, ere the Danes could understand the meaning of this sudden movement, had formed themselves into their wedge, raised a mighty shout, and advanced against the enemy. The onslaught was irresistible. The great wedge, with its thick fringe of spears, burst its way straight through the Danish centre carrying all before it. Then at another note of Edmund's bugle it broke up into two bodies, which moved solidly to the right and left, crumpling up the Danish lines.

Alfred now gave the order for a general advance, and the Saxon ranks, with a shout of triumph, flung themselves upon the disordered Danes. Their success was instant and complete. Confounded at the sudden break up of their line, bewildered by these new and formidable tactics, attacked in front and in flank, the Danes broke and fled. The Saxons pursued them hotly, Edmund keeping his men well together in case the Danes should rally. Their rout, however, was too complete; vast numbers were slain, and the remnant of their army did not pause until they found themselves within the shelter of their camp at Chippenham.

No quarter was given by the Saxons to those who fell into their hands, and pressing upon the heels of the flying Danes the victorious army of King Alfred sat down before Chippenham. Every hour brought fresh reinforcements to the king's standard. Many were already on their way when the battle was fought; and as the news of the victory spread rapidly every man of the West Saxons capable of bearing arms made for Chippenham, feeling that now or never must a complete victory over the Danes be obtained.

No assault was made upon the Danish camp. Confident in his now vastly superior numbers, and in the enthusiasm which reigned in his army, Alfred was unwilling to waste a single life in an attack upon the entrenchments, which must ere long surrender from famine. There was no risk of reinforcements arriving to relieve the Danes. Guthorn had led to the battle the whole fighting force of the Danes in Wessex and East Anglia. This was far smaller than it would have been a year earlier; but the Northmen, having once completed their work of pillage, soon turned to fresh fields of adventure. Those whose disposition led them to prefer a quiet life had settled upon the land from which they had dispossessed the Saxons; but the principal bands of rovers, finding that England was exhausted and that no more plunder could be had, had either gone back to enjoy at home the booty they had gained, or had sailed to harry the shores of France, Spain, and Italy.

Thus the position of the Danes in Chippenham was desperate, and at the end of fourteen days, by which time they were reduced to an extremity by hunger, they sent messengers into the royal camp offering their submission. They promised if spared to quit the kingdom with all speed, and to observe this contract more faithfully than those which they had hitherto made and broken. They offered the king as many hostages as he might wish to take for the fulfilment of their promises. The haggard and emaciated condition of those who came out to treat moved Alfred to pity.

So weakened were they by famine that they could scarce drag themselves along. It would have been easy for the Saxons to have slain them to the last man; and the majority of the Saxons, smarting under the memory of the cruel oppression which they had suffered, the destruction of home and property, and the slaughter of friends and relations, would fain have exterminated their foes. King Alfred, however, thought otherwise.

Guthorn and the Danes had effected a firm settlement in East Anglia, and lived at amity with the Saxons there. They had, it is true, wrested from them the greatest portion of their lands. Still peace and order were now established. The Saxons were allowed liberty and equal rights. Intermarriages were taking place, and the two peoples were becoming welded into one. Alfred then considered that it would be well to have the king of this country as an ally; he and his settled people would soon be as hostile to further incursions of the Northmen as were the Saxons themselves, and their interests and those of Wessex would be identical.

Did he, on the other hand, carry out a general massacre of the Danes now in his power he might have brought upon England a fresh invasion of Northmen, who, next to plunder, loved revenge, and who might come over in great hosts to avenge the slaughter of their countrymen. Moved, then, by motives of policy as well as by compassion, he granted the terms they asked, and hostages having been sent in from the camp he ordered provisions to be supplied to the Danes.

The same night a messenger of rank came in from Guthorn saying that he intended to embrace Christianity. The news filled Alfred and the Saxons with joy. The king, a sincere and devoted Christian, had fought as much for his religion as for his kingdom, and his joy at the prospect of Guthorn's conversion, which would as a matter of course be followed by that of his subjects, was deep and sincere.

To the Saxons generally the temporal consequence of the conversion had no doubt greater weight than the spiritual. The conversion of Guthorn and the Danes would be a pledge far more binding than any oaths of alliance between the two kingdoms. Guthorn and his followers would be viewed with hostility by their countrymen, whose hatred of Christianity was intense, and East Anglia would, therefore, naturally seek the close alliance and assistance of its Christian neighbour.

Great were the rejoicings in the Saxon camp that night. Seldom, indeed, has a victory had so great and decisive an effect upon the future of a nation as that of Ethandune. Had the Saxons been crushed, the domination of the Danes in England would have been finally settled. Christianity would have been stamped out, and with it civilization, and the island would have made a backward step into paganism and barbarism which might have delayed her progress for centuries.

The victory established the freedom of Wessex, converted East Anglia into a settled and Christian country, and enabled King Alfred to frame the wise laws and statutes and to establish on a firm basis the institutions which raised Saxon England vastly in the scale of civilization, and have in no small degree affected the whole course of life of the English people.

CHAPTER XII: FOUR YEARS OF PEACE

SEVEN weeks afterwards Guthorn, accompanied by thirty of his noblest warriors, entered Alfred's camp, which was pitched at Aller, a place not far from Athelney. An altar was erected and a solemn service performed, and Guthorn and his companions were all baptized, Alfred himself becoming sponsor for Guthorn, whose name was changed to Athelstan. The Danes remained for twelve days in the Saxon camp. For the first eight they wore, in accordance with the custom of the times, the chrismal, a white linen cloth put on the head when the rite of baptism was performed; on the eighth day the solemn ceremony known as the chrism, the loosing or removal of the cloths, took place at Wedmore. This was performed by the Ealdorman Ethelnoth.

During these twelve days many conferences were held between Alfred and Athelstan as to the future of the two kingdoms. While the Danes were still in the camp a witenagemot or Saxon parliament was held at Wedmore. At this Athelstan and many of the nobles and inhabitants of East Anglia were present, and the boundary of the two kingdoms was settled. It was to commence at the mouth of the Thames, to run along the river Lea to its source, and at Bedford turn to the right along the Ouse as far as Watling Street. According to this arrangement a considerable portion of the kingdom of Mercia fell to Alfred's share.

The treaty comprehended various rules for the conduct of commerce, and courts were instituted for the trial of disputes and crimes. The Danes did not at once leave Mercia, but for a considerable time lay in camp at Cirencester; but all who refused to become Christians were ordered to depart beyond the seas, and the Danes gradually withdrew within their boundary.

Guthorn's conversion, although no doubt brought about at the moment by his admiration of the clemency of Alfred, had probably been for some time projected by him. Mingling as his people did in East Anglia with the Christian Saxons there, he must have had opportunities for learning the nature of their tenets, and of contrasting its mild and beneficent teaching with the savage worship of the pagan gods. By far the greater proportion of his people followed their king's example; but the wilder spirits quitted the country, and under their renowned leader Hasting sailed to harry the shores of France. The departure of the more turbulent portion of his followers rendered it more easy for the Danish king to carry his plans into effect.

After the holding of the witan Edmund and Egbert at once left the army with their followers, and for some months the young ealdorman devoted himself to the work of restoring the shattered homes of his people, aiding them with loans from the plunder he had gained on the seas, Alfred having at once repaid him the sums which he had lent at Athelney. As so many of his followers had also brought home money after their voyage, the work of rebuilding and restoration went on rapidly, and in a few months the marks left of the ravages by the Danes had been well-nigh effaced.

Flocks and herds again grazed in the pastures, herds of swine roamed in the woods, the fields were cultivated, and the houses rebuilt. In no part of Wessex was prosperity so speedily re-established as in the district round Sherborne governed by Edmund. The Dragon was thoroughly overhauled and repaired, for none could say how soon fresh fleets of the Northmen might make their appearance upon the southern shores of England. It was not long, indeed, before the Northmen reappeared, a great fleet sailing up the Thames at the beginning of the winter. It ascended as high as Fulham, where a great camp was formed. Seeing that the Saxons and East Anglians would unite against them did they advance further, the Danes remained quietly in their encampment during the winter, and in the spring again took ship and sailed for France.

For the next two years England enjoyed comparative quiet, the Danes turning their attention to France and Holland, sailing up the Maas, Scheldt, Somme, and Seine. Spreading from these rivers they carried fire and sword over a great extent of country. The Franks resisted bravely, and in two pitched battles defeated their invaders with great loss. The struggle going on across the Channel was watched with great interest by the Saxons, who at first hoped to see the Danes completely crushed by the Franks.

The ease, however, with which the Northmen moved from point to point in their ships gave them such immense advantage that their defeats at Hasle and Saucourt in no way checked their depredations. Appearing suddenly off the coast, or penetrating into the interior by a river, their hordes would land, ravage the country, slay all who opposed them, and carry off the women and children captives, and would then take to their ships again before the leaders of the Franks could assemble an army.

Alfred spent this time of repose in restoring as far as possible the loss and damage which his kingdom had suffered. Many wise laws were passed, churches were rebuilt, and order restored; great numbers of the monks and wealthier people who had fled to France in the days of the Danish supremacy now returned to England, which was for the time freer from danger than the land in which they had sought refuge; and many Franks from the districts exposed to the Danish ravages came over and settled in England.

Gradually the greater part of England acknowledged the rule of Alfred. The kingdom of Kent was again united to that of Wessex; while Mercia, which extended across the centre of England from Anglia to Wales, was governed for Alfred by Ethelred the Ealdorman, who was the head of the powerful family of the Hwiccas, and had received the hand of Alfred's daughter Ethelfleda. He ruled Mercia according to its own laws and customs, which differed materially from those of the West Saxons, and which prevented a more perfect union of the two kingdoms until William the Conqueror welded the whole country into a single whole. But Ethelred acknowledged the supremacy of Alfred, consulted him upon all occasions of importance, and issued all his edicts and orders in the king's name. He was ably assisted by Werfrith, the Bishop of Worcester. The energy and activity of these leaders enabled Mercia to keep abreast of Wessex in the onward progress which Alfred laboured so indefatigably to promote.

Edmund, when not occupied with the affairs of his earldom, spent much of his time with the king, who saw in him a spirit of intelligence and activity which resembled his own. Edmund was, however, of a less studious disposition than his royal master; and though he so far improved his education as to be able to read and write well, Alfred could not persuade him to undertake the study of Latin, being, as he said, well content to master some of the learning of that people by means of the king's translations.

At the end of another two years of peace Edmund was again called upon to take up arms. Although the Danes attempted no fresh invasion some of their ships hung around the English coast, capturing vessels, interfering with trade, and committing other acts of piracy.

Great complaints were made by the inhabitants of the seaports to Alfred. The king at once begged Edmund to fit out the Dragon, and collecting a few other smaller ships he took his place on Edmund's ship and sailed in search of the Danes. After some search they came upon the four large ships of the Northmen which had been a scourge to the coast.

The Saxons at once engaged them, and a desperate fight took place. The Dragon was laid alongside the largest of the Danish vessels; and the king, with Edmund and Egbert by his side, leapt on to the deck of the Danish vessel, followed by the crew of the Dragon. The Danish ship was crowded with men who fought desperately, but the discipline even more than the courage of Edmund's crew secured for them the victory. For a time each fought for himself; and although inspired by the presence of the king they were able to gain no advantage, being much out-numbered by the Northmen.

Edmund, seeing this, sounded on his horn the signal with which in battle he ordered the men to form their wedge. The signal was instantly obeyed. The Saxons were all fighting with boarding-pikes against the Northmen's swords and axes, for they had become used to these weapons and preferred them to any other.

The instant Edmund's horn was heard, each man desisted from fighting and rushed to their leader, around whom they instantly formed in their accustomed order. The Danes, astonished at the sudden cessation of the battle, and understanding nothing of the meaning of the signal or of the swift movement of the Saxons, for a minute lowered their weapons in surprise.

Before they again rushed forward the formation was complete, and in a close body with levelled spears the Saxons advanced, Egbert as usual leading the way, with Edmund and the king in the centre.

In vain the Danes strove to resist the onset; in spite of their superior numbers they were driven back step by step until crowded in a close mass at one end.

Still the Saxon line of spears pressed on. Many of the Danes leapt into the sea, others were pushed over or run through, and in a few minutes not a Northman remained alive in the captured vessel.

In the meantime the battle was raging in other parts. Two of the small vessels were engaged with one of the Danes at close quarters, while the other ships hung around the remaining Danish vessels and kept up volleys of arrows and javelins upon them.

The Dragon at once went to the assistance of the two Saxon ships, whose crews were almost overpowered by the Northmen. Laying the ship alongside, Edmund boarded the Danes. The Northmen rushed back from the decks of the Saxon ship to defend their own vessel; and the Saxons, regaining courage, at once rallied and followed them. The combat was short but desperate. Attacked on three sides, the Danes were speedily overcome and were slaughtered to a man.

An attack was next made upon the two remaining vessels. These resisted for some time, but they were overwhelmed by the missiles from the Saxon flotilla; and the greater portion of their crews being killed or wounded, their commanders prayed for mercy, which was granted them by Alfred; and with the four captured vessels the fleet returned to England.

On reaching port Alfred begged Edmund to continue for a while with the Dragon, to cruise along the coasts and to stop the depredations of the Danes; and for some weeks the Dragon kept the seas. She met with considerable success, capturing many Danish galleys. Some of these contained rich spoil, which had been gathered in France, for cruising in the seas off Dover Edmund intercepted many of the Danish vessels on their homeward way from raids up the Seine, Garonne, and other French rivers.

One day in the excitement of a long pursuit of a Danish galley, which finally succeeded in making her escape, Edmund had paid less attention than usual to the weather, and, on giving up the chase as hopeless, perceived that the sky had become greatly overcast, while the wind was rising rapidly.

"We are in for a storm from the north, Egbert," he said, "and we must make for the mouth of the Thames for shelter."

The sails were lowered, and the Dragon's head turned west. Before two hours had passed the sea had risen so greatly that it was no longer possible to row.

"What had we best do?" Edmund asked the chief of the sailors. "Think you that we can make Dover and shelter under the cliffs there?"

"I fear that we cannot do so," the sailor replied, "for there are terrible sands and shallows off the Kentish coast between the mouth of the Thames and Dover, and the wind blows so strongly that we can do nought but run before it."

"Then let us do so," Edmund replied; "anything is better than being tossed at the mercy of the waves."

A sail was hoisted, and the Dragon flew along before the wind. The storm increased in fury, and for some hours the vessel ran before it. She was but a short distance from the French coast, and as the wind veered round more to the west her danger became great.

"I fear we shall be cast ashore," Edmund said to the sailor.

"Fortunately," the man answered, "we are but a mile or two from the mouth of the Seine, and there we can run in and take shelter."

It was an anxious time until they reached the mouth of the river, for they were continually drifting nearer and nearer to the coast. However, they cleared the point in safety, and, turning her head, ran up the river and soon anchored under the walls of Havre. As she came to an anchor armed men were seen crowding the walls.

"They take us for Danes," Egbert said. "We had best hoist the Dragon, and they will then know that we are a Saxon ship."

Soon after the flag was hoisted the gates of the town were seen to open, and an officer and some men issued out. These launched a boat and rowed out to the ship. The officer mounted to the deck. He was evidently in considerable fear, but as he saw the Saxons standing about unarmed he was reassured. "Is this really a Saxon ship," he asked, "as its flag testifies?"

"It is so," Edmund replied; "it is my vessel, and I am an ealdorman of King Alfred. We have been chasing the Danish pirates, but this storm having arisen, we were blown down the French coast and forced to seek shelter here."

"The governor bids you welcome," the officer said, "and bade me invite you to land."

"That will I gladly; the more so since my ship has suffered some damage in the gale, her bulwarks having been partly shattered; and it will need a stay of a few days here to repair her for sea. Will you tell the governor that in a short time I will land with my kinsman Egbert and accept his hospitality?"

An hour later Edmund and Egbert landed and were at once conducted to the governor, who welcomed them cordially.

They found there many whom they had known at the court of King Alfred. The wealthier men, the bishops and thanes, had for the most part journeyed to Paris or to other towns in the interior to escape the dreaded Northmen; but there were many detained at Havre from want of funds to journey farther.

"It is a sad pity," the governor said as they talked over the troubled state of Western Europe, "that your English king and our Frankish monarch did not make common cause against these sea robbers. They are the enemies of mankind. Not only do they ravage all our coasts, but they have entered the Mediterranean, and have plundered and ravaged the coasts of Provence and Italy, laying towns under ransom, burning and destroying."

"I would that I could meet some of their ships on their way back from Italy," Edmund said. "I warrant that we should obtain a rare booty, with gems of art such as would delight King Alfred, but are thrown away on these barbarians; but I agree with you that 'tis shameful that the coasts of all Europe should be overrun with these pirates."

"Yes," the governor replied, "if every country in Christendom would unite against their common foe, and send a quota of ships and men, we would drive the Black Raven from the seas, and might even land on the Danish shores and give them a taste of the suffering they have inflicted elsewhere. As it is, all seem paralysed. Local efforts are made to resist them; but their numbers are too great to be thus withstood. I wonder that the pope does not call Christendom to arms against these pagan robbers, who not only destroy towns and villages, but level to the ground the holy shrines, and slay the ministers of God on the altars."

CHAPTER XIII: THE SIEGE OF PARIS

ON the following morning Edmund, who had returned to his ship to sleep, was aroused by loud shouts on deck. Hurrying from his cabin he saw a vast fleet of ships approaching the mouth of the river. They were of all sizes--from great sailing ships to rowing galleys. It needed but a glance at them to assure him that they were the dreaded ships of the Northmen, for the Black Raven floated at many of the mast-heads.

From the town the sounds of horns and great shoutings could be heard, showing that there too the approaching fleet had just been discerned as the morning fog lifted from the sea. Edmund held a hurried consultation with his kinsman. It was now too late to gain the sea, for the Danish ships had already reached the mouth of the river. To attempt to escape by fighting would be madness, and they hesitated only whether to run the ship ashore, and, leaving her there, enter the town and share in its defence, or to proceed up the river with all speed to Rouen, or even to Paris.

The latter course was decided upon, for the Danish ships would contain so vast a number of men that there was little hope that Havre could resist their attack, nor was it likely that Rouen, which, on the previous year had been captured and sacked, would even attempt another resistance, which would only bring massacre and ruin upon its inhabitants. Paris alone, the capital of the Frankish kings, seemed to offer a refuge. The deliberation was a short one, and by the time the men had taken their places at the oars their leaders had decided upon their course.

The anchor ropes were cut, for not a moment was to be lost, the leading ships of the Danes being already less than half a mile distant. The tide was flowing, and the Dragon swept rapidly up the river. Some of the Danish galleys followed for a while, but seeing that the Dragon had the speed of them, they abandoned the pursuit, and at a more easy stroke the rowers continued their work until they reached Rouen.

Here the tide failed them, and they moored against the bank under the walls.

Edmund and Egbert went on shore. They found the city in a state of wild confusion. Saying that they had important news, and must see the governor, they were led to the council-chamber, where the leading men of the town were assembled. After stating who he and his companion were, Edmund announced the arrival of a great Danish fleet at the mouth of the river.

"Your news, sir, is terrible for our poor country," the governor said, "but to us it scarce brings any additional horror, although it will probably decide the question which we are engaged in discussing. We have news here that a great Danish army which landed at Abbeville is marching hitherward, and we are met to discuss whether the town should resist to the last or should open its gates at their approach. This news you bring of the arrival of a fresh army of these sea robbers at Havre renders our case desperate. So fierce is their attack that we could hardly hope successfully to resist the approaching army, but against it and this fleet you tell us of resistance could only bring about our utter destruction. That, at least, is my opinion, the other members of the council must speak for themselves."

The other members, who were the principal merchants and traders of the town, were unanimously of the same opinion.

"Better," they said, "to give up all our worldly goods to the Northmen than to be slaughtered pitilessly with our wives and families."

"Such being your decision," Edmund said, "my kinsman and myself will proceed up the river to Paris; hitherto, as we hear, the Northmen have not ventured to attack that city, and should they do so, it will doubtless resist to the last."

Accordingly the two Saxons returned at once to the Dragon, and as soon as the tide turned unmoored and proceeded up the river. Three days after leaving Rouen they arrived in sight of Paris. The capital of the Franks was but a small city, and was built entirely upon the island situated just at the confluence of the Seine and Marne. It was surrounded by a strong and lofty wall.

On the approach of a vessel differing entirely from anything they had before seen the citizens flocked to the walls. The Golden Dragon floating at the mast-head showed them that the vessel did not belong to the Danes, and some of the more experienced in these matters said at once that she must be a Saxon ship. The Count Eudes, who had been left by the king in command of Paris, himself came to the walls just as the Dragon came abreast of them. Edmund ordered the rowers to pause at their work.

"Who are you?" the Count Eudes shouted. "Whence do you come and with what intent?"

"My name is Edmund. I am an ealdorman of King Alfred of the Saxons. When at sea fighting the Northmen a tempest blew me down your coast, and I took refuge in the port of Havre. Four days since at daybreak a vast fleet of Northmen entered the river. We rowed up to Rouen hoping to be able to find safe shelter there; but the citizens being aware that a great army of the sea robbers was marching against their town, and being further intimidated by the news I brought them, decided upon surrendering without resistance. Therefore we have continued our journey hither, being assured that here at least the Danish wolves would not have their way unopposed. We have fought them long in our native land, and wish for nothing better than to aid in the efforts of the Franks against our common enemy."

"You are welcome, sir earl," the Count Eudes said, "though the news you bring us is bad indeed. We have heard how valiantly the thanes of King Alfred have fought against the invaders, and shall be glad indeed of your assistance should the Northmen, as I fear, come hither."

So saying the count ordered the gates to be opened, and the Dragon having been moored alongside, Edmund and Egbert with their crew entered the town, where the leaders were received with great honour by the count. He begged them to become guests at the castle, where quarters were also assigned to the crew. A banquet was at once prepared, at which many of the principal citizens were present.

As soon as the demands of hunger were satisfied the count made further inquiries as to the size of the fleet which had entered the Seine, and as to the army reported to be marching against Rouen.

"I doubt not," he said, when the Saxons had given him all the particulars in their power, "that it is the armament of Siegfroi who has already wrought such destruction. More than once he has appeared before our walls, and has pillaged and ravaged the whole of the north of France. The last time he was here he threatened to return with a force which would suffice to raze Paris to the ground, and doubtless he is coming to endeavour to carry out his threat; but he will not find the task an easy one, we shall resist him to the last; and right glad am I that I shall have the assistance of two of the Saxon thanes who have so often inflicted heavy defeats upon these wolves of the sea. Your vessel is a strange one, and differs from those that I have hitherto seen, either Dane or Saxon. She is a sailing ship, and yet appears to row very fast."

"She is built," Edmund said, "partly upon the design of King Alfred himself, which were made from paintings he possessed of the war galleys of Italy, which country he visited in his youth. They were carried out by a clever shipwright of Exeter; and, indeed, the ship sails as well as she rows, and, as the Danes have discovered to their cost, is able to fight as well as she can sail and row. Had we been fairly out to sea before the Danish fleet made its appearance we could have given a good account of ourselves, but we were caught in a trap."

"I fear that if the Northmen surround the city your ship will be destroyed."

"I was thinking of that," Edmund said, "and I pray you to let me have some men who know the river higher up. There must assuredly be low shores often overflowed where there are wide swamps covered with wood and thickets, which the enemy would not enter, seeing that no booty could be obtained there. The ship was built in such a spot, and we could cut a narrow gap from the river and float her well in among the trees so as to be hidden from the sight of any passing up the river in galleys, closing up the cut again so that none might suspect its existence."

"That could be done easily enough," the count said; "there are plenty of spots which would be suitable, for the banks are for the most part low and the ground around swampy and wooded. To-morrow I will tell off a strong body of men to accompany you in your ship, and aid your crew in their work."

Twenty miles up the Seine a suitable spot was found, and the crew of the Dragon, with the hundred men whom the Count Eudes had lent for the purpose, at once set about their work. They had but little trouble, for a spot was chosen where a sluggish stream, some fifteen feet wide, drained the water from a wide-spreading swamp into the river. The channel needed widening but a little to allow of the Dragon entering, and the water was quite deep enough to permit her being taken some three hundred yards back from the river.

The trees and underwood were thick, and Edmund was assured that even when winter, which was now approaching, stripped the last leaf from the trees, the Dragon could not be seen from the river. Her masts were lowered, and bundles of brushwood were hung along her side so as to prevent the gleam of black paint being discerned through the trees.

The entrance to the stream was filled up to a width of three or four feet, and the new work turfed with coarse grass similar to that which grew beside it. Bushes were planted close to the water's edge, and stakes were driven down in the narrow channel to within a few inches of the surface of the water.

Certain now that no Danish boats would be likely to turn aside from the river to enter this channel into the swamp, the party embarked in some boats which had been towed up by the Dragon and returned down the river to Paris.

The afternoon before starting all the valuable booty which had been captured from the Danes was landed and placed in security in the castle, and upon his return to Paris Edmund disposed of this at good prices to the traders of the city.

A fortnight after they had returned to Paris the news was brought in that a vast fleet of Northmen was ascending the river. The next morning it was close at hand, and the citizens mounting the walls beheld with consternation the approaching armament. So numerous were the ships that they completely covered the river. The fleet consisted of seven hundred sailing ships, and a vastly greater number of rowing galleys and boats. These vessels were crowded with men, and their fierce aspect, their glittering arms, and their lofty stature, spread terror in the hearts of the citizens.

"This is truly a tremendous host!" the Count Eudes said to Edmund, who stood beside him on the walls.

"It is indeed," Edmund replied. "Numerous as are the fleets which have poured down upon the shores of England, methinks that none approached this in strength. It is clear that the Northmen have united their forces for a great effort against this city; but having at home successfully defended fortifications, which were not to be named in comparison with those of Paris, against them, I see no reason to doubt that we shall be able to beat them off here."

The Danes landed on the opposite bank and formed a vast camp there, and the following morning three of their number in a small boat rowed across the river and said that their king Siegfroi desired to speak with Goslin, archbishop of Paris, who stood in the position of civil governor. They were told that the archbishop would receive the king in his palace.

An hour later a stately figure in glittering armour was seen to take his place in a long galley, which, rowed by twenty men, quickly shot across the stream. Siegfroi landed, and, accompanied by four of his leading warriors, entered the gates, which were opened at his approach. The chief of the Northmen was a warrior of lofty stature. On his head he wore a helmet of gold, on whose crest was a raven with extended wings wrought in the same metal. His hair fell loosely on his neck; his face was clean shaved in Danish fashion, save for a long moustache. He wore a breastplate of golden scales, and carried a shield of the toughest bull's-hide studded with gold nails.

He was unarmed, save a long dagger which he wore in his belt. He and his followers, who were all men of immense stature, walked with a proud and assured air between the lines of citizens who clustered thickly on each side of the street, and who gazed in silence at these dreaded figures. They were escorted by the chamberlain of the archbishop, and on arriving at his palace were conducted into the chamber where Goslin, Count Eudes, and several of the leading persons of Paris awaited them.

Siegfroi bent his head before the prelate.

"Goslin," he said, "I beg you to have compassion upon yourself and your flock if you do not wish to perish. We beseech you to turn a favourable ear to our words. Grant only that we shall march through the city. We will touch nothing in the town, and we undertake to preserve all your property, both yours and that of Eudes."

The archbishop replied at once:

"This city has been confided to us by the Emperor Charles, who is, after God, the king and master of the powers of the earth. Holding under his rule almost all the world, he confided it to us, with the assurance that we should suffer no harm to come to the kingdom, but should keep it for him safe and sure. If it had happened that the defence of these walls had been committed to your hands, as it has been committed to mine, what would you have done had such a demand been made upon you? Would you have granted the demand?"

"If I had granted it," Siegfroi replied, "may my head fall under the axe and serve as food for dogs. Nevertheless, if you do not grant our demands, by day we will overwhelm your city with our darts, and with poisoned arrows by night. You shall suffer all the horrors of hunger, and year after year we will return and make a ruin of your city."

Without another word he turned, and followed by his companions, strode through the streets of Paris, and taking his place in the boat returned to his camp.

At daybreak the next morning the Norsemen were seen crowding into their ships. The trumpets sounded loudly, and the citizens seized their arms and hastened to the walls. The Norsemen crossed the river, and directed their attack against a tower which stood at the head of the bridge connecting the city and island with the farther bank. Those who landed were provided with picks, crowbars, and other implements for effecting a breach, and their approach was protected by a cloud of arrows and javelins from the fleet which covered the surface of the river.

The French leaders soon assembled at the threatened point. Chief among these were Eudes, his brother Robert, the Count Ragenaire, and the Abbe Ebble, a nephew of the archbishop. The Franks bore themselves bravely, and in spite of the rain of arrows defended the walls against the desperate attacks of the Northmen.

The fortifications in those days were very far from having attained the strength and solidity which a few generations later were bestowed upon them. The stones of which they were constructed were comparatively small, and fastened together by mortar, consequently they could ill resist even an assault by manual weapons. Covered by their shields the Northmen worked untiringly at the foundations, and piece by piece the walls crumbled to the ground. Every effort, however, to enter at the breaches so made was repulsed, and Siegfroi kept back his warriors, determined to delay the grand assault until the next day. By nightfall the tower was in ruins, scarce a portion of the walls remaining erect. Many of the besieged had been killed. The archbishop was wounded with an arrow. Frederic, a young soldier who led the troops of the church was killed.

The besiegers had suffered much more severely, great numbers having been killed by the stones and missiles hurled down by the defenders while engaged in the demolition of the walls. At nightfall the Danes carried off their wounded and recrossed the river, confident that next day they would succeed in their assault. As soon as darkness had set in Count Eudes collected the citizens, and these, bearing beams and planks, crossed the bridge to the tower, and set to work. Outside the circle of ruins holes were dug and the beams securely fixed. Planks were nailed to these, and earth heaped up behind them.

All night the work continued, and by morning a fortification much higher than the original tower had been erected all round the ruin. The Danes again crossed the river in their ships, and the assault was renewed. Javelins and great stones were hurled at the fortification, and clouds of arrows from the shipping fell within them. Covered with portable roofs constructed of planks the Danes strove to destroy the wall. The besieged poured upon them a blazing mixture of oil, wax, and pitch. Numbers of the Danes were burned to death, while others, maddened by the pain, threw themselves into the river.

Over and over again Siegfroi led his warriors to the attack, but the defenders, headed by Eudes and the brave Abbe Ebble, each time repelled them. The abbe particularly distinguished himself, and he is reported to have slain seven Danes at once with one javelin, a blow which may be considered as bordering on the miraculous. But the number of the defenders of the tower was small indeed to that of the enemy, and the loss which they inflicted upon the Danes, great as it was, was as nothing in so vast a host.

The flames of the machines, lighted by the pitch and oil, communicated to the planks of the fortification, and soon these too were on fire. As they burned, the earth behind them gave way, and a breach was formed. Encouraged by this result the Danes brought up faggots, and in several places lighted great fires against the fortifications. The defenders began to lose all hope, when a tremendous storm of rain suddenly burst over Paris quenching the fire.

The besieged gained heart, reinforcements crossed from the town, and the Danes again withdrew to their ships, having lost in the day's fighting three hundred men. After this repulse the Northmen desisted for a time from their attack. They formed a strong fortified camp near the church of St. Germain, and then spread over the country slaying and burning, sparing none, man, woman, or child. From the walls of Paris the smoke could be seen rising over the whole country, and every heart was moved with rage and sorrow.

Edmund and his party had taken no part in the defence of the tower. Its loss would not have involved that of the town, and Eudes requested him to keep his band in reserve in order that they might remain intact until the Danes should make a breach in the walls of the city itself, when the sudden reinforcement of a party of such well-trained warriors might decide the result.

While a portion of the Danish host were engaged upon the work of devastation, a large number were employed upon the construction of three great towers. These were built on wheels, and were each large enough to hold sixty men. They far overtopped the walls, and the citizens viewed with alarm the time when an assault should be delivered under the protection of these formidable machines. Eighteen ships of equal size were moored by the bank six deep. Great planks were laid across them, and a sloping platform having been formed, the towers were by the efforts of thousands of men moved up and placed on the ships.

"If we do not destroy those towers, Egbert," Edmund said one day as he saw them slowly moving into their position on board the ships, "all is lost, for from their summits the Northmen with their bows and javelins will be able to clear the walls, while those below effect a breach at their leisure."

"That is true enough, Edmund, but I do not see any way to destroy them. Unfortunately we have no boats, or we might fill some of them with combustibles, and tow them down until near enough for the stream to carry them upon those vessels; but even then the chance were small indeed, for the Danes would swarm out in their boats and manage to tow or push them so that they would not touch the ships."

"I should think, Egbert, that if we could get some skins or planks we and our band might, when it is quite dark, sally out and take to the water at the lower end of the island and float down quietly for a mile or two, and then gain the further bank; then we might march along quietly until we reach those ships. The Danes know that we have no boats, and will not fear an attack. We must not do it until an hour or two before morning, when, after spending the early hours of the night as usual in feasting and drinking, they will sleep heavily. Just before we are ready to begin a small party can unmoor two or three of the boats by the bank and push them out, one to the outside of each tier of six vessels, so that we may have a means of retreat across the river. When that is done we will make a rush on board the ships, cut down any Danes we may find there, and set fire to all the vessels. We must hold the gangways to the shore until the flames get well alight, and then take to the boats and return."

"I think the plan is a good one, Edmund, and may well be carried out without great loss. There are plenty of empty wine skins at present in Paris. I will at once set about collecting a hundred of them. We will fasten to each a stout cord so as to form a loop to go over the head and shoulders, then we had best attach them all together by one long cord, by which means we shall float in a body."

"Fortunately the night is very dark and I think that we shall succeed. Say nothing about it, Egbert, and tell the men to keep silent. The good people of Paris shall know nothing of the matter until they see the flames dancing round the towers which they hold in so much dread."

The Saxons received with satisfaction the news of the intended expedition. They had been disappointed at being kept back from taking any part in the fighting during the two days' attack upon the tower, and longed for an opportunity to inflict a blow upon their hated enemy the Danes. The wine skins were fitted up with ropes as Egbert had suggested, and soon after nightfall the party, armed with spear and sword, and carrying each his float, sallied out from the gates, as Edmund was by this time so well known among the citizens that the gate was opened without demur on his order.

They crept along the foot of the wall until they reached the lower extremity of the island. Across the river innumerable fires blazed high, and the songs and shouts of the Danes rose loud in the air. Numbers of figures could be seen moving about or standing near the fires, the tents of the chiefs were visible some distance back, but the number of these as well as of the fires was much less than it had been on the first arrival of the Northmen, owing to the numbers who had gone to the camp round St. Germain.

The night was very dark and a light rain was falling. Before taking to the water Edmund bade his men strip off the greater portion of their clothes and fasten them in a bundle on their heads, as it would be some time after they landed before they could advance upon the camp, and the cold and dripping garments would tend to lessen their spirits and courage.

When all was ready they stepped into the water, and keeping in a body, drifted down the stream. The wine skins floated them well above the water, the stream was running strong, and the lights of the Danish fires were soon left behind.

In half an hour Edmund and Egbert deemed that they were now far beyond a point where they might chance upon any Danish stragglers. The word was therefore given, and all made for the bank. The stream had already drifted them in that direction, and they soon reached the shore. Here the skins which had proved so useful were left behind, and putting on their dry clothes, they felt comparatively comfortable. Edmund ordered them to lay down their spears and swords by their sides, and to swing their arms violently. This they continued to do until they were nearly breathless, by which time the blood was coursing warmly in their veins.

They were now in December, and the water was extremely cold, and Egbert congratulated Edmund upon having made the men strip, for had they been compelled to remain in their wet garments while waiting for the Danish fires to die down, they would scarce have been in a fit state to fight when the moment for so doing had arrived.

Three hours elapsed before the glare of the distant fires began to subside, another half hour passed, and then the band were formed up and moved along on the bank of the river.

CHAPTER XIV: THE REPULSE
OF THE NORTHMEN

WHEN within half a mile of the Danish camp Edmund and Egbert left the band and advanced alone. They were pretty confident that they should find but few of the Danes near the bank of the river, for the arrows from the walls of Paris carried some distance beyond it, and the Northmen consequently encamped some hundred yards away. They had to pick their way carefully, for the ships were moored along the bank, their ropes being fastened to great stakes driven into the ground.

There were lights on board the vessels, many of the crews remaining on board. They made their way along until they reached the spot they aimed at. Here lay the three sets of vessels, each six deep; their masts had been removed, and the great towers rose high into the darkness above the platforms extending over their decks.

The planks forming the gangways up which the towers had been moved had been taken away, save one which gave access to each tier, and Edmund doubted not that it was intended that they should the next morning move across the river in tow of the numerous row-boats. The two Saxons did not attempt to go on board, as they had now found out all they wanted, and might mar all by disturbing some sleeper upon the platform. They accordingly returned to the spot where the band were awaiting them.

"I propose, Egbert," Edmund said, "that as we go along we cut the mooring-ropes of all the vessels. We must do it quietly so as not to excite any alarm, and they will know nothing of it until they find themselves drifting down the river in a mass. Then there will be great jostling and carrying away of bowsprits and bulwarks, and the confusion and shouting which will arise will tend to confuse the Danes and to distract their attention from us."

Egbert agreed to the proposal, and as soon as they reached the first ships the Saxons began their work, sawing with their knives and daggers through the ropes. The vessels lay four or five deep and there were many cables to cut, but the keen knives of the Saxons made short work of these. Before beginning their work they had spread along the bank, leaving only two men abreast of each ship, so that in the course of two or three minutes the cables for the length of forty ships were severed, and these and their consorts beyond them began to drift out into the stream.

The Saxons ran quickly on ahead and repeated the work until the whole of the vessels below those forming the platform for the towers were adrift in the stream; but by this time those in the ships at the lower end of the tiers had taken the alarm, and shouts of wonder and anger rose on the air. The nine Saxons told off for the purpose leaped into three small boats and rowed out into the stream, while the rest of the band, divided into three parties, dashed across the planks on to the platforms. The Danes here had already been alarmed by the uproar from the vessels adrift, and although unable to see what was passing judged that something was wrong, and had called to their comrades sleeping in the holds to come up.

Some of these bearing torches came up on deck just as the Saxons, pouring across the planks which connected the ships with the shore, fell upon them. Taken utterly by surprise, the Danes could offer no effective resistance. The Saxons, charging with levelled spears, drove those above headlong into the water; then, having made themselves masters of the platforms, they dashed below and despatched the Danes they found there. The torches were now applied to the contents of the holds. These were for the most part crammed with the booty which the Norsemen had gained at Havre, Rouen, and other places, and the flames speedily shot up. By this time the Danes in the camp, alarmed by the shouting from the drifting ships and the sounds of conflict from the towers, came flocking down in haste. The planks had already been thrown overboard. The Danes strove by pulling at the ropes to haul the vessels nearer to land. Some ran towards their ships, others jumped into boats, and pushing out to the platforms strove to get on board them; but by this time the flames were rising high through the hatchways. According to previous agreement Edmund and the leaders of the other two parties, seeing that the flames had now firm hold, cut the ropes which fastened them to the bank, and as soon as the stream began to swing them out leaped into the boats and rowed for the opposite shore.

The uproar was now tremendous; and shouts of rage rose from the Northmen, who were amazed and puzzled by the appearance of the Saxons, whose attire differed but slightly from their own; and the general belief among them was that this sudden alarm was the result of treachery among themselves. There was no time to waste in conjecture; the three groups of ships were now masses of flame, in the midst of which the lofty towers rose high. The shouts of the sailors in the vessels crowded together in helpless confusion in the stream below rose higher and higher as the blazing vessels drifted down and threatened to overtake them.

Some tried to hoist their sails; others got out long oars and strove to sweep their vessels towards the shore, but they were huddled too closely in the stream; the yards and rigging of many having become interlocked with each other. The Northmen leaped into the rowing boats by the bank above where the tower-ships had been moored, and rowing down endeavoured to tow them to the bank; but they were now in a blaze from end to end, the heat was so great that it was difficult to approach them, and all endeavours to fasten ropes to them were frustrated, as these were instantly consumed. The Northmen, finding their efforts unavailing, then turned their attention to trying to tow the ships below to the banks.

In some cases they were successful. A few of the vessels also at the lower end of the mass succeeded in getting up their sails and drawing out from their fellows, for the wind was blowing down stream. This, however, proved the destruction of the rest of the ships, for the great towers rising amid the lofty pillars of flames acted as sails and bore the fire-ships down upon the helpless crowd of vessels.

Soon they reached those nearest to them, and the flames, borne forward by the wind, sprang from vessel to vessel. There was no longer any hope of saving a single ship; and the crews, climbing hastily across from one to the other till they reached those nearest to the shore, leaped overboard. Although now more than half a mile below the city the flames lit up the walls with a bright glare, and the shouts of the exulting Franks rose loud and continuous.

The sudden shouting which had broken out among the Danes had alarmed the watchmen, who, ignorant of the cause, called the citizens to arms, and these on reaching the walls had stood astonished at the spectacle. The flames were already rising from the three groups of ships which they had regarded with so much anxiety on the previous evening, and by the light they could see the river below covered with a mass of drifting vessels. Then they saw the tower-ships float away from the bank, and the figures on their decks leap into three small boats, which at once rowed with all speed across the river.

That they were friends who had wrought this destruction was certain, and Count Eudes threw open the gate, and with the Abbe Ebble ran down to meet them. They were astonished when Edmund with his Saxons leaped to land.

"What miracle is this?" the count exclaimed.

"A simple matter, Sir Count," Edmund answered. "My kinsman and I, seeing that the townspeople were troubled by yonder towers, determined to destroy them. We have succeeded in doing so, and with them I trust fully half of the Danish fleet will perish."

"You are the saviour of our town, my brave young Saxon," Count Eudes cried, embracing him. "If Paris is saved it will be thanks to the valiant deed that you have accomplished this night. But let us to the walls again, where we may the better see whether the Danes can remove their ships from those great furnaces which are bearing down upon them."

The sight from the walls, when the fire-ships reached the fleet and the flames spread, was grand in the extreme, for in half an hour nigh three hundred vessels were in flames. For some time the three towers rose like pillars of fire above the burning mass; then one by one they fell with a crash, which could be plainly heard, although they were now near a mile away.

Paris was wild with joy at the destruction of the towers which had menaced it, and the conflagration of nigh half the Danish fleet, laden with the spoil of northern France. Edmund and his Saxons were conducted in triumph by a shouting crowd to the palace of the archbishop, where Goslin, in the name of the city, returned them the heartiest thanks for the services which they had rendered. The wealthy citizens vied with each other in bestowing costly presents upon them, bonfires were lighted in the streets, and till morning the town gave itself up to revelry and rejoicing.

A month elapsed before the Danes recovered from the blow which had been dealt them and resumed the assault. Part of this time had been spent in manufacturing great shields of bull's hide. These were strongly constructed, and were each capable of covering six men. On the 29th of January their preparations were complete, and at daybreak the warders on the wall saw them pouring down into their ships and galleys. As the fleet crossed the river its aspect was singular. The decks were covered by the black shields, above which appeared a forest of spears, sparkling in the morning sunlight. As they reached the shore the Northmen sprang to land, while from the decks of the vessels a storm of missiles flew towards the walls. Vast numbers of catapults, which they had manufactured since their last attack, hurled masses of stone, heavy javelins, and leaden bullets, while thousands of arrows darkened the air.

The bells of the church sounded the alarm, which called every citizen capable of bearing arms to the walls. The archbishop took his place at the spot most threatened by the enemy, with his nephew, the valiant abbe, by his side. The Counts Eudes, Robert, Ragenaire, Utton, and Herilang stood foremost among the defenders.

The Saxons, as before, were held in reserve, but to Edmund and Egbert had been assigned, at their urgent request, the command of the defence of the tower. It was against this point that the Danes again made their most desperate effort. Their main body advanced against it, and smaller parties attacked the city at other points, while the rowing galleys, divided into two bodies, strove to destroy the bridge, and so isolate the defenders of the post.

Around the tower the combat was desperate. The assailants were well-nigh hidden under their great bucklers. Their shouts, and the constant clashing of arms which they maintained, made a terrific uproar; a storm of missiles from the fleet poured upon the tower, while from the crevices between the shields the bowmen shot incessantly at the defenders. The very number of the Danes hindered their attack, for the tower was so small that comparatively few could approach at once.

It had been greatly strengthened since the last assault, and through the loopholes in the walls the archers did their best to answer the storm of missiles poured into the fort. Edmund and Egbert went among them, begging them not to fire at random, but to choose moments when the movements of the assailants opened a space in the roof of shields which covered them.

Whenever this took place a dozen arrows fell true to the mark. Some of those bearing the shield would be struck, and these falling, a gap would be caused through which the arrows of the defenders flew thickly, causing death and confusion until the shield could be raised in its place again. Boiling liquids were poured over those who approached the walls, and huge stones crushed the shields and their bearers.

Eudes and his men valiantly defended the wall, and the Danes in vain strove to scale it. All day long the battle continued, but at nightfall the tower still remained in the hands of the defenders, the deep ditch which they had dug round it having prevented the Danes from working at the wall, as they had done in the previous assault.

When darkness came on the Danes did not retire, but lay down in the positions they occupied, under their shields. In the morning many ships were seen crossing the river again, and the defenders saw to their surprise numbers of captives who had been collected from the surrounding country, troops of oxen, ship-loads of branches of trees, trusses of hay and corn, and faggots of vines landed. Their surprise became horror when they saw the captives and the cattle alike slaughtered as they landed. Their bodies were brought forward under cover of the shields and thrown into the moat, in which, too, were cast the hay, straw, faggots, and trees.

At the sight of the massacre the archbishop prayed to the Virgin to give him strength, and drawing a bow to its full strength, let fly an arrow, which, great as was the distance, flew true to its mark and struck the executioner full in the face. This apparent miracle of the Virgin in their favour re-animated the spirit of the defenders; and a solemn service was instantly held in the church in her honour, and prayers were offered to her to save Lutece, which was the original name of Paris, and was still cherished by its inhabitants.

The Danes were occupied all day at their work of filling up the moat. The besieged were not idle, but laboured at the construction of several mangonels capable of casting huge blocks of stone. In the morning the Danes planted their battering-rams, one on each side of the tower, and recommenced the assault. The new machines of the defenders did great havoc in their ranks, their heavy stones crashing through the roof of bucklers and crushing those who held them, and for a time the Norsemen desisted from the attack.

They now filled three of their largest vessels with combustibles, and placing them on the windward side of the bridge, set them alight. The people of Paris beheld with afright these fire-ships bearing down upon the bridge, and old and young burst into tears and cries at the view of the approaching destruction, and, led by the archbishop, all joined in a prayer to St. Germain, the patron saint of Paris, to protect the city. The exulting Danes replied to the cries of those on the walls with triumphant shouts. Thanks, as the Franks believed, to the interposition of St. Germain, the fireships struck against the pile of stones from which the beams supporting the bridge in the centre were raised. Eudes and his companions leaped down from the bridge and with hatchets hewed holes in the sides of the ships at the water-line, and they sank without having effected any damage to the bridge.

It was now the turn of the Franks to raise triumphant shouts, while the Danes, disheartened, fell back from the attack, and at night recrossed the river, leaving two of their battering-rams as tokens of the triumph of the besieged. Paris had now a respite while the Danes again spread over the surrounding country, many of them ascending the river in their ships and wasting the country as far as Burgundy.

The monastery of St. Germain and the church in which the body of the saint was buried still remained untouched. The bands of Northmen who had invaded England had never hesitated to plunder and destroy the churches and shrines of the Christians, but hitherto some thought of superstition had kept the followers of Siegfroi from assailing the monastery of St. Germain.

One soldier, bolder than the rest, now approached the church and with his spear broke some of the windows. The Abbe D'Abbon, an eye-witness and minute historian of the siege of Paris, states that the impious Dane was at once struck dead. The same fate befell one of his comrades, who mounted to the platform at the top of the church and in descending fell off and was killed. A third who entered the church and looked round lost his sight for ever. A fourth entering it fell dead; and a fifth, who, more bold than all, tried to break into the tomb of the saint, was killed by a stone which fell upon him.

One night after a continuance of heavy rain the Seine, being greatly swollen, swept away the centre of the bridge connecting the tower with the town. At daybreak the Northmen, seeing what had taken place, hastened across the river and attacked the tower. The garrison was but a small one, no more than twenty men having slept there. For a time these repulsed every effort of the Danes, but gradually their numbers were lessened until at last fourteen only remained. Their names have come down to us. Besides Edmund and Egbert there were Hermanfroi, Herivee, Herilard, Odoacre, Herric, Arnold, Sohie, Gerbert, Elvidon, Havderad, Ermard, and Gossuin. These resisted so valiantly that the Danes, after losing large numbers in the vain attempt to storm the walls, brought up a wagonful of grain; this they rolled forward to the gate of the tower and set it on fire.

The flames rapidly spread from the gates to the walls, which were all of wood, and soon the whole were a sheet of flames. The little band of defenders retreated on to the end of the bridge, and there, when the flames had sufficiently abated to allow them to pass, the Northmen attacked them. Edmund and Egbert were both good swimmers, but this was an accomplishment which but few of the Franks possessed, and none of the remnant of the garrison were able to swim. For a long time the little band repulsed all the efforts of the Danes, but were gradually driven back foot by foot until they reached the edge of the chasm. Here they made a last desperate stand, but were at length cut down or driven over by sheer weight of numbers. Egbert and Edmund had disencumbered themselves of all their defensive armour, and at the last moment, throwing off their helmets and relinquishing their spears, they plunged into the stream, diving deeply to avoid the arrows of the Northmen.

The fact of the river being in flood, which had caused the destruction of the tower, now proved the cause of their safety. Had the water been clear, the Danes on the bridge above could have marked their progress and poured a storm of arrows upon them as they came to the surface; but its yellow and turbid waters concealed them from sight, and each time they rose to the surface for air they were enabled to take a rapid breath and dive again before their enemies could direct and launch their arrows at them.

As they drifted far down the stream, they reached the land beyond bowshot of the Danes, and they soon entered the town amid the loud acclamations of the citizens. The Danes now for the most part drew off from the neighbourhood, and the Abbe Ebble led out a sortie, which reached the Danish camp, and driving back those whom they found within it, set it on fire and effected their retreat to Paris without loss, in spite of the efforts of the enemy, who rapidly assembled at the sight of the flames.

The Danes had brought in from the surrounding country such vast quantities of cattle, sheep, and goats, that their camps would not suffice to hold them, and they turned the church of St. Germain into a stable and crowded it with these animals. The saint, as the Abbe D'Abbon relates, indignant at this desecration, sent a terrible plague among the cattle, and when the Danes in the morning entered the church it contained nothing but carcasses in the last state of decomposition.

The valiant defence of Paris had given time for the rest of France to arm, and the Danes scattered over the country now met with a stout resistance. The North-men were defeated in their efforts to capture Le Mans, Chartres, and other towns, and were defeated in several battles near Chartres by Godefroi and Odon.

In March Henri advanced with a strong force to the relief of Paris, and arriving at night attacked the camp of the Danes, slew great numbers, and captured a vast booty; and then, having supplied Paris with a considerable amount of provisions, retired with his band before the Danes had time to assemble in sufficient strength to oppose him. Shortly afterwards the Danes expressed the desire of Siegfroi to hold parley with the Count Eudes. Siegfroi and a number of his warriors landed, and Eudes left the city and advanced to meet them. No sooner had he reached them than he was attacked by the Northmen, but drawing his sword he defended himself with immense bravery until the garrison ran down to his succour, and the Danes were driven back to their ship with loss of nearly half of their party.

The Danes now left the church of St. Germain L'Auxerrois and surrounded the monastery of St. Germain des Pres, but the monks there paid him sixty pounds of pure silver to leave them in peace. Siegfroi now wished to abandon the siege which had already cost him so dear, but the Northmen, furious at their losses, determined upon another assault.

"Very well," the king said; "have your way then. Attack Paris on all sides, hew down its towers, and make breaches in its walls; for once I will remain a specta-tor."

The Danes crossed the river and landed on the island, but owing to the absence of large numbers on other expeditions, and the heavy losses which they had suf-fered, their numbers were no longer so overwhelming, and Count Eudes led out his forces to oppose them outside the walls. This time Edmund headed his band of Saxons, who until now had only taken part as archers in the defence.

The combat was a furious one. In spite of the valour of Eudes and Ebble the Danes pressed hard upon the Franks, and were driving them back towards the gates when Edmund led his Saxons, in the close phalanx in which they had so often met the Danes in the field, to the front. With irresistible force the wedge burst its way through the ranks of the Danes, bearing all before it with its wedge of spears. Into the gap thus formed Eudes and Ebble with their bravest men threw themselves, and the Danes, severed in two, were driven back towards their ships. But for some hours the rain had been falling heavily and the river was rapidly rising and had already overflowed a portion of the island. Thus the Danes had great difficulty in getting on board their ships again, and great numbers were killed in doing so.

There was no longer any resistance to Siegfroi's wishes. A parley was held with the city, and a further sum being added to that contributed by the monks of St. Germain des Pres the Danes drew off from the town.

At this time the long confinement of so many men within the walls had caused a pestilence to break out in Paris. The Archbishop Goslin, the Bishop Everard of Sens, the Prince Hugues, and many others died. The 16th of April was the day on which the Parisians were accustomed to go in solemn procession to the church of St. Germain. The Northmen, knowing this, in mockery filled a wagon with grain and organized a mock procession. The bullocks who drew the chariot suddenly became lame; numbers of other bullocks were attached, but although goaded by spears their united efforts were unable to drag the wagon an inch, and the Danes were obliged at last to abandon their intention.

The same day St. Germain is reported to have further shown his power. One of the Northmen, condemned for some offence to be executed, fled to the church for refuge, and was there slain by his countrymen; but all who took part in the deed at once fell dead. The Northmen, struck by these miracles, placed a certain number as guard over the church to prevent any from touching aught that it contained. One of these men, a Dane of great stature, spread his bed in the church and slept there; but to the astonishment of his comrades he was found in the morning to have shrunk to the size of a new-born infant, at which stature he remained for the rest of his life.

A miracle of an opposite kind was at the same time performed in the town. A valiant warrior had from the effects of fever fallen into an extreme weakness, and was devoured with grief at the thought that he should no longer be able to take share in the defence of the town. To him St. Germain appeared at night and told him that his prayers had been heard, and that his strength should be restored to him. On awakening in the morning he found that he was as vigorous and as robust as ever.

Another day when the soldiers were carrying the banner of the saint round the walls of the town, followed by the citizens chanting hymns, one of the bearers of the holy relics, named Gozbert, was struck by a stone from a catapult. The man who had fired it fell dead, while Gozbert continued his promenade in no way injured by the blow. The Abbe D'Abbon vouches for these miracles on the part of St. Germain in defence of his faithful city.

CHAPTER XV: FRIENDS IN TROUBLE

ALTHOUGH for a time the Northmen abstained from grand assaults, continued skirmishes took place. Sometimes parties landed beneath the walls, and strove to carry off the cattle which the besieged turned out to gather a little fresh food there. Sometimes the citizens, led by Eudes or Ebble, would take boat and cross, and endeavour to cut off small parties of the enemy. They had now sufficient boats at their disposal for expeditions of this kind; for, in their last defeat, the Danes had in their haste left several boats behind them. Of one of the largest of these Edmund took possession, and going out in her at night, several times succeeded in capturing Danish vessels, sometimes while they were rowing along the river unsuspicious that any foes were near, sometimes by boarding them as they lay alongside the bank.

As the vessels so captured were too large to be dragged ashore, and could have been easily recaptured by the Danes, they were, after being emptied of their contents, always burned. The plague continued its ravages, and the city became straitened for provisions. Count Eudes therefore determined to go to King Charles to urge him to hurry to the succour of the town. Almost all the chiefs of the defence had fallen victims to the pest, or had been killed in battle with the Danes, and the count at his departure committed the defence of the city to the Abbe Ebble and Edmund. He then crossed the stream at night, and made his way successfully through the Danes.

The abbe and Edmund vied with each other in keeping up the spirits of the garrison with successful little forays with the Danes, frequently crossing the river to the one bank or the other, sometimes with parties of only five or six men, and falling upon similar bodies of the enemy. Several times they pounced upon small herds of the enemy's cattle, and driving them into the river, directed them in their boats across the stream.

In the commencement of July Eudes appeared on the slopes on Mont Martre with three battalions of soldiers. The enemy, who were for the most part on the other side of the Seine, crossed the river. A desperate battle ensued. A portion of the garrison crossed in boats to the assistance of their friends, Edmund leading over his band of Saxons. With these he fell upon the rear of the Danes engaged in fighting with the force under the count, and the Northmen, attacked on both sides, gave way and took to flight. They were hotly pursued by the Franks.

The reinforcements entered Paris triumphantly by the bridge, which had long since been repaired. But the siege was not yet over. When the news of the victory of Eudes spread, the Danes again drew together from all parts, and crossing the river, attacked the city on every side. The onslaught was more furious than any which had preceded it. The Danes had provided themselves with large numbers of mangonels and catapults. Every man capable of bearing arms was upon the walls; but so furious was the attack, so vast the number of the assailants, so prodigious were the clouds of missiles which they rained upon the walls, that the besieged almost lost heart.

The relics of St. Genevieve were taken round the walls. In several places the Danes had formed breaches in the walls, and although the besieged still struggled, hope had well-nigh left them, and abject terror reigned in the city. Women ran about the streets screaming, and crying that the end was at hand. The church bells tolled dismally, and the shouts of the exultant Danes rose higher and higher. Again a general cry rose to St. Germain to come to the aid of the town. Just at this moment Edmund and Egbert, who had till now held the Saxons in reserve, feeling that a desperate effort must be made, formed up their band, and advancing to the principal breach, passed through the ranks of the disheartened Franks, and with levelled pikes charged headlong down into the crowd of Danes. The latter, already exhausted by their efforts, were at once borne back before the serried pikes of their fresh assailants. In vain their chiefs at that point tried to rally them; nothing could withstand the impetus of the Saxon attack.

Astonished at seeing the tide of battle swept away from the breach, the French believed that St. Germain had wrought a miracle in their favour, and taking heart poured out in the rear of the Saxons. The news of the miracle spread rapidly. Through the breaches, and from every gate, they poured out suddenly upon the Danes, who, struck with consternation at this sudden onslaught by a foe whom they had already regarded as beaten, hesitated, and soon took to flight. Vast numbers were cut down before they could reach their vessels. A great portion fled towards the bridge and endeavoured to cross there; but their numbers impeded them, and the Saxons and Franks, falling upon their rear, effected a terrible slaughter.

Two days after the battle a force of six hundred Franks arrived from the Emperor Charles. The Danes sought to oppose their entrance to the city, but were defeated with a loss of three thousand men. The siege was now virtually over, and in a short time the emperor himself with a great army arrived. It was now November, and after some negotiations the Danes agreed upon the receipt of seven hundred pounds of silver to retire to Burgundy and to leave the country at the beginning of March.

Having wasted Burgundy, however, they again returned to Paris. Consternation seized the capital when the fleet of the Northmen was seen approaching. A treaty was, however, made, for the wind had fallen just when the Danish fleet, which had but lately arrived and was descending the river, was abreast of Paris. As soon as the wind became favourable the Northmen broke the truce, slew a number of Franks who had mingled among them, and passed up the Marne.

In the meantime Emperor Charles had died and Count Eudes had been chosen his successor. When the Danes again advanced against Paris he speedily sent reinforcements. The town had already repulsed an attack. Eudes himself on St. John's Day was advancing with 1000 men-at-arms when he was attacked by 10,000 mounted Danes and 9000 footmen. The combat was desperate but the Franks were victorious. Eudes, however, had other difficulties. Burgundy and Aquitaine revolted, and in order to secure peace to the kingdom he made a treaty with the Danes, giving over to them the province of Normandy.

Edmund and Egbert had no part in the second siege of Paris. As soon as the place was relieved by the Emperor Charles they prepared to depart. Taking boats they ascended the river, and to their joy found the Dragon safe in the hiding place where she had been lying for nearly a year. She was brought out into the stream and floated down to Paris, where by the order of Count Eudes she was thoroughly repaired and redecorated.

The Franks, convinced that next only to the assistance of St. Germain they owed the safety of their city to the valour of the Saxons, loaded them with presents;

and these, with the gifts which they had previously received after the destruction of the three towers, and the sums for which the booty captured from the Danes had been sold, made up a great treasure.

Upon the day before they had arranged to sail a Danish boat was seen rowing down the stream. It approached the Dragon and the helmsman asked:

"Is this ship the Dragon? and has it for a captain Edmund the Saxon?"

"I am Edmund," he replied, "and this is the Dragon. What would you with me?"

"I am sent by the Jarl Siegbert, who lies wounded near, to beg that you will come to him immediately, as he is in a sore strait and needs your assistance."

"I will come at once," Edmund said. "Put one of your men on board to show me where he is, for I shall be there before you."

Edmund's horn sounded the signal, and messengers were sent to the town to order the crew at once to repair on board the Dragon. Edmund landed and took leave of the Frankish leaders. The provisions and stores were hastily carried on board, and then, amidst the enthusiastic cheers of the inhabitants, who thronged the walls and shore, the oars were got out and the Dragon proceeded at the top of her speed up the river.

On the way Edmund questioned the Dane, and found that Siegbert had been wounded in the last assault upon Paris. He had not been present at the first part of the siege, having but recently arrived from Norway. His daughter Freda had accompanied him. "Yes," she was still unmarried, although many valiant Northmen had sought her hand, chief among them the brave leader Sweyn "of the left hand;" but there had been a fray on the previous night in Siegbert's camp, and it was said--but for that he could not vouch--that Freda had been carried off.

The news filled Edmund with anxiety. Ever since the day he left her on her father's galley his thoughts had turned often to the Danish maiden, and the resolution to carry out his promise and some day seek her again had never for a moment wavered. He had seen many fair young Saxons, and could have chosen a bride where he would among these, for few Saxons girls would have turned a deaf ear to the wooing of one who was at once of high rank, a prime favourite with the king, and regarded by his countrymen as one of the bravest of the Saxon champions; but the dark-haired Freda, who united the fearlessness and independence of a woman with the frankness and gaiety of a child, had won his heart.

It was true she was a Dane and a pagan; but her father was his friend, and would, he felt sure, offer no objections on the ground of the enmity of the races. Since Guthorn and his people had embraced Christianity, the enmity between the races, in England at least, was rapidly declining. As to her religion, Edmund doubted not that she would, under his guidance and teaching, soon cast away the blood-stained gods of the Northmen and accept Christianity.

In the five years of strife and warfare which had elapsed since he saw her Edmund had often pictured their next meeting. He had not doubted that she would remain true to him. Few as were the words which had been spoken, he knew that when she said, "I will wait for you even till I die," she had meant it, and that she was not one to change. He had even been purposing, on his return to England, to ask King Alfred to arrange through Guthorn for a safe pass for him to go to Norway. To hear, then, that she had been carried off from her father's side was a terrible blow, and in his anxiety to arrive at Siegbert's tent Edmund urged the rowers to their fullest exertions.

It was three hours after leaving Paris when the Dane pointed to a village at a short distance from the river and told him that Siegbert was lying there. The Dragon was steered to shore, and Edmund leaping out followed the Dane with rapid footsteps to the village. The wounded jarl was lying upon a heap of straw.

"Is it really you, Edmund?" he exclaimed as the young Saxon entered. "Glad am I indeed that my messenger did not arrive too late. I heard of you when we first landed-- how the Danes, when they sailed up the Seine, had seen a Saxon galley of strange shape which had rowed rapidly up the river; how the galley herself had never again been seen; but how a young Saxon with his band had performed wonders in the defence of Paris, and had burned well-nigh half the Danish fleet.

"They said that the leader was named Edmund, for they had heard the name shouted in battle; and especially when he, with one other alone, escaped from the burning tower and swam the river. So I was sure that it was you. Then, a week back, my men told me of a strange ship which had passed down the river to Paris, and I doubted not that it was your Dragon, which had been hidden somewhere during the siege. I thought then of sending to tell you that I was lying here wounded; but Freda, who had always been talking of you, suddenly turned coy and said that you might have forgotten us, and if you wanted us you would come to us in Norway."

"But where is Freda?" Edmund, who had been listening impatiently, exclaimed. "One of your men told me that she had been carried off. Is it true?"

"Alas! it is true," Siegbert replied; "and that is why I sent for you. I have never been good friends with Bijorn since the wounding of his son, but after a time the matter blew over. Sweyn, who though but with one arm, and that the left, has grown into a valiant warrior, is now, Bijorn being dead, one of our boldest vikings. A year since he became a declared suitor for Freda's hand. In this, indeed, he is not alone, seeing that she has grown up one of our fairest maidens, and many are the valorous deeds that have been done to win a smile from her; but she has refused all suitors, Sweyn with the others. He took his refusal in bad part, and even ventured to vow she should be his whether she willed it or not. Of course I took the matter up and forbade all further intimacy, and we had not met again till the other day before Paris. We had high words there, but I thought no more of it. A few days afterwards I was struck by a crossbow bolt in the leg. It smashed my knee, and I shall never be able to use my leg again. I well-nigh died of fever and vexation, but Freda nursed me through it. She had me carried on a litter here to be away from the noise and revelry of the camp. Last night there was a sudden outcry. Some of my men who sprang to arms were smitten down, and the assailants burst in here and tore Freda, shrieking, away. Their leader was Sweyn of the left hand. As I lay tossing here, mad with the misfortune which ties me to my couch, I thought of you. I said, 'If any can follow and recapture Freda it is Edmund.' The Danes had for the most part moved away, and there were few would care to risk a quarrel with Sweyn in a matter which concerned them not closely; but I felt that I could rely upon you, and that you would spare no pains to rescue my child."

"That will I not!" Edmund exclaimed; "but tell me first what you think are his plans. Which way has he gone, and what force has he with him?"

"The band he commands are six shiploads, each numbering fifty men. What his plans may be I know not, but many of the Danes, I know, purposed, when the war was finished here, to move east through Burgundy. Some intended to build boats on the banks of the Rhine and sail down on that river, others intended to journey further and to descend by the Elbe. I know not which course Sweyn may adopt. The country between this and the Rhine swarms with Danes. I do not suppose that

Sweyn will join any other party. Having Freda with him, he will prefer keeping apart; but in any case it would not be safe for you to journey with your band, who would assuredly become embroiled with the first party of Danes they met; and even if they be as brave as yourself they would be defeated by such superior numbers."

"You do not think that Sweyn will venture to use violence to force Freda to become his wife?"

"I think he will hardly venture upon that," Siegbert said, "however violent and headstrong he may be. To carry off a maiden for a wife is accounted no very evil deed, for the maiden is generally not unwilling; but to force her by violence to become his wife would be a deed so contrary to our usages that it would bring upon him the anger of the whole nation. Knowing Sweyn's disposition, I believe that were there no other way, he would not hesitate even at this, but might take ship and carry her to some distant land; but he would not do this until all other means fail. He will strive to tire her out, and so bring her in her despair to consent to wed him."

Edmund was silent for three or four minutes; then he said: "I must consult my kinsman Egbert. I will return and tell you what I purpose doing."

On leaving the cottage Edmund found Egbert walking up and down outside awaiting the result of the interview. He had been present when the Dane had told of Freda's abduction, and knew how sore a blow it was to the young ealdorman, for Edmund had made no secret to him of his intention some day to wed the Danish jarl's daughter. Edmund in a few words related to him the substance of Siegbert's narrative, and ended by saying: "Now, Egbert, what is best to be done?"

"'Tis of no use asking me, Edmund; you know well enough that it is you that always decide and I agree. I have a hand to strike, but no head to plan. Tell me only what you wish, and you may be sure that I will do my best to execute it."

"Of course we must follow," Edmund said; "of that there is no question. The only doubt is as to the force we must take. What Siegbert said is true. The Danish bands are so numerous to the east that we should be sure to fall in with some of them, and fight as we might, should be destroyed; and yet with a smaller number how could we hope to rescue Freda from Sweyn's hands?"

Edmund walked up and down for some time.

"I think," he went on at last, "the best plan will be to take a party of but four at most. I must choose those who will be able to pass best as Danes. With so small a number I may traverse the country unobserved. I will take with me two of Siegbert's men, who, when we get nigh to Sweyn's band, may join with him and tell me how things are going, and how Sweyn treats his captive. If I find he is pushing matters to an extreme I must make some desperate effort to carry her off; but if, as is more probable, he trusts to time to break her resolution, I shall follow at a short distance."

"Shall I go with you, Edmund?"

"I think it will be better not, Egbert. Your beard would mark you as a Saxon at once."

"But that I can cut off," Egbert said. "It would be a sacrifice truly, but I would do it without hesitation."

"Thanks, dear kinsman, but I think it would be of more purpose for you to remain in command of the Dragon. She may meet many foes, and it were best that you were there to fight and direct her. I pray you at once to descend the Seine and sailing round the north coast of France, place the Dragon at the mouth of the Rhine. Do not interfere with any Danish ships that you may see pass out, but keep at a distance. Should Sweyn descend the Rhine I will, if possible, send a messenger down before him, so do you look out for small boats; and if you see one in which the rower hoists a white flag at the end of his oar, you will know he is my messenger. If I find Sweyn goes on towards the Elbe I will also send you word, and you will then move the Dragon to the mouth of that river.

"Lastly, if you receive no message, but if you mark that in a Danish vessel when passing you a white cloth is waved from one of the windows of the cabins in the poop, that will be a signal to you that the vessel is Sweyn's, and that Freda is a captive on board. In that case you will of course at once attack it. Let us ask Siegbert. He has sailed up both the Rhine and the Elbe, and can tell us of some quiet port near the mouth of each river where you may lay the Dragon somewhat out of sight of passers-by, while you can yet note all ships that go down the river. My messengers will then know where to find you." Having settled this point they returned to Siegbert, and Edmund told him what he thought of doing.

"I can advise no better," Siegbert said. "Assuredly you cannot prevail by force. At present I have only ten of my followers with me; the rest, after I was wounded, and it was plain that a long time must elapse before I could again lead them in the field, asked me to let them follow some other chief, and as they could not be idle here I consented. I have ten men with me, but these would be but a small reinforcement. As you say, your Saxons would be instantly known, and the Northmen have suffered so at their hands during the siege that the first party you met would set upon you."

"I will take two only of your men," Edmund said. "Choose me two who are not known by sight to Sweyn. I wish one to be a subtle fellow, who will act as a spy for me; the other I should choose of commanding stature; and the air of a leader. He will go with my party, and should we come upon Danes he will assume the place of leader, and can answer any questions. There is far too much difference between the Saxon and Danish tongue for me and my men to pass as Danes if we have many words to say. I shall take four of my men, all full grown, strong, and good fighters. They have but little hair upon their chins at present, and they can shave that off. Now, jarl, I want five Danish dresses, for your costume differs somewhat from ours. Have you horses? If not, I must send back to Paris to buy some."

"I have plenty to mount you and your party."

"Good," Edmund said; "I will go down to my ship and pick my men."

In half an hour the party were ready to start. Egbert had received from Siegbert particulars of villages at the mouths of the Rhine and Elbe, and he promised Edmund that a watch should be kept night and day at the mouth of the Rhine until a messenger arrived. Edmund had already ascertained that Sweyn had left a fortnight before with his following, and had marched towards Champagne. There probably he had halted his main body, returning only with a party of horsemen to carry off Freda.

"I would I could go with you," Siegbert groaned as Edmund said adieu to him. "I would ride straight into his camp and challenge him to mortal combat, but as it is I am helpless."

"Never fear, good Siegbert," Edmund said cheerfully; "when your leg is cured travel straight homeward, and there, I trust, before very long to place Freda safe and unharmed in your arms. If I come not you will know that I have perished."

A minute later, after a few parting words with Egbert, Edmund mounted his horse, and followed by his six companions, rode off at full speed. He knew that it would be useless making any inquiries about Sweyn and his party. But few of the inhabitants of the country were to be seen about, for the Danes had burned every house within very many miles of Paris, and the peasants would assuredly not have paid any special attention to a party of Danes, for whenever they saw the dreaded marauders even at a distance they forsook their homes and fled to the forests. The party therefore rode eastward until nightfall, then picketed their horses, and having lit a fire, made their supper from the store of provisions they had brought with them, and then lay down to sleep for the night.

At daybreak they again started and continued their journey until it was necessary to halt to give their horses a rest. They had passed several parties of Danes, for these in great numbers, after the siege of Paris had been given up, were journeying towards Burgundy. There was but slight greeting as they passed; but on one occasion a horseman rode out from one of the bands and entered into conversation with the two Danes who rode at the head of the party. They told them that they were followers of the Jarl Siegbert, and were riding to join the rest of his band, who were with the company of Jarl Eric, as Siegbert would be long before he would be able to move, and had therefore kept only a few of his followers with him.

"Eric is a long way ahead," the Dane said; "he must be full as far as Nancy by this time. Those who left first," he grumbled, "will have the pick of the country. We were fools to linger so long before Paris." Then turning his horse, he rode back to his comrades, and the party continued their way.

They avoided all towns and large Danish encampments on the way, but made inquiries from all small parties they met after the party of Sweyn. They learned without difficulty the place where he had been encamped a few days before, but on their arriving in the neighbourhood they found that the place was deserted, nor could any tell them the direction in which the Northmen had travelled.

CHAPTER XVI: FREDA

FOR some days Edmund and his party scoured the country round, journeying now in one direction, now in another, but without hearing ought of Sweyn's party. Certainly they had not gone along the track which the main body of the Danes had followed; but the question was whether they had turned rather to the south in order to cross the mountain ranges between them and the Rhine, or had turned north and journeyed through the great forest of Ardennes, and so to some of the other rivers which run down into the North Sea.

The latter was in some respects the most likely course to have been chosen. By taking it Sweyn would avoid altogether the track which the majority of his countrymen were taking, and this would naturally be his object. Siegbert had many powerful friends, and the carrying off of the jarl's daughter from the side of her wounded father would be regarded as a grave offence; and Sweyn might well wish to keep clear of his countrymen until he had forced Freda to become his wife. Even then it would not be safe for him for a long time to return to his country. Striking through the Ardennes he would come down upon the Scheldt, the Moselle, the Maas, or other rivers flowing into the North Sea direct, or into the Rhine.

Edmund knew nothing of these streams; but the Danes with him said there were several rivers so situated, for they had sailed up them. Where they took their rise they knew not, but it would probably be in or beyond the forest of Ardennes.

"Then in that way we will search," Edmund said. "If they come upon a river they will doubtless set to work to build galleys to carry them to the sea, for with only three hundred men Sweyn will not venture to march by land through a country which has but lately suffered heavily at the hands of the Danes. It will take him a month or six weeks to cut down trees and build his ships; therefore we may hope to find him before he is ready to embark. First we will push through the forest to the other side; there we will question the inhabitants concerning the position of the nearest rivers; then we will divide into parties and go on the search, appointing a place of rendezvous where we may rejoin each other. It can hardly be that we shall fail to find them if they have taken that way."

Before entering the forest they obtained a considerable store of provisions; for they had no idea of its extent, and had no time to spend in hunting game. The forest of Ardennes was at that time of immense size, extending from Verdun and Metz on the south, to Liege and Aix on the north.

Men of the present day would have found it impossible to find their way through, but would speedily have been lost in its trackless recesses; but the Saxons and Danes were accustomed to travel in forests, and knew the signs as well as did the Red-skins and hunters of the American forests. Therefore they felt no hesitation in entering the forest without a guide.

The danger which might beset them was of a different kind. Immense numbers of the inhabitants of France, Champagne, and Burgundy had taken refuge in the forests, driving their flocks and herds before them. Here they lived a wild life, hoping that the emperor would ere long clear the country of the invaders. No mercy could be expected if Edmund and his party fell in with a number of these fugitives. They would have no time to tell their story, but would be attacked at once as a party of plundering Danes.

Knowing that the horses would be an encumbrance to them in the forest, they were sold to the last party of Northmen they encountered before entering it, and they pursued their way on foot. The greatest caution was observed; every sound was marked, and at the call of a human voice, the low of cattle, or the bleating of sheep, they turned their course so as to avoid encounter with the inhabitants of the forest. They lit no fires at night, and scarce a word was spoken on the march. Several times they had to take refuge in thickets when they heard the sound of approaching voices, and it needed all their knowledge of woodcraft to maintain their direction steadily towards the north. At last, after six days' journey, they issued out into the open country beyond the forest and soon arrived at a cottage.

The peasant was struck with terror and astonishment at the appearance of seven Danes; and he could with difficulty be made to understand that their object was neither plunder nor murder, but that they wished only information from him of the situation and direction of the various rivers of the country. After learning from him all that he knew Edmund arrived at the conclusion that Sweyn would probably attempt to descend either by a branch of the Moselle, and so to the Rhine on the right, or by one of the Maas on the left of the place at which they had emerged from the forest.

Edmund decided to strike the Maas, and to follow its course up into the forest, taking with him one of the Danes and two of his Saxons, and to send the others to search the banks of the tributary of the Moselle. Before starting he sent the peasant to the nearest village to purchase garments of the country for the whole party. He had already told the man that they were not Danes but Saxons, the bitter enemies of the Northmen, and that he had been aiding in the defence of Paris against them.

The peasant did not doubt what Edmund told him, for the conduct of his visitors was so opposed to all that he had heard of the doings of the Danes that he well believed they could not belong to that nation. He was away some hours, and returned with the required dresses. Having put these on, and laying aside their helmets and shields, the two parties started, the Danes alone carrying with them their former garments. The next day Edmund arrived at the river, and at once followed its course upwards, for Sweyn and his party would be building their ships in the forest.

They had not proceeded many miles before they heard the sound of axes. Edmund gave an exclamation of delight. It was almost certain that he had hit upon Sweyn's track, for it was unlikely that any of the inhabitants of the country would have gone so far into the forest for timber. They now moved with the greatest caution, and as they approached the place whence the sound proceeded Edmund halted the two Saxons and bade them conceal themselves. The Dane resumed his own garments and put on his helmet and shield; and then, taking advantage of every clump of undergrowth, and moving with the greatest caution, he and Edmund made their way forward. Presently they came within sight of an animated scene.

A large number of trees had been felled by the banks of the river and three hundred Northmen were busily at work. The frames of two great galleys had already been set up, and they were now engaged in chopping out planks for their sides. Two huts were erected in the middle of the clearing. One was large, and Sweyn's banner floated from a spear before it. The other which stood close by was much smaller, and Edmund doubted not that this was appropriated to Freda.

Nothing more could be done now--their object was so far attained; and retiring they joined the two Saxons and made their way along the river bank till they reached the edge of the forest. One of the Saxons was now sent off to the peasant's hut, where he was to remain until the return of the other party, and was then to bring them on to the spot which Edmund had chosen for his encampment. This was in the heart of a large clump of underwood extending down to the river.

The brushwood was so thick that it was entered with difficulty, and no passer-by would dream that a party was hidden within it. Near the stream Edmund and his companions with their swords soon cleared away a circle, and with the boughs constructed an arbour. A thin screen of bushes separated them from the river, but they could see the water, and none could pass up or down unperceived.

The Saxon was charged to bring with him on his return a considerable supply of provisions, for it would have been dangerous to wander in the woods in pursuit of game. The Northmen had, Edmund noticed, some cattle with them; but they would be sure to be hunting in the woods, as they would wish to save the cattle for provision on their voyage. It was nightfall before the hut was completed; and as they had journeyed far for many days Edmund determined to postpone an attempt to discover what was passing in Sweyn's camp until the following evening.

The day passed quietly, and towards evening Edmund and the Dane started for Sweyn's camp. When they approached it they saw many fires burning, and the shouting and singing of the Norsemen rang through the forest. They waited until the fires burnt down somewhat and they could see many of the Danes stretching themselves down by them. Then Edmund's companion proceeded to the camp.

Anxious as Edmund was himself to learn what was doing, he restrained his impatience, for it was safer that the Northman should go alone. In the dull light of the dying fires his features would be unnoticed, and his tongue would not betray him if spoken to. Siegbert had commended him as a crafty and ready fellow, and Edmund felt that he would be able to gather more information than he could do himself. From his place of concealment he kept his eyes fixed on the Northman's figure. Presently he saw him enter the clearing, and sauntering slowly across it throw himself down near a fire by which a party of Danes were still sitting talking.

One by one these lay down, and when the last had done so the Northman rose quietly and stole out again into the forest. When he rejoined Edmund the latter set forward with him, and not a word was spoken until they were some distance from the camp; then Edmund stopped.

"What have you learned?" he asked.

"All that there is to learn, I think," the Northman replied. "The lady Freda is, as you supposed, a captive in the little hut. Two men only keep watch over it by day, but at night six lie around it, two being always on foot. They speak in admiration of her courage and spirit. She has sworn to Sweyn that she will slay herself if he attempts to use violence to force her to marriage with him, and they doubt not that she will keep her word. However, they believe that she will grow tired out at last when she finds that there is no hope whatever of a rescue. The ships are being built for a long sea voyage, for Sweyn is going to lead them to join the Viking Hasting in the Mediterranean, and has promised his men the plunder of countries ten times richer than France or England. With so long an expedition in view, they may well think that the Lady Freda's resolution will soon give way, and that she may come to see that the position of the wife of a bold viking is a thousand times preferable to that of a captive. Many of the men loudly express their wonder why she would refuse the love of so valiant a warrior as Sweyn."

The news was at once good and bad. Edmund did not fear Freda's resolution giving way for a long time, but the news that Sweyn intended to carry her upon so distant an expedition troubled him. It was of course possible that he might intercept them with the Dragon at the mouth of the Maas, but it was uncertain whether the ship would arrive at the mouth of the Rhine in time to be brought round before the Northmen descended. The length of her voyage would depend entirely on the wind. Were this favourable when she reached the mouth of the Seine, a week would carry her to her destination. Should it be unfavourable there was no saying how long the voyage would last.

The risk was so great that Edmund determined to make an effort to rouse the country against the Danes, and to fall upon them in their encampment; but the task would he knew be a hard one, for the dread of the Danes was so great that only in large towns was any resistance to them ever offered. However he determined to try, for if the Northmen succeeded in getting to the sea the pursuit would indeed be a long one, and many weeks and even months might elapse before he could again come up to them.

On the following day the rest of the party arrived, and leaving the forest Edmund proceeded with them through the country, visiting every village, and endeavouring to rouse the people to attack the Danes, but the news that the dreaded marauders were so near excited terror only. The assurances of Edmund that there was much rich plunder in their camp which would become the property of those who destroyed them, excited but a feeble interest. The only point in the narrative which excited their contentment was the news that the Danes were building ships and were going to make their way down to the sea.

"In Heaven's name let them go!" was the cry; "who would interfere with the flight of a savage beast? If they are going down the river they will scarcely land to scatter and plunder the country, and he would be mad indeed who would seek them when they are disposed to let us alone."

Finding his efforts vain in the country near the forest Edmund went down the river to the town of Liege, which stood on its banks. When it became known that a band of Northmen was on the upper river, and was likely to pass down, the alarm spread quickly through the town, and a council of the principal inhabitants was summoned. Before these Edmund told his story, and suggested that the fighting men of the town should march up the river and fall upon the Danes in their camp.

"It is but two days' march--the Northmen will be unsuspicious of danger, and taken by surprise may be easily defeated." The proposition, however, was received with absolute derision.

"You must be mad to propose such a thing, young Saxon, if Saxon indeed you are, but for aught we know you may be a Northman sent by them to draw us into an ambush. No; we will prepare for their coming. We will man our walls and stand on the defensive, and if there be, as you say, but three hundred of them, we can defend ourselves successfully; and we may hope that, seeing our strength, and that we are prepared for their coming, the Northmen will pass by without molesting us; but as for moving outside our walls, it would be worse than folly even to think of such a thing."

After this rebuff Edmund concluded that he could hope for no assistance from the inhabitants of the country, but must depend upon himself and the Dragon alone. He at once despatched two of his men, a Dane and a Saxon, with orders to journey as rapidly as possible to the rendezvous, where the Dragon was to be found at the mouth of the Rhine, and to beg Egbert to move round with all speed to the Maas.

Having done this, he purchased a small and very fast rowing-skiff at Liege, and taking his place in this with his four remaining followers, he rowed up the river. It took them three days before they reached the edge of the forest. On reaching their former hiding-place, they landed. The bushes were carefully drawn aside, and the boat hauled up until completely screened from sight of the river, and Edmund and the Dane at once started for the encampment of the Northmen.

They had been ten days absent, and in that time great progress had been made with the galleys. They looked indeed completely finished as they stood high and lofty on the river bank. The planks were all in their places; the long rows of benches for the rowers were fastened in; the poop and forecastle were finished and decked. A number of long straight poles lay alongside ready to be fashioned into oars; and Edmund thought that in another two or three days the galleys would be ready for launching. They were long and low in the waist, and were evidently built for great speed. Edmund did not think that they were intended to sail, except perhaps occasionally when the wind was favourable, as an aid to the rowers. Each would carry a hundred and fifty men, and there were thirty seats, so that sixty would row at once.

"They are fine galleys," the Dane whispered. "Sweyn has a good eye for a boat."

"Yes," Edmund said, "they look as if they will be very fast. With oars alone they would leave the Dragon behind, but with sails and oars we should overhaul them in a wind. I wish it had been otherwise, for if, when they reach the mouth of the river, there is no wind, they may give the Dragon the slip. Ah!" he exclaimed, "there is Freda."

As he spoke a tall maiden came out from the small hut. The distance was too great for Edmund to distinguish her features, but he doubted not from the style of her garments that it was Siegbert's daughter. There were other women moving about the camp, for the Danes were generally accompanied by their wives on their expeditions; but there was something in the carriage and mien of the figure at the door of the hut which distinguished it from the rest. She did not move far away, but stood watching the men at work on the ships and the scene around. Presently a tall figure strode down from the vessels towards her.

"There is Sweyn!" Edmund exclaimed, seeing that the warrior possessed but one arm.

"Ah! you know him by sight then?" The Dane said.

"I should do so," Edmund answered grimly, "seeing that it was I who smote off that right arm of his. I regret now that I did not strike at his head instead."

The Dane looked with admiration and surprise at his leader. He had heard of the fight between the Saxon champion and Sweyn, which had cost the latter his right arm, but until now he had been ignorant of Edmund's identity with Sweyn's conqueror.

Freda did not seek to avoid her captor, but remained standing quietly until he approached. For some time they conversed; then she turned and left him and re-entered her hut. Sweyn stood looking after her, and then with an angry stamp of the foot returned to the galleys.

"I would give much to be able to warn her that I am present and will follow her until I rescue her from Sweyn," Edmund said. "Once at sea and on her way south she may well despair of escape, and may consent, from sheer hopelessness, to become his wife. Were it not that her hut is so strongly guarded at night I would try to approach it, but as this cannot be done I must take my chance in the day. To-morrow I will dress myself in your garments and will hide in the wood as near as I can to the hut; then if she come out to take the air I will walk boldly out and speak with her. I see no other way of doing it."

On the following morning, attired in the Dane's clothes and helmet, Edmund took his place near the edge of the wood. It was not until late in the afternoon that Freda made her appearance. The moment was propitious; almost all the men were at work on the ships and their oars. The women were cooking the evening meal, and there was no one near Freda, with the exception of the two armed Danes who sat on the trunk of a fallen tree on guard, a short distance away. Edmund issued boldly from the wood, and, waiting till Freda's steps, as she passed backwards and forwards, took her to the farthest point from the guards, he approached her.

"Freda," he said, "do not start or betray surprise, for you are watched."

At the sound of his voice the girl had paused in her steps, and exclaimed in a low voice, "Edmund!" and then, obeying his words, stood motionless.

"I am near you, dear, and will watch over you. I have not strength to carry you away; but my ship will be at the mouth of the river as you pass out. Hang a white cloth from the window of your cabin in the poop as a signal. If we fail to rescue you there we will follow you wheresoever you may go, even to Italy, where I hear you are bound. So keep up a brave heart. I have seen your father, and he has sent me to save you. See, the guards are approaching, I must go."

Edmund then made for the forest. "Stop there!" the guards cried. "Who are you, and whence do you come?"

Edmund made no answer, but, quickening his steps, passed among the trees, and was soon beyond pursuit. This, indeed, the Danes did not attempt. They had been surprised at seeing, as they supposed, one of their party addressing Freda, for Sweyn's orders that none should speak with her were precise. He had given this command because he feared, that by the promise of rich rewards she might tempt some of his followers to aid her escape. They had, therefore, risen to interrupt the conversation, but it was not until they approached that it struck them that the Northman's face was unfamiliar to them, and that he was not one of their party, but Edmund had entered the wood before they recovered from their surprise. Their shouts to him to stop brought Sweyn to the spot.

"What is it?" he asked.

"A strange Northman has come out of the wood, and spoken to the lady Freda."

Sweyn turned to his captive. She stood pale and trembling, for the shock of the surprise had been a severe one.

"Who is this whom you have spoken to?" he asked. Freda did not answer.

"I insist upon knowing," Sweyn exclaimed angrily.

Freda recovered herself with an effort, and, raising her head, said, "Your insistence has small effect with me, as you know, Jarl Sweyn; but as there is no reason for concealment I will tell you. He is a messenger whom my dear father has sent to me to tell me that some day he hopes to rescue me from your hands."

Sweyn laughed loudly.

"He might have saved himself the trouble," he said. "Your good father lies wounded near Paris, and by the time he is able to set out to your rescue we shall be with Hasting on the sunny waters of Italy, and long ere that you will, I hope, have abandoned your obstinate disposition, and consented to be my wife."

Freda did not answer at once. Now that there was a hope of rescue, however distant, she thought it might be as well to give Sweyn some faint hope that in time she might yield to his wishes. Then she said:

"I have told you often, jarl, that I will never be your wife, and I do not think that I shall ever change my mind. It may be that the sunny skies you speak of may work a wonderful change in me, but that remains to be seen." Sweyn retired well satisfied. Her words were less defiant than any she had hitherto addressed to him. As to the message of her father, who could know nothing of his intention to sail to the Mediterranean, he thought no further of it.

Three days later the galleys were launched, and after a day spent in putting everything in its place they started on their way down the river. They rowed many miles, and at night moored by the bank. After darkness had fallen a small boat rowed at full speed past them. It paid no attention to the summons to stop, enforced though it was by several arrows, but continued its way down the river, and was soon lost in the darkness. Sweyn was much displeased. As they rowed down they had carefully destroyed every boat they found on the river, in order that the news of their coming might not precede them.

"The boat must have been hauled up and hidden," he said; "we might as well have stopped and landed at some of the villages and replenished our larder. Now we shall find the small places all deserted, and the cattle driven away from the river. It is an unfortunate mischance."

As the Northmen anticipated they found the villages they passed the next day entirely deserted by their inhabitants, and not a head of cattle was to be seen grazing near the banks. In the afternoon they came to Liege. The gates were shut, and the walls bristled with spears. The galleys passed without a stay. Sweyn had other objects in view. Any booty that might be obtained without severe fighting he would have been glad enough to gather in; but with a long sea-voyage before him he cared not to burden his galleys, and his principal desire was to obtain a sufficient supply of provisions for the voyage. For several days the galleys proceeded down the river. The villages were all deserted, and the towns prepared for defence.

When he arrived within a day's journey of the sea he was forced to halt. Half the crews were left in charge of the ships, and with the others he led a foray far inland, and after some sharp fighting with the natives succeeded in driving down a number of cattle to the ships and in bringing in a store of flour.

Edmund had kept ahead of the galleys, stopping at every town and village and warning the people of the approach of the marauders. He reached the mouth of the river two days before them, but to his deep disappointment saw that the Dragon had not arrived at the rendezvous. On the following afternoon, however, a distant sail was seen, and as it approached Edmund and his followers gave a shout of joy as they recognized the Dragon, which was using her oars as well as sails and was approaching at full speed. Edmund leaped into the boat and rowed to meet them, and a shout of welcome arose from the Dragon as the crew recognized their commander.

"Are we in time?" Egbert shouted.

"Just in time," Edmund replied. "They will be here to-morrow." Edmund was soon on board, and was astonished at seeing Siegbert standing by the side of his kinsman.

"What is the news of Freda?" the jarl asked eagerly.

"She is well and keeps up a brave heart," Edmund replied. "She has sworn to kill herself if Sweyn attempts to make her his wife by violence. I have spoken to her and told her that rescue will come. But how is it that you are here?"

"After you had left us your good kinsman Egbert suggested to me that I should take passage in the Dragon. In the first place I should the sooner see my daughter; and in the next, it would be perilous work, after the Danish army had left, for a small party of us to traverse France."

"I would I had thought of it," Edmund said; "but my mind was so disturbed with the thought of Freda's peril that it had no room for other matters. And how fares it with you?"

"Bravely," the Northman replied. "As soon as I sniffed the salt air of the sea my strength seemed to return to me. My wound is well-nigh healed; but the joint has stiffened, and my leg will be stiff for the rest of my life. But that matters little. And now tell me all your adventures. We have heard from the messenger you sent how shrewdly you hunted out Sweyn's hiding-place."

CHAPTER XVII: A LONG CHASE

THE following morning the weather was still and dull. Not a breath of wind ruffled the surface of the river.

"This is unfortunate," Edmund said to his companion. "Sweyn's galleys will row faster than we can go with oars alone, and though they may not know the Dragon they will be sure that she is not one of their own ships. We must hope that they may attack us."

The day passed on without a sight of the galleys, but late in the afternoon they were seen in the distance. The Dragon was moored near the middle of the rivet. Her oars were stowed away, and the crews ordered to keep below the bulwarks, in hopes that the Danes, seeing but few men about and taking her for an easy prize, might attack her. When they approached within half a mile the Danish galleys suddenly ceased rowing.

"What is that strange-looking vessel?" Sweyn asked the Northmen standing round him.

"I know her," one of them said, "for I have twice seen her before to my cost. The first time she chased us hotly at the mouth of the Thames, destroying several of the vessels with which we were sailing in convoy. The next time was in the battle where King Alfred defeated us last year, nearly in the same water. She is a Saxon ship, wondrous fast and well-handled. She did more damage in the battle than any four of her consorts."

"Were it not that I have other game in view," Sweyn said, "we would fight her, for we are two to one and strongly manned, and the Saxon can scarce carry more men than one of our galleys; but she is not likely to be worth the lives she would cost us to capture her; therefore we will e'en let her alone, which will be easy enough, for see that bank of sea-fog rolling up the river; another ten minutes and we shall not see across the deck. Give orders to the other galley to lay in oars till the fog comes, then to make for the left bank of the river and to drift with the tide close inshore. Let none speak a word, and silence be kept until they hear my horn. I will follow the right bank till we reach the mouth."

Freda was standing near and heard these orders with a sinking heart. She had no doubt that Edmund was on board the Saxon ship, and she had looked forward with confidence to be delivered from her captor; but now it seemed that owing to the evil change of the weather the hope was to be frustrated.

Edmund and the Saxons had viewed with consternation the approach of the sea-fog. The instant it enveloped the ship the oars were got out and they rowed in the direction of the Danish vessels, which they hoped would drop anchor when the fog reached them. Not a word was spoken on board the Dragon. Edmund, Egbert, and Siegbert stood on the forecastle intently listening for any sound which would betray the position of the Danes, but not a sound was to be heard. They had, they calculated, already reached the spot where the Dane should have been anchored when from the left, but far away astern, a loud call in a woman's voice was heard.

"That must be Freda!" Edmund exclaimed. "Turn the ship; they have passed us in the fog."

The Dragon's head was turned and she was rowed rapidly in the direction of the voice. No further sound was heard. Presently there was a sudden shock which threw everyone on to the deck. The Dragon had run high on the low muddy bank of the river. The tide was falling; and although for a few minutes the crew tried desperately to push her off they soon found that their efforts were in vain, and it was not until the tide again rose high nine hours later that the Dragon floated. Until morning broke nothing could be done, and even when it did so matters were not mended, for the fog was still dense.

The disappointment of Edmund and Siegbert at the escape of the Danes was extreme. Their plans had been so well laid that when it was found that the Dragon had arrived in time no doubts were entertained of the success of the enterprise, and to be foiled just when Freda seemed within reach was a terrible disappointment.

"My only consolation is," Edmund said as he paced the deck impatiently side by side with Egbert, "that this fog which delays us will also hinder the Danes."

"That may be so or it may not," Egbert answered. "It is evident that some on board the Danish ships must have recognized us, and that they were anxious to escape rather than fight. They draw so little water that they would not be afraid of the sandbanks off the mouth of the river, seeing that even if they strike them they can jump out, lighten the boats, and push them off; and once well out at sea it is probable that they may get clearer weather, for Siegbert tells me that the fog often lies thick at the mouths of these rivers when it is clear enough in the open sea."

When the tide again began to run out Edmund determined at all risks to proceed to sea. The moorings were cast off from the shore and the Dragon suffered to drift down. Men with poles took their stations in her bows and sounded continually, while at her stern two anchors were prepared in readiness to drop at a moment's notice. Several times the water shoaled so much that Edmund was on the point of giving orders to drop the anchors, but each time it deepened again.

So they continued drifting until they calculated that the tide must be nearly on the turn, and they then dropped anchor. It was much lighter now than it had been in the river, but was still so misty that they could not see more than a hundred yards or so round the vessel. No change took place until night, and then Edmund, who had been too excited and anxious to sleep on the previous night, lay down to rest, ordering that he should be woke if any change took place in the weather. As the sun rose next morning the fog gradually lifted, and they were able to see where they were. Their head pointed west; far away on their left could be seen a low line of coast. Not a sail was in sight, and indeed sails would have been useless, for the water was still unruffled by a breath of wind. The anchors were at once got up and the oars manned, and the ship's head turned towards shore.

Two hours' rowing took them within a short distance of land, and keeping about a mile out they rowed to the west. The men, knowing how anxious was their leader to overtake the Danish galleys, rowed their hardest, relieving each other by turns, so that half the oars were constantly going. Without intermission they rowed until night set in, and then cast anchor. When the wind came--it was not until the third day--it was ahead, and instead of helping the Dragon it greatly impeded its progress.

So far they had seen nothing of the galleys, and had the mortification of knowing that in spite of all their efforts these were probably gaining ground upon them every day. Even without wind the galleys would row faster than the Dragon, and being so fully manned would be able to keep all their oars going; but against the wind their advantage would be increased greatly, for lying low in the water they would offer but little resistance to it, and would be able to make way at a brisk pace, while the Dragon could scarce move against it.

The Saxon ship was off Calais when the breeze sprang up, and as it increased and their progress became slower and slower Edmund held a consultation with his companions and it was determined to run across the channel and lie in the mouth of the Thames till the wind turned. So long as it continued to blow they would lag farther and farther behind the chase, who might, moreover enter any of the rivers in search of shelter or provisions, and so escape their pursuers altogether. Siegbert had never been up the Mediterranean, but he had talked with many Danes who had been. These had told him that the best course was to sail west to the extremity of England, then to steer due south until they came upon the north coast of Spain. They would follow this to its western extremity; and then run south, following the land till they came to a channel some ten miles wide, which formed the entrance to the Mediterranean.

They decided, therefore, to follow this course in hopes of interrupting the galleys there; they would thus avoid the dangerous navigation of the west coast of France, where there were known to be many islands and rocks, around which the tides ran with great fury. For a fortnight the Dragon lay windbound; then came two days of calm; and then, to their delight, the pennon on the top of the mast blew out from the east.

They were lying in the mouth of the Colne, and would therefore have no difficulty in making the Foreland; and with her sail set and her oars out the Dragon dashed away from her moorings. Swiftly they ran round the south-easterly point of England and then flew before the breeze along the southern coast. On the third day they were off Land's End and hauled her head to the south. The east wind held, the Bay of Biscay was calm, and after a rapid voyage they sighted the high lands of Spain ahead. Then they sheered to the west till they rounded its extremity and then sailed down the coast of Spain. They put into a river for provisions, and the natives assembled in great numbers on the banks with the evident intention of opposing a landing; but upon Egbert shouting that they were not Danes but Saxons, and were ready to barter for the provisions they required, the natives allowed them to approach. There was no wrangling for terms. Cattle were purchased, and the water-tanks filled up, and a few hours after entering the river the Dragon was again under way. Rounding the southern point they followed the land. After a day's sailing they perceived land on their right, and gave a shout of joy at the thought that they had arrived at the entrance of the straits. At nightfall they dropped anchor.

"What are you looking at, Siegbert?" Edmund asked, seeing the jarl looking thoughtfully at the anchor-chain as the ship swung round.

"I am thinking," the jarl said, "that we must have made some error. Do you not see that she rides, just as we were sailing, with her head to the north-east? That shows that the current is against us."

"Assuredly it does," Edmund said; "but the current is a very slack one, for the ropes are not tight."

"But that agrees not," Siegbert said, "with what I have been told. In the first place, this channel points to the northeast, whereas, as I have heard, the straits into the Mediterranean run due east. In the next place, those who have been through have told me that there are no tides as in the northern seas, but that the current runs ever like a river to the east."

"If that be so," Edmund said, "we must have mistaken our way, for here what current there is runs to the west. To-morrow morning, instead of proceeding farther, we will cross to the opposite side, and will follow that down until we strike upon the right channel."

In the morning sail was again made, and crossing what was really the Bay of Cadiz they sailed on till they arrived at the mouth of the straits. There was no doubt now that they were right. The width of the channel, its direction, and the steady current through it, all corresponded with what Siegbert had heard, and proceeding a mile along it they cast anchor.

They soon opened communications with the natives, who, although speaking a tongue unknown to them, soon comprehended by their gestures and the holding up of articles of barter that their intentions were friendly. Trade was established, and there was now nothing to do but to await the coming of the galleys.

"I would," Edmund said, as, when evening was closing, he looked across the straits at the low hills on the opposite side, "that this passage was narrower. Sweyn will, doubtless, have men on board his ship who have sailed in these seas before, and will not need to grope his way along as we have done. If he enters the straits at night we shall see nothing of him, and the current runs so fast that he would sweep speedily by. It is possible, indeed, that he has already passed. If he continued to row down the shores of France all the time we were lying wind-bound he would have had so long a start when the east wind began to blow, that, although the galleys carry but little sail, they might well have been here some days before us. Sweyn would be anxious to join Hasting as soon as he could. The men would be thirsting for booty, and would make but short halt anywhere. I will stay but a week. If in that time they come not we will enter this southern sea and seek the fleet of Hasting. When we find that we shall find Sweyn; but I fear that the search will be a long one, for these people speak not our tongue, and we shall have hard work in gaining tidings of the whereabouts of the Northmen's fleet."

Day and night a vigilant watch was kept up from the mast-head of the Dragon, but without success. Each day they became more and more convinced that Sweyn must be ahead of them, and on the morning of the seventh they lifted their anchor and proceeded through the straits. Many had been the consultations between Edmund and his friends, and it had been determined at last to sail direct for Rome. Siegbert knew that by sailing somewhat to the north of east, after issuing from the passage, they would in time arrive at Italy.

At Rome there was a monastery of Saxon monks, and through them they would be able to obtain full information as to the doings and whereabouts of the squadron of Hasting. Scarcely were they through the straits than the wind, veering to the south-east, prevented them from making the course they had fixed upon, but they were able to coast along by the shore of Spain. They put into several small ports as they cruised up, but could obtain no intelligence of the Danes, being unable to converse except by signs.

When they reached Marseilles they were pleased to meet with Franks, with whom they could converse, and hired a pilot acquainted with the coasts of the Mediterranean. They learned that Hasting and his fleet had harried the coasts of Provence and Italy; that the Genoese galleys had had several engagements with them, but had been worsted.

The Danish fleet was now off the coast of Sicily, and the Northmen were ravaging that rich and fertile island. They were reported to have even threatened to ascend the Tiber and to burn Rome. Having obtained the services of a man who spoke both the Italian and Frankish tongues, Edmund started again. He first went to Genoa, as he thought that the people there might be despatching another fleet against the Northmen in which case he would have joined himself to them. On his arrival there he was well entertained by the Genoese when they learned, through the interpreter, who they were, and that they had come from England as enemies of the Danes.

Edmund and his Saxons were much surprised at the splendour of Genoa, which immensely surpassed anything they had hitherto seen in the magnificence of its buildings, the dress and appearance of its inhabitants, the variety of the goods displayed by the traders, and the wealth and luxury which distinguished it. It was indeed their first sight of civilization, and Edmund felt how vastly behind was Northern Europe, and understood for the first time Alfred's extreme eagerness to raise the condition of his people. On the other hand, the Genoese were surprised at the dress and appearance of the Saxons.

The crew of the Dragon were picked men, and their strength and stature, the width of their shoulders, and the muscles of their arms, and, above all, their fair hair and blue eyes, greatly astonished the Genoese. Edmund and his companions might have remained in Genoa and received entertainment and hospitality from its people for a long time; but after a stay of a day or two, and having obtained the various stores necessary for their voyage, Edmund determined to proceed. Three of the young Genoese nobles, fired by the story which they heard of the adventures which the Dragon had gone through, and desirous of taking part in any action which she might fight against the Danes, begged leave to accompany them.

Edmund gladly acceded to the request, as their presence would be of great utility in other ports at which the Dragon might touch. At Genoa Edmund procured garments for his men similar to those worn by the Italian soldiers and sailors, and here he sold to the gold and silversmiths a large number of articles of value which they had captured from the Danes, or with which the Count Eudes and the people of Paris had presented them.

The Dragon differed but little in appearance from the galleys of the Genoese, and Edmund determined when he approached the shores where the Northmen were plundering to pass as a Genoese ship, for should the news come to Sweyn's ears that a Saxon galley was in the Mediterranean it might put him on his guard, as he would believe that she was specially in pursuit of his own vessel.

On arriving at the mouth of the Tiber the Dragon ascended the river and anchored under the walls of the imperial city. The Genoese nobles had many friends and relations there, and Edmund, Egbert, and Siegbert were at once installed as guests in a stately palace.

The pope, upon hearing that the strange galley which had anchored in the river was a Saxon, sent an invitation to its commander to visit him, and Edmund and his kinsman were taken by their Italian friends to his presence. The pope received them most graciously, and after inquiring after King Alfred and the state of things in England, asked how it was that a Saxon ship had made so long a voyage.

Edmund explained that he was in search of a Danish damsel who had once shown him great kindness, and who had been carried off from her father by one of the vikings of Hasting's fleet. When he said that they had taken part in the defence of Paris the holy father told him that he now recognized his name, for that a full account of the siege had been sent to him by one of the monks there, and that he had spoken much of the valour of a Saxon captain and the crew of his galley, to whom indeed their successful resistance to the Northmen was in no slight degree due.

"Would I could aid you, my son, in your enterprise against these northern pirates. The depredations which they are committing on the shores of Italy are terrible indeed, and we are powerless to resist them; they have even threatened to ascend the Tiber and attack Rome, and though I trust that we might resist their attacks, yet rather than such misfortune as a siege should fall upon my people I have paid a large sum of money to the leader of the Northmen to abstain from coming hither; but I know that the greed of these pirates does but increase with their gains, and that ere long we may see their pagan banner floated before our walls. A few galleys I could man and place under your orders, but in truth the people of this town are not skilled in naval fighting. I have already endeavoured to unite the states of Genoa, Pisa, and Venice against them, for it is only by common effort that we can hope to overwhelm these wolves of the sea."

Edmund expressed his thanks to the pope for his offer, but said that he would rather proceed with the Dragon alone.

"She is to the full as swift as the Northmen's vessels," he said; "and although I would right gladly join any great fleet which might be assembled for an attack upon them, I would rather proceed alone than with a few other ships. Not being strong enough to attack their whole armament I must depend upon stratagem to capture the galley of which I am specially in pursuit, and will with your permission set out as soon as I have transformed my ship so that she will pass muster as a galley of Genoa or Venice."

The holy father gave orders that every assistance should be afforded to Edmund to carry out his designs, and the next morning a large number of artisans and work-men took possession of the Dragon. She was painted from stem to stern with bright colours. Carved wood-work was added to her forecastle and poop, and a great deal of gilding overlaid upon her. The shape of her bow was altered, and so transformed was she that none would have known her for the vessel which had entered the Tiber, and she would have passed without observation as a galley of Genoa.

A number of prisoners accustomed to row in the state galleys were placed on board to work the oars, thus leaving the whole of the crew available for fighting purposes, and a state officer was put in command of these galley-slaves. The ship was well stored with provisions, and after a farewell interview with the pope, Ed-mund and his companions returned on board ship, and the Dragon took her way down the river.

The fleet of the Northmen was at Palermo, and keeping under the land, the Saxon ship sailed down the coast of Calabria, and at night crossed near the mouth of the straits to the shore of Sicily. They entered a quiet bay, and Edmund dressed as a Dane, with the two Northmen who had accompanied him from Paris, landed and journeyed on foot to Palermo.

Everywhere they came upon scenes similar to those with which they were familiar in France. Villages burned and destroyed, houses deserted, orchards and crops wasted, and a country destitute of inhabitants, all having fled to the moun-tains to escape the invader. They did not meet with a single person upon their jour-ney. When they approached Palermo they waited until nightfall, and then boldly entered the town. Here the most intense state of misery prevailed. Many of the inhabitants had fled before the arrival of the Danes, but those who remained were kept in a state of cruel subjection by their conquerors, who brutally oppressed and ill-used them, making free with all their possessions and treating them as slaves.

The Danes entered into conversation with some of their countrymen, and professing to have that evening but newly arrived from home, learned much of the disposition of the fleet of the Northmen. They pretended that they were desirous of joining the galleys under the command of Sweyn, and were told that these had arrived three weeks before, and were now absent with some others on the southern side of the island.

Having obtained this information, Edmund and his companions started without delay to rejoin the Dragon. Upon reaching her she at once put to sea. Palermo was passed in the night, and the vessel held her way down the western coast of Sicily. She was now under sail alone, and each night lay up at anchor in order that she might not pass the Danish galleys unobserved. On the third day after passing Palermo, several galleys were seen riding off a small port. The wind was very light, and after a consultation with his friends Edmund determined to simulate flight so as to tempt the Danes to pursue, for with so light a breeze their smaller galleys would row faster than the Dragon; besides, it was possible that Sweyn might be on shore.

It was early morning when the Danish galleys were seen, and apparently the crews were still asleep, for no movement on board was visible, and the Dragon sailed back round a projecting point of land and then cast anchor. It was so important to learn whether Sweyn was with Freda on board his ship, or whether, as was likely, he had established himself on shore, that it was decided it would be better to send the two Danes to reconnoitre before determining what plan should be adopted.

CHAPTER XVIII: FREDA DISCOVERED

THE spies upon their return reported that Sweyn had taken up his abode in the mansion of the Count of Ugoli, who was the lord of that part of the country. Most of the Danes lived on shore in the houses of the townspeople. Many of these had been slain, and the rest were treated as slaves. The lady Freda was also on shore, and it was thought that she would ere long become the bride of the Viking.

"Think you that there will be any possibility of surprising the house and carrying her off?"

"I think not," the Dane said, "for Sweyn's men are on the alert, and keep good guard, for the people of this part of the island, being maddened by their exactions and cruelty, have banded themselves together; and although they cannot withstand the strong parties which go out in search of plunder they cut off stragglers, and have made several attacks on small parties. It is thought that they may even venture an attack upon the place at night, therefore sentries are set, and a portion of the force remains always under arms in readiness to sally out in case of alarm."

"I would fain go myself," Edmund said, "and see how matters stand, and try to communicate with Freda. It may be that her long resistance has tired her out, and that she is at the point of consenting to become Sweyn's bride."

"I think not that," Siegbert replied. "When Freda has once made up her mind she is not given to change."

"I doubt not her resolution," Edmund said; "but none can blame her if, after all these months, she has begun to despair of rescue; nay, it is even probable that, having Sweyn, who is assuredly a brave and enterprising Viking, always near her, she may have come to love him."

"No, Edmund," Siegbert replied. "I am sure you need have no fear that she has softened towards Sweyn. But how do you think of proceeding if you land?"

"I will take with me this Dane, and if one of the Genoese nobles will go with me I will take him, and also the man we brought from Marseilles, who acts as an interpreter between us and the Italians."

"But why hamper yourself with two men, who would be even more likely to be detected by the Danes than would you yourself?"

"I shall leave them in the outskirts of the place," Edmund replied. "I would fain see if I can enter into any negotiations with the natives. Perhaps we may arrange that they shall attack the place on the land side, while the Dragon falls upon the galleys, and in any case we may need an interpreter with the people."

One of the young Genoese, upon being asked whether he would take part in the adventure, at once consented, and the four men, attiring themselves as Danes, speedily landed in the Dragon's boat. The bay in which the ship was lying was some ten miles along the shore from the town. The spies had made their way along the sea-coast by night, but as it was morning when Edmund landed, he thought that it would be safer to make a detour so as to arrive near the landward side of the town and so enter it after dark.

They had not proceeded far when they came upon the ruins of a village. It had been destroyed by fire, and the freshness of the charred beams showed that it had been done but a short time before, probably not many days. Marks of blood could be seen in the roadway, but no bodies were visible, and Edmund supposed that, after the Danes had retired, the survivors must have returned and buried their dead. They had not proceeded far when the Dane pointed out to Edmund a half-naked lad who was running with the swiftness of a deer over a slope of some little distance.

"He is going too fast for us to catch him," Edmund said carelessly; "and as, even if we did so, he could give us no information of any use, for you may be sure he has not ventured near the town, we may well let him go on in his way."

For three or four miles further they pursued their course. The country, which was exceedingly fertile, and covered with corn-fields and vineyards, appeared entirely deserted. Here and there a wide blackened tract showed where, from carelessness or malice, a brand had been thrown into the standing corn.

"The Danes are ever the same," Edmund said. "Well may they be called the sea-wolves. It would be bad enough did they only plunder and kill those who oppose them; but they destroy from the pure love of destroying, and slay for the pleasure of slaying. Why are these robbers permitted to be the scourge of Europe?"

"Why indeed?" the Genoese repeated when the interpreter had translated Edmund's exclamation to him. "'Tis shame and disgrace that Christendom does not unite against them. They are no more invincible now than they were when Caesar overran their country and brought them into subjection. What the Romans could do then would be easy for the Christian powers to do now if they would but make common cause against these marauders--nay, Italy alone should be able at any rate to sweep the Mediterranean free of their pirate galleys; but Venice and Genoa and Pisa are consumed by their own petty jealousies and quarrels, while all our sea-coasts are ravaged by these wolves of the ocean."

"Ah! what is that?" he exclaimed, breaking off, as an arrow struck smartly against his helmet.

They were at the moment passing through a small wood which bordered the road on both sides. The first arrow seemed but a signal, for in an instant a score of others flew among the party. It was well that they carried with them the long Danish shields, which nearly covered their whole body. As it was, several slight wounds were inflicted, and the interpreter fell dead with an arrow in his forehead.

Immediately following the flight of arrows a crowd of peasants armed with staves, axes, and pikes dashed out from the wood on both sides and fell upon them, uttering shouts of "Death to the marauders!" "Kill the sea-wolves!"

So great was the din, that, although the Genoese shouted loudly that they were not Danes but friends, his words were unheard in the din; and attacked fiercely on all sides, the three men were forced to defend themselves for their lives. Standing back to back in the form of a triangle, they defended themselves valiantly against the desperate attacks of their assailants.

Several of these were cut down, but so furious was the attack of the maddened peasants that the defenders were borne down by the weight of numbers, and one by one beaten to the ground. Then the peasants rained blows upon them as if they had been obnoxious wild beasts, and in spite of their armour would speedily have slain them had not the Genoese, with a great effort, pulled from his breast a cross, which was suspended there by a silken cord, and held it up, shouting, "We are Christians, we are Italians, and no Danes."

So surprised were the peasants at the sight that they recoiled from their victims.

The Dane was already insensible. Edmund had just strength to draw his dagger and hold up the cross hilt and repeat the words, "We are Christians." It was the sight of the cross rather than the words which had arrested the attacks of the peasants. Indeed, the words of the Genoese were scarce understood by them, so widely did their own patois differ from the language of polished Italy.

The fact, however, that these Danes were Christians seemed so extraordinary to them that they desisted from their attack. The Danes, they knew, were pagans and bitterly hostile to Christianity, the monasteries and priests being special objects of their hostility. The suggestion of one of the peasants, that the cross had no doubt been taken from the body of some man murdered by the Danes, revived the passion of the rest and nearly cost the prisoners their lives; but an older man who seemed to have a certain authority over the others said that the matter must be inquired into, especially as the man who had the cross, and who continued to address them in Italian, clearly spoke some language approaching their own. He would have questioned him further, but the Genoese was now rapidly losing consciousness from the pain of his wounds and the loss of blood.

The three prisoners were therefore bound, and being placed on rough litters constructed of boughs, were carried off by the peasants. The strength and excellence of Edmund's armour had enabled him to withstand the blows better than his companions, and he retained his consciousness of what was passing. For three hours their journey continued. At the end of that time they entered a wood high up on the hillside. There was a great clamour of voices round, and he judged that his conductors had met another party and that they were at the end of their journey.

The litters were now laid down and Edmund struggled to his feet. Before him stood a tall and handsome man in the attire of a person of the upper class. The old peasant was explaining to him the manner of their capture of the prisoners, and the reason why they had spared their lives.

"How is it," the noble asked when he had finished, turning to Edmund, "that you who are Danes and pagans, plunderers and murderers, claim to be Christians?"

Edmund did not understand the entire address, but he had already picked up a little Italian, which was not difficult for him from his acquaintance with French.

"We are not Danes," he said; "we are their enemies, I am a Saxon earl, and this my friend is a noble of Genoa."

"A Saxon!" the Italian exclaimed in surprise; "one of the people of King Alfred, and this a Genoese noble! How is it that you are masquerading here as Danes?"

"I speak but a few words of Italian," Edmund said, "but my friend will tell you the whole story when he recovers. I pray you to order aid to be given to him at once."

Although still at a loss to understand how it had come about, the Count of Ugoli--for it was that noble himself- saw that his prisoner's statement must be a true one. In their native patois he hastily told the peasants that there must be some mistake, and that although their prisoners seemed to be Danes they were really Christians and friends. He bade them then instantly to strip off their armour, to bind up their wounds, and to use all their efforts to restore them to life.

At his bidding one of the peasants brought a wine-skin, and filling a large cup with the liquid, offered it to Edmund. The latter drained it at a draught, for he was devoured by a terrible thirst. After this he felt revived, and soon had the satisfaction of seeing his comrades recovering under the ministrations of the peasants, who chafed their hands, applied cool poultices of bruised leaves to their bruises, and poured wine down their throats.

In half an hour the Genoese was sufficiently recovered to be able to sit up and to give a full account of their presence there, and of their object in assuming the disguise of Danes. He then told the count that Edmund intended to reconnoitre the place alone, and that he hoped he and his people would attack the town, while the Saxons in their galley made an assault from the sea. The count replied that the peasantry could not be induced to take such a step.

"I will, however, aid your friend," he said, "by a feigned attack to-morrow evening when he is there. This may help him to escape, and if the Danes sally out next day in pursuit there will be the fewer for him to cope with."

When Edmund awoke the next morning he found himself able to walk and move without difficulty and with but little pain, thanks to the care of the peasants, and in the afternoon, being furnished by the count with a guide, he started for the town.

When he arrived within a short distance he dismissed his guide and lay down in some bushes till nightfall, then he rose and made his way into the town, passing unobserved between the watch-fires made by the parties of Danes encamped in its outskirts to protect it against surprise. Once in the town, he walked boldly on, having no fear of recognition or question.

Sounds of carousing came through the open casements, but few people were in its streets. He made his way down to the sea-shore, which he followed until he came to a large and stately mansion standing in beautifully laid out gardens at the end of the town. Several tents were erected in the garden; and although the night was not cold great fires had been lighted, around which the Danes were carousing.

Avoiding these Edmund walked up to the open windows. The first room he looked into was deserted, but in the next, which was a large apartment, a number of Danes were seated at table. At its head sat Sweyn with Freda on his right hand. Around were a number of his leading men, the captains of the galleys and their wives. The meal was over, and the winecup was passing round. A number of attendants moved about the room, and many of the warriors who had supped elsewhere stood around the table, joining in the conversation and taking their share of the wine.

Edmund saw at once that he could not hope for a more favourable opportunity, and he accordingly entered the mansion, and, passing through the open door, joined the party within, keeping himself in rear of those standing round the table, so that the light from the lamps placed there should not fall upon his face.

Just as he had taken his place, Sweyn called out: "Let us have a song. Odoacre the minstrel, do you sing to us the song of the Raven."

A minstrel bearing a small harp advanced into the centre of the horse-shoe table, and after striking a chord, began to sing, or rather to chant one of the favourite songs of the sea-rovers.

A shout of applause rose from the Danes as the minstrel ceased, and holding their goblets high above their heads, they drank to the Raven.

While the singing was going on Edmund quietly made his way round to one of the open windows. It was the hour at which the count had promised to make his attack, and he listened eagerly for any sound which might tell that the peasants had begun their work. Other songs followed the first, and Edmund began to be afraid that the courage of the peasants had failed at the last moment.

Suddenly he saw lights appear at five or six points in the distance, and, putting his head out, he thought he could hear distant cries and shouts. The lights grew brighter, and soon broad tongues of flame shot up. Shouts at once arose from the guards without. Some of the revellers hearing these went to the windows to see what was happening, and gave a cry of alarm. "Sweyn, we must be attacked; fires are rising in the outskirts of the town."

"These cowards would never venture to disturb us," Sweyn said scornfully; "of all the foes we have ever met none were so feeble and timid as these Italians."

"But see, Sweyn, the flames are rising from eight points; this cannot be accident."

Sweyn rose from his seat and went to the window.

"No, by Wodin," he exclaimed, "there is mischief here; let us arm ourselves, and do you," he said, turning to a young man, "run swiftly to the outposts, and learn what is the meaning of this."

Scarcely, however, had he spoken when a man ran breathlessly into the hall.

"Haste to the front, jarl," he said to Sweyn, "we are attacked. Some of the enemy creeping in between our fires set fire to the houses in the outskirts, and as we leapt to our feet in astonishment at the sudden outbreak, they fell upon us. Many of my comrades were killed with the first discharge of arrows, then they rushed on in such numbers that many more were slain, and the rest driven in. How it fares with the other posts I know not, but methinks they were all attacked at the same moment. I waited not to see, for my captain bade me speed here with the news."

"Sound the horn of assembly," Sweyn said. "Do you, Oderic, take twenty of the guard without, and at once conduct the ladies here to the boats and get them on board the galleys. Let all others hasten to the scene of attack. But I can hardly even now believe that this coward herd intend to attack us in earnest."

In the confusion which reigned as the warriors were seizing their shields and arms, Edmund approached Freda, who had with the rest risen from her seat.

"The Dragon is at hand," he whispered; "in a few hours we will attack Sweyn's galley; barricade yourself in your cabin until the fight is over."

Freda gave a little start as Edmund's first words reached her ear. Then she stood still and silent. She felt her hand taken and pressed, and glancing round, met Edmund's eye for a moment just as he turned and joined the Danes who were leaving the hall. A minute later Oderic entered with the guard, and at once escorted the women down to the boats, and rowed them off to the galleys.

Sweyn and the main body of the Danes rushed impetuously to the outskirts of the town. The fighting was already at an end, the peasants having withdrawn after their first success. Two or three of the parties round the watch-fires had been annihilated before they could offer any effectual resistance, others had beaten off the attack, and had fallen back in good order to the houses, losing, however, many men on the way from the arrows which their assailants shot among them.

Sweyn and the Norsemen were furious at the loss they had suffered; but as pursuit would have been useless, there was nothing to be done for the present, and after posting strong guards in case the attack should be renewed, the Danish leaders returned to the banqueting hall, where, over renewed draughts of wine, a council was held.

Most of those present were in favour of sending out a strong expedition on the following day to avenge the attack; but Sweyn argued that it might be that the natives had assembled from all parts of the island, and that this sudden attack, the like of which had not been attempted before, was perhaps made only to draw them out into an ambush or to attack the town in their absence. Therefore he urged it was better to delay making an expedition for a short time, when they would find the enemy unprepared.

After some discussion Sweyn's arguments prevailed, and it was determined to postpone the expedition for a few days.

CHAPTER XIX: UNITED

NO sooner did Edmund find himself outside the mansion than he separated himself from the Danes, and following the sea-shore, set out on his return to the Dragon. The tide was out, and although the night was dark he had no difficulty in finding his way along the shore, keeping close to the margin of the waves. When he approached the headland he was forced to take to the land, as the waves beat against the foot of the rock. Guided by the stars he made his way across the cape and came down on to the shore of the bay.

A light was burning on the poop of the Dragon, and his hail was at once answered. A few minutes later a boat touched the shore beside him, and he was soon on board the ship, and at once held council with Egbert and Siegbert, to whom he related all that had happened. He learned from them that his two wounded comrades had been brought down to the beach that evening by the country people, and had told them how narrow an escape they had had of death at the hands of the enraged peasants.

After a discussion of all the different plans upon which they might act, it was determined that the attempt to rescue Freda should be made at once, as they considered it certain that Sweyn with a large portion of his band would set out at daybreak to take vengeance upon the natives.

The plan decided upon was that they should proceed along the shore, and that if the Danish galleys, being undermanned, did not put out in pursuit, they should sail in and attack them. The Danes were indeed greatly superior in force, for they had counted the ships, the smallest of which would carry a hundred men. Still in the absence of a portion of their crews, and from the effects of surprise, they thought that success was possible.

The next morning sail was hoisted, and the Dragon made her way along the coast. The hour was later than that at which she had shown herself on the previous day. She sailed on until within two miles of the town, and then suddenly turned her head seaward, as if she had only then perceived the Danish vessels. The instant she did so a great bustle was observed among them. Many boats were seen pushing off from shore crowded with men, oars were got out, and sails loosed.

"From the number of men who are crowding on board," Egbert said, "I believe that Sweyn cannot have started in pursuit of the natives; in that case we shall have a hard fight of it."

"So much the better," Siegbert exclaimed. "I should consider our task was half accomplished if we rescued Freda without punishing Sweyn. Let them come," he said, shaking his battle-axe at the galleys. "Though my leg is stiff my arms are not, as Sweyn shall learn if I meet him."

The Dragon's oars were now put out and the galley-slaves began to row, the Saxons concealing themselves behind the bulwarks. In a few minutes the whole of the Danish galleys were unmoored and started in the pursuit of the supposed Italian vessel. The breeze was light, but somewhat helped the Dragon. Four of the Northmen vessels were large ships with sails, and these speedily fell behind, but the others with their oars gained slowly on the Dragon.

Edmund saw with satisfaction that the two galleys of Sweyn, which he at once recognized, were somewhat faster than their consorts, and the slaves were made to row as hard as they could in order to prolong the chase as much as possible, by which means Sweyn's galleys would be the further separated from the others.

After the pursuit had been continued for some miles Sweyn's galleys were but a few hundred yards in the rear, and were nearly a quarter of a mile ahead of those of their comrades, which had gained but little upon the Dragon since the chase began. Edmund ordered the men to cease rowing, as if despairing of escape. The Genoese took their station on the poop, and as Sweyn's galley came rushing up they shouted to it that they would surrender if promised their lives. The Northmen answered with a shout of triumph and derision, and dashed alongside.

Sweyn's own galley was slightly in advance of the others. Edmund ordered the oars to be pulled in as the Northmen came up, so as to allow them to come alongside. Not a word was spoken on board the Dragon till the Danes, leaving their oars, swarmed up the side headed by Sweyn himself. Then Edmund gave a shout, the Saxons leaped to their feet, and raising their battle-cry fell upon the astonished

Danes.

Those who had climbed up were instantly cut down or hurled back into their own galley, and the Saxons leaping down, a tremendous fight ensued. Edmund with Siegbert and half his crew boarded the Dane close to the poop, and so cut the Northmen off from that part of the vessel, while Egbert with the rest boarded farther forward. The Danes would have been speedily overpowered had not the second galley arrived upon the spot; and these, seeing the combat which was raging, at once leaped upon Sweyn's galley. With this accession of force, although numbers of the Danes had fallen in the first attack, they still outnumbered the Saxons.

Sweyn, heading his men, made a desperate effort to drive back Edmund's party. His men, however, fought less bravely than usual. Their astonishment at finding the ship which they had regarded as an easy prize manned by Saxons was overwhelming, and the sight of Siegbert, whom many of them knew, in the front rank of their enemies added to their confusion.

Sweyn himself, as he recognized Edmund, at once made at him, and, wielding a heavy axe in his left hand, strove to cut him down; and Edmund, strong and skilful as he was, had great difficulty in parrying the blows which the Northman rained upon him. The combat, however, was decided by Siegbert, who hurled his javelin at Sweyn, the weapon passing completely through his body.

Sweyn fell on the deck with a crash.

The Northmen, dispirited at the fall of their leader, hesitated, and as the Saxons sprang upon them turned and fled into the other galley. The door of the poop opened and Freda flew into her father's arms.

"Quick, Siegbert, to the Dragon!" Edmund cried, and shouted orders to his men. "There is not a moment to be lost. The other galleys are just upon us!"

The Saxons rushed back to the Dragon; the oars were thrust out again, and the vessel got under weigh just as the other Danish galleys arrived on the spot. While some of the Saxons poured volleys of arrows and javelins into the Northmen, the others at Edmund's order leaped down and double-banked the oars. The increase of power was soon manifest, and the Dragon began to draw away from the Danes. Gradually their galleys fell back out of bow-shot, and after continuing the chase for some little time longer they abandoned it as hopeless and lay upon their oars to rest.

A shout of triumph rose from the Saxons, and then Edmund, who had hitherto been fully occupied with the command of the vessel, turned to Freda, who was still standing by her father.

"I have been a long time in fulfilling my promise, Freda," he said; "but as your father will tell you I have done my best. Thank God, who has given me success at last!"

"I never doubted that you would come, Edmund," she said, "and the knowledge has enabled me to stand firm against both the entreaties and threats of Sweyn. How can I thank you for all you have done for me?"

"I have spoken to your father, Freda; and he has promised me your hand if you, indeed, are willing to bestow it. I promised to come for you if you would wait, nearly five years ago, and I have never thought of any other woman."

"I have waited for you, Edmund," she said simply, "and would never have wed another had you not come. You are my hero, and methinks I have loved you ever since the day when you boarded our ship off the mouth of the Humber."

"Take her, Edmund," Siegbert said; "you have nobly won her, and there is no one to whom I could be so well content to intrust her. I now join your hands in token of betrothal."

The crew of the Dragon, who had been watching the scene, raised a shout of gladness as they saw Siegbert place Freda's hand in that of Edmund. They had guessed that their lord must have an affection for this Danish maiden in whose pursuit they had come so far, and were delighted at the happy issue of the expedition.

"I trust, Freda," Edmund said to her after a while, "that you have thought of the talk we had about religion, and that you will forsake the barbarous gods of your people and become a Christian, as so many of your people have done in England, and that you will be wedded to me not in the rude way of the Danes, but in a Christian church."

"I have thought much of it," she said, "and have come to think that your God of peace must be better than the gods of war; but I would fain know more of Him before I desert the religion of my fathers."

"That shall you," Edmund said. "With your father's permission I will place you for a short time in a convent in Rome, and one of the Saxon monks shall teach you the tenets of our faith. It will be but for a short time, dear; and while you are there we will try and capture some of Hasting's galleys, filled with plunder, for my men have come far, and I would fain that they returned with an ample booty."

Freda and Siegbert agreed to the plan, and the latter said, "I too will tarry in Rome while you are away, Edmund. I could fight against Sweyn, for it was in a private quarrel, but I cannot war against my countrymen. I too will talk with your Saxon monks, and hear about this new religion of yours, for I think that as I have no others to love or care for I shall return to England with you, and, if you will have me, take up my abode in your English home so as to be near you and my daughter."

The Dragon returned to Rome. There Edmund procured lodgings for Siegbert and Freda, and the Saxon monks gladly arranged to visit them and instruct them in the doctrines of Christianity. The Dragon sailed again for the coast of Sicily and was absent a month, during which time she captured a number of Danish galleys, most of which were laden with rich booty. Then she returned to Rome. A few days later a solemn service was held, at which Freda and Siegbert were baptized as Christians, and after this was done a marriage service was held, and Edmund and Freda married with the rites of the Christian Church. The pope himself was present at the services and bestowed his blessing upon the newly married couple, the novelty of the occasion drawing a vast crowd of spectators.

A few days later the Dragon again put to sea, and after a speedy voyage with favourable weather arrived in England without further adventure. Edmund's arrival at home was the occasion of great rejoicings. The news of the share which the Dragon and her crew had taken in the defence of Paris had reached England, but none knew what had become of her from that time, and when months had passed without tidings of her being received it was generally supposed that she must have been lost.

Her return laden with rich booty excited the greatest enthusiasm, and the king himself journeyed to Sherborne to welcome Edmund on his arrival there.

"So this is the reason," he said smiling, when Edmund presented Freda to him, "why you were ever so insensible to the attractions to our Saxon maidens! Truly the reason is a fair one and fully excuses you, and right glad am I to welcome your bonnie bride to our shores."

Alfred remained three days at Sherborne and then left Edmund to administer the affairs of his earldom, for which a substitute had been provided in his absence. The large plunder which the Dragon had brought home had enriched all who had sailed in her, and greatly added to the prosperity which prevailed in Edmund's district.

He found that in his absence Alfred had introduced many changes. The administration of justice was no longer in the hands of the ealdormen, judges having been appointed who journeyed through the land and administered justice. Edmund highly approved of the change, for although in most cases the ealdormen had acted to the best of their powers they had a great deal of other business to do; besides, their decisions necessarily aggrieved one party or the other and sometimes caused feuds and bad feelings, and were always liable to be suspected of being tinged with partiality; whereas the judges being strangers in the district would give their decisions without bias or favour.

Freda had, as was the custom, taken a new name in baptism, but at Edmund's request her name had only been changed to the Christian one of Elfrida, and Edmund to the end of his life continued to call her by her old name. She speedily became as popular in the earldom as was her husband.

Siegbert, who had been christened Harold, took kindly to his new life. Between him and Egbert a great friendship had sprung up, and Edmund built for their joint use a house close to his own.

In 884 Alfred heard that the Danes of East Anglia were in correspondence with their countrymen at home and in France, and that there was danger that the peace of England would be disturbed. The thanes were therefore bidden to prepare for another struggle, to gather sufficient arms in readiness for all the able-bodied men in their district, and to call out their contingents from time to time to practise in the use of arms.

The ealdormen whose seats of government bordered on the sea were ordered to construct ships of war, so that any Danish armament might be met at sea. Edmund was appointed to command this fleet, and was instructed to visit the various ports to superintend the construction of the ships, and when they were completed to exercise their crews in naval maneuvers.

The winter of 884 was spent by Edmund in the performance of these duties. The Dragon was again fitted out, and in her he cruised from port to port. Freda, who was passionately fond of the sea, accompanied him, as did Siegbert and Egbert. It was not until May in 885 that the threatened invasion took place. Then the news came to the king that the Danes had landed in large numbers near Rochester and had laid siege to the town. The king instantly summoned his fighting array, and in a few days moved at the head of a large army towards Kent. Rochester was defending itself valiantly. The Danes erected a great tower opposite to the principal gate, and overwhelming the defenders on the walls with their missiles endeavoured to force their way in by battering down the gate.

The inhabitants, however, piled great masses of stone behind it, and even when the gate was battered in the Danes, with all their efforts, were unable to force an entrance. The Saxon army advanced with such celerity that the Danes had received no news of their coming until they were close at hand. Then one of their foraging parties arrived with the intelligence that a great Saxon army was upon them. The Danes were seized with a sudden panic, and fled precipitately to their ships, leaving behind them the horses they had brought from France, their stores, and all the prisoners and spoil they had gathered in their incursions in the neighbourhood of Rochester. Seeing how well the Saxons were prepared for resistance the greater portion of the Danes crossed to France, but sixteen of their vessels entered the Stour and joined their allies of East Anglia.

Alfred ordered his fleet to assemble in the Medway, and in a fortnight the vessels from all the southern ports arrived. They were filled with fighting men, and sailed to attack the Danes in the Stour, after which the force was to land and to inflict a severe punishment upon East Anglia. On hearing of the gathering of the Saxon fleet Athelstan sent across to France and begged the Danes to come to his assistance, but none of their vessels had arrived when the Saxon fleet reached the mouth of the Stour.

The fighting force on board the Danish ships had been largely reinforced by their countrymen of East Anglia, and in a close body they rowed out to give battle to the Saxons. A desperate fight ensued, but after a struggle, which continued for many hours, the Danes were completely defeated, the whole of their vessels were captured, and all on board put to the sword.

On the following day the army landed and ravaged the surrounding country and returned to the ships with much booty. As they sailed out of the river they saw a vast fleet of the enemy approaching. Athelstan had assembled his ships from all the ports of East Anglia, and had been joined by a large reinforcement of his countrymen from France. The Saxons were greatly outnumbered, but a portion of the fleet fought with great bravery. Some of the ships, however, being manned with newly-collected crews unaccustomed to naval war, lost heart, and made but a poor resistance.

Alfred was on board the Dragon, which sank several of the Danish galleys, and with some of her consorts continued the fight until nightfall, beating off every attempt of the Danes to board them. Seeing that several of the ships had been captured, that others had taken to flight, and that there was no longer a hope of victory, Alfred gave the signal, and the Dragon and her remaining consorts fought their way through the Danish fleet and made their escape.

The valour which the Saxons had shown in these two sea-fights, and the strength of the army with which Alfred had so speedily marched to the relief of Rochester, greatly impressed the enemy, and although Rollo came across from Normandy to the assistance of Athelstan, the Danes concluded that it was better to leave the Saxons to themselves.

Alfred in the following spring again assembled his army and laid siege to London, which was still in the possession of the Danes. Athelstan did not venture to march to its assistance, and the town, which had long been in the Northmen's hands, was captured. The greater portion of the city was burned in the siege. Alfred ordered it to be rebuilt, invited its former inhabitants to return, and offered privileges to all who would take up their abode there. The walls were rebuilt, and the city placed in a position of defence. Alfred then handed it over to Ethelred, the ealdorman of Mercia.

Peace was now made with Athelstan, and for some years remained unbroken. In 893 a Danish fleet of 250 ships sailed across from Boulogne and landed in the Weald of Kent, which was then covered with a great forest, and there wintered, while the viking Hasting with eighty ships sailed up the Thames and built a strong fort at Milton.

Alfred stationed his army in a strong position half-way between the forest and the Danish camp at Milton, so that he could attack either army when they moved out of their stronghold. The Danes for many months remained in the forest, issuing out occasionally to plunder in the open country of Kent, Sussex, and Hampshire, but they met with a stout resistance from the Saxons who had remained in the towns and country.

After Easter, having collected a considerable amount of spoil, and finding the resistance ever increasing, the Danes moved northwards from their forest, intending to march into Essex. The king's forces at once set off to intercept them, and overtook them at Farnham, where the Northmen were completely defeated. All their booty was recaptured, with their horses and stores. Those who escaped fled across the Thames and took refuge on an island in the Colne. The Saxons besieged them there; but when the Danes were about to surrender from want of provisions the news arrived that the Northmen of Northumbria and East Anglia, with 240 ships, had landed suddenly in Devonshire, and had laid siege to Exeter.

The siege of the island was at once raised, and King Alfred marched against the new arrivals, and advancing with great speed fell upon them and defeated them. Then hastily returning he came to London and, joined by a strong force from Mercia, marched against Milton, where Hasting had been joined by the great number of the Danes who had formed the army in the Weald. Hasting himself was away, but his army marched out to meet the Saxons.

A great battle was fought, but the Danes could not resist the ardour of their assailants. Their army was routed and their fortress stormed. All the booty within it fell into the hands of the victors, together with the wives and families of the Danes, among whom were the wife and two sons of Hasting. The Danish fleet also was captured, and was burned or taken to London. Another great fleet of the East Angles and Northumbrians sailed up the Thames, and landing, the Northmen marched across to the Severn, but were defeated and destroyed by Ethelred of Mercia.

Exeter was again invested by a Danish fleet, and again saved by Alfred. The Danes, as they retired along the south coast, landed near Chichester, where they suffered a heavy defeat from the South Saxons.

In the following year a fresh fleet sailed up the Thames and thence up the Lea, where they constructed a fortress twenty miles above London.

Alfred caused two fortresses to be erected on the Lea below them, with vast balks of timber entirely obstructing the river. The Danes, finding their retreat cut off, abandoned their ships and marched across England to Cwatbridge on the Severn.

Their fleet fell into the hands of the Londoners, who burned and broke up all the smaller ships and carried the rest down to London. The Danes were so disconcerted by the many and severe defeats which had befallen them that they now abandoned the idea of again conquering England, and taking ship, sailed for France.

Four years later, in 901, King Alfred died, having reigned twenty-nine years and six months. During his reign England had made immense advances in civilization, and in spite of the devastation wrought by the Danish occupation of Wessex during the early years of his reign, and the efforts required afterwards to oppose them, the wealth and prosperity of the country vastly increased during his reign. Abbeys and monasteries had multiplied, public buildings been erected, towns rebuilt and beautified, and learning had made great advances. The laws of the country had been codified and regulated, the administration of justice placed on a firm basis. The kingly authority had greatly increased, and the great ealdormen were no longer semi-independent nobles, but officers of the crown. Serfdom, although not entirely abolished, had been mitigated and regulated. Arts and manufactures had made great progress.

Edmund and Freda survived King Alfred many years, and their district continued to be one of the most prosperous and well-ruled in the kingdom. Their descendants continued to hold the office of ealdorman until the invasion by William the Conqueror, and the holder of the office at that time fell, with numbers of his followers, at the battle of Hastings. For very many years after that event the prow of the Dragon was kept in the great hall of Sherborne as a memorial of the valiant deeds performed against the Danes by Ealdorman Edmund.

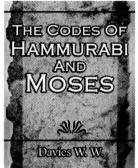

The Codes Of Hammurabi And Moses
W. W. Davies

QTY

The discovery of the Hammurabi Code is one of the greatest achievements of archaeology, and is of paramount interest, not only to the student of the Bible, but also to all those interested in ancient history...

Religion   **ISBN:** *1-59462-338-4*

Pages:132
MSRP $12.95

The Theory of Moral Sentiments
Adam Smith

QTY

This work from 1749. contains original theories of conscience amd moral judgment and it is the foundation for systemof morals.

Philosophy   **ISBN:** *1-59462-777-0*

Pages:536
MSRP $19.95

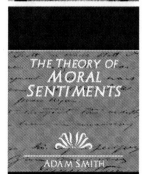

Jessica's First Prayer
Hesba Stretton

QTY

In a screened and secluded corner of one of the many railway-bridges which span the streets of London there could be seen a few years ago, from five o'clock every morning until half past eight, a tidily set-out coffee-stall, consisting of a trestle and board, upon which stood two large tin cans, with a small fire of charcoal burning under each so as to keep the coffee boiling during the early hours of the morning when the work-people were thronging into the city on their way to their daily toil...

Childrens   **ISBN:** *1-59462-373-2*

Pages:84
MSRP $9.95

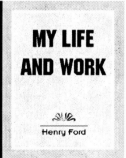

My Life and Work
Henry Ford

QTY

Henry Ford revolutionized the world with his implementation of mass production for the Model T automobile. Gain valuable business insight into his life and work with his own auto-biography... "We have only started on our development of our country we have not as yet, with all our talk of wonderful progress, done more than scratch the surface. The progress has been wonderful enough but..."

Biographies/   **ISBN:** *1-59462-198-5*

Pages:300
MSRP $21.95

www.bookjungle.com *email: sales@bookjungle.com fax: 630-214-0564 mail: Book Jungle PO Box 2226 Champaign, IL 61825*

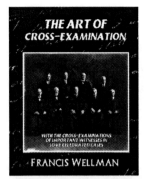

The Art of Cross-Examination
Francis Wellman

QTY

I presume it is the experience of every author, after his first book is published upon an important subject, to be almost overwhelmed with a wealth of ideas and illustrations which could readily have been included in his book, and which to his own mind, at least, seem to make a second edition inevitable. Such certainly was the case with me; and when the first edition had reached its sixth impression in five months, I rejoiced to learn that it seemed to my publishers that the book had met with a sufficiently favorable reception to justify a second and considerably enlarged edition. ...

Pages:412

Reference   ISBN: *1-59462-647-2*   *MSRP $19.95*

On the Duty of Civil Disobedience
Henry David Thoreau

QTY

Thoreau wrote his famous essay, On the Duty of Civil Disobedience, as a protest against an unjust but popular war and the immoral but popular institution of slave-owning. He did more than write—he declined to pay his taxes, and was hauled off to gaol in consequence. Who can say how much this refusal of his hastened the end of the war and of slavery ?

Law   ISBN: *1-59462-747-9*   **Pages:48**
MSRP $7.45

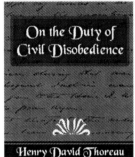

Dream Psychology
Psychoanalysis for Beginners

Sigmund Freud

Dream Psychology Psychoanalysis for Beginners
Sigmund Freud

QTY

Sigmund Freud, born Sigismund Schlomo Freud (May 6, 1856 - September 23, 1939), was a Jewish-Austrian neurologist and psychiatrist who co-founded the psychoanalytic school of psychology. Freud is best known for his theories of the unconscious mind, especially involving the mechanism of repression; his redefinition of sexual desire as mobile and directed towards a wide variety of objects; and his therapeutic techniques, especially his understanding of transference in the therapeutic relationship and the presumed value of dreams as sources of insight into unconscious desires.

Pages:196

Psychology   ISBN: *1-59462-905-6*   *MSRP $15.45*

The Miracle of Right Thought
Orison Swett Marden

QTY

Believe with all of your heart that you will do what you were made to do. When the mind has once formed the habit of holding cheerful, happy, prosperous pictures, it will not be easy to form the opposite habit. It does not matter how improbable or how far away this realization may see, or how dark the prospects may be, if we visualize them as best we can, as vividly as possible, hold tenaciously to them and vigorously struggle to attain them, they will gradually become actualized, realized in the life. But a desire, a longing without endeavor, a yearning abandoned or held indifferently will vanish without realization.

Pages:360

Self Help   ISBN: *1-59462-644-8*   *MSRP $25.45*

www.bookjungle.com *email: sales@bookjungle.com fax: 630-214-0564 mail: Book Jungle PO Box 2226 Champaign, IL 61825*

QTY

The Rosicrucian Cosmo-Conception Mystic Christianity by *Max Heindel* ISBN: *1-59462-188-8* **$38.95**
The Rosicrucian Cosmo-conception is not dogmatic, neither does it appeal to any other authority than the reason of the student. It is: not controversial, but is: sent forth in the, hope that it may help to clear... New Age/Religion Pages 646

Abandonment To Divine Providence by *Jean-Pierre de Caussade* ISBN: *1-59462-228-0* **$25.95**
"The Rev. Jean Pierre de Caussade was one of the most remarkable spiritual writers of the Society of Jesus in France in the 18th Century. His death took place at Toulouse in 1751. His works have gone through many editions and have been republished... Inspirational/Religion Pages 400

Mental Chemistry by *Charles Haanel* ISBN: *1-59462-192-6* **$23.95**
Mental Chemistry allows the change of material conditions by combining and appropriately utilizing the power of the mind. Much like applied chemistry creates something new and unique out of careful combinations of chemicals the mastery of mental chemistry... New Age Pages 354

The Letters of Robert Browning and Elizabeth Barret Barrett 1845-1846 vol II ISBN: *1-59462-193-4* **$35.95**
by *Robert Browning* and *Elizabeth Barrett* Biographies Pages 596

Gleanings In Genesis (volume I) by *Arthur W. Pink* ISBN: *1-59462-130-6* **$27.45**
Appropriately has Genesis been termed "the seed plot of the Bible" for in it we have, in germ form, almost all of the great doctrines which are afterwards fully developed in the books of Scripture which follow... Religion/Inspirational Pages 420

The Master Key by *L. W. de Laurence* ISBN: *1-59462-001-6* **$30.95**
In no branch of human knowledge has there been a more lively increase of the spirit of research during the past few years than in the study of Psychology, Concentration and Mental Discipline. The requests for authentic lessons in Thought Control, Mental Discipline and... New Age/Business Pages 422

The Lesser Key Of Solomon Goetia by *L. W. de Laurence* ISBN: *1-59462-092-X* **$9.95**
This translation of the first book of the "Lernegton" which is now for the first time made accessible to students of Talismanic Magic was done, after careful collation and edition, from numerous Ancient Manuscripts in Hebrew, Latin, and French... New Age/Occult Pages 92

Rubaiyat Of Omar Khayyam by *Edward Fitzgerald* ISBN:*1-59462-332-5* **$13.95**
Edward Fitzgerald, whom the world has already learned, in spite of his own efforts to remain within the shadow of anonymity, to look upon as one of the rarest poets of the century, was born at Bredfield, in Suffolk, on the 31st of March, 1809. He was the third son of John Purcell... Music Pages 172

Ancient Law by *Henry Maine* ISBN: *1-59462-128-4* **$29.95**
The chief object of the following pages is to indicate some of the earliest ideas of mankind, as they are reflected in Ancient Law, and to point out the relation of those ideas to modern thought. Religion/History Pages 452

Far-Away Stories by *William J. Locke* ISBN: *1-59462-129-2* **$19.45**
"Good wine needs no bush, but a collection of mixed vintages does. And this book is just such a collection. Some of the stories I do not want to remain buried for ever in the museum files of dead magazine-numbers an author's not unpardonable vanity..." Fiction Pages 272

Life of David Crockett by *David Crockett* ISBN: *1-59462-250-7* **$27.45**
"Colonel David Crockett was one of the most remarkable men of the times in which he lived. Born in humble life, but gifted with a strong will, an indomitable courage, and unremitting perseverance... Biographies/New Age Pages 424

Lip-Reading by *Edward Nitchie* ISBN: *1-59462-206-X* **$25.95**
Edward B. Nitchie, founder of the New York School for the Hard of Hearing, now the Nitchie School of Lip-Reading, Inc, wrote "LIP-READING Principles and Practice". The development and perfecting of this meritorious work on lip-reading was an undertaking... How-to Pages 400

A Handbook of Suggestive Therapeutics, Applied Hypnotism, Psychic Science ISBN: *1-59462-214-0* **$24.95**
by *Henry Munro* Health/New Age/Health/Self-help Pages 376

A Doll's House: and Two Other Plays by *Henrik Ibsen* ISBN: *1-59462-112-8* **$19.95**
Henrik Ibsen created this classic when in revolutionary 1848 Rome. Introducing some striking concepts in playwriting for the realist genre, this play has been studied the world over. Fiction/Classics/Plays 308

The Light of Asia by *sir Edwin Arnold* ISBN: *1-59462-204-3* **$13.95**
In this poetic masterpiece, Edwin Arnold describes the life and teachings of Buddha. The man who was to become known as Buddha to the world was born as Prince Gautama of India but he rejected the worldly riches and abandoned the reigns of power when... Religion/History/Biographies Pages 170

The Complete Works of Guy de Maupassant by *Guy de Maupassant* ISBN: *1-59462-157-8* **$16.95**
"For days and days, nights and nights, I had dreamed of that first kiss which was to consecrate our engagement, and I knew not on what spot I should put my lips..." Fiction/Classics Pages 240

The Art of Cross-Examination by *Francis L. Wellman* ISBN: *1-59462-309-0* **$26.95**
Written by a renowned trial lawyer, Wellman imparts his experience and uses case studies to explain how to use psychology to extract desired information through questioning. How-to/Science/Reference Pages 408

Answered or Unanswered? by *Louisa Vaughan* ISBN: *1-59462-248-5* **$10.95**
Miracles of Faith in China Religion Pages 112

The Edinburgh Lectures on Mental Science (1909) by *Thomas* ISBN: *1-59462-008-3* **$11.95**
This book contains the substance of a course of lectures recently given by the writer in the Queen Street Hall, Edinburgh. Its purpose is to indicate the Natural Principles governing the relation between Mental Action and Material Conditions... New Age/Psychology Pages 148

Ayesha by *H. Rider Haggard* ISBN: *1-59462-301-5* **$24.95**
Verily and indeed it is the unexpected that happens! Probably if there was one person upon the earth from whom the Editor of this, and of a certain previous history, did not expect to hear again... Classics Pages 380

Ayala's Angel by *Anthony Trollope* ISBN: *1-59462-352-X* **$29.95**
The two girls were both pretty, but Lucy who was twenty-one who supposed to be simple and comparatively unattractive, whereas Ayala was credited, as her Bombwhat romantic name might show, with poetic charm and a taste for romance. Ayala when her father died was nineteen... Fiction Pages 484

The American Commonwealth by *James Bryce* ISBN: *1-59462-286-8* **$34.45**
An interpretation of American democratic political theory. It examines political mechanics and society from the perspective of Scotsman James Bryce Politics Pages 572

Stories of the Pilgrims by *Margaret P. Pumphrey* ISBN: *1-59462-116-0* **$17.95**
This book explores pilgrims religious oppression in England as well as their escape to Holland and eventual crossing to America on the Mayflower, and their early days in New England... History Pages 268

QTY

The Fasting Cure *by Sinclair Upton*   ISBN: *1-59462-222-1*   **$13.95**

In the Cosmopolitan Magazine for May, 1910, and in the Contemporary Review (London) for April, 1910, I published an article dealing with my experiences in fasting. I have written a great many magazine articles, but never one which attracted so much attention... New Age/Self Help/Health Pages 164

Hebrew Astrology *by Sepharial*   ISBN: *1-59462-308-2*   **$13.45**

In these days of advanced thinking it is a matter of common observation that we have left many of the old landmarks behind and that we are now pressing forward to greater heights and to a wider horizon than that which represented the mind-content of our progenitors... Astrology Pages 144

Thought Vibration or The Law of Attraction in the Thought World   ISBN: *1-59462-127-6*   **$12.95**

by William Walker Atkinson   Psychology/Religion Pages 144

Optimism *by Helen Keller*   ISBN: *1-59462-108-X*   **$15.95**

Helen Keller was blind, deaf, and mute since 19 months old, yet famously learned how to overcome these handicaps, communicate with the world, and spread her lectures promoting optimism. An inspiring read for everyone... Biographies/Inspirational Pages 84

Sara Crewe *by Frances Burnett*   ISBN: *1-59462-360-0*   **$9.45**

In the first place, Miss Minchin lived in London. Her home was a large, dull, tall one, in a large, dull square, where all the houses were alike, and all the sparrows were alike, and where all the door-knockers made the same heavy sound... Childrens/Classic Pages 88

The Autobiography of Benjamin Franklin *by Benjamin Franklin*   ISBN: *1-59462-135-7*   **$24.95**

The Autobiography of Benjamin Franklin has probably been more extensively read than any other American historical work, and no other book of its kind has had such ups and downs of fortune. Franklin lived for many years in England, where he was agent... Biographies/History Pages 332

Name	
Email	
Telephone	
Address	
City, State ZIP	

☐ **Credit Card**   ☐ **Check / Money Order**

Credit Card Number	
Expiration Date	
Signature	

Please Mail to: Book Jungle
                        PO Box 2226
                        Champaign, IL 61825
or Fax to: 630-214-0564

ORDERING INFORMATION

web: *www.bookjungle.com*
email: *sales@bookjungle.com*
fax: *630-214-0564*
mail: *Book Jungle PO Box 2226 Champaign, IL 61825*
or PayPal *to sales@bookjungle.com*

Please contact us for bulk discounts

DIRECT-ORDER TERMS

**20% Discount if You Order
Two or More Books**
Free Domestic Shipping!
Accepted: Master Card, Visa,
Discover, American Express

CPSIA information can be obtained at www.ICGtesting.com
Printed in the USA
265826BV00003B/290/A

9 781604 245776